One Billion Secrets

RUTHLESS BILLIONAIRES 1

LYDIA MICHAELS

One Billion Secrets

RUTHLESS BILLIONAIRES

Book One

LYDIA MICHAELS

Lydia Michaels Books, LLC

www.LydiaMichaelsBooks.com
USA | CANADA | SPAIN | EUROPE | NEW ZEALAND |
AUSTRALIA

ONE BILLION SECRETS
Ruthless Billionaires 1
Billionaire Romance
Contemporary Romance
Copyright © 2023 Lydia Michaels
Lydia Michaels Books, LLC
Second E-book Publication: © Lydia Michaels 2023
Cover Design by Lydia Michaels Books, LLC

For Amy —one of the strongest women I know.

Part One

Isadora

Prologue

"If the only mark I leave upon this earth is the indelible caress of my whispered name within the downbeats of your heart, I will be satisfied."

Fiona Summerville
Only Dark Around the Edges

THERE IS a moment in every woman's life, be her a queen or a pawn, when she is taken so off guard the game is forever changed. Isadora Patras should have been shockproof by now, but as the pieces fell, exposing her once again to the excruciating agony of loss, her hard earned fortitude slipped and she surrendered. Game over.

Her lungs constricted around each draw of perfumed air as she pivoted away from her brother, Lucian. Dizzy, she flinched, each onlooker's stare stabbing through her thin veneer of composure. Too many strangers.

"Isadora?"

She couldn't whisper a single excuse to Lucian as she turned. She needed to escape. Keeping her head down she rushed toward the doorway, against the current of bodies approaching.

Her life flashed painfully through her mind with kaleidoscope glimpses of her past, tilted and jagged. Broken. Upside down and disjointed. Lumbering strides clumsily carried her away from the crowd. She struggled for elegance when everything inside of her begged to run. Escape.

A cry built in her throat, but she swallowed it back. Patrases didn't cry—not even the female ones—according to her father.

A thousand unfinished sentiments danced on her tongue as the agony inside seeped past her lips in a clipped whimper. The pain in her heart climbed as the sob in her throat built, each step announcing the end of her courage, the acceptance of her loss.

A piercing buzz sounded in her ears as reality truly set in. She wasn't going to make it. She was going to fall apart, right here, in front of all these people and the last of her dignity would be stolen, just as so many other things had been.

I can't handle this...

The excruciating sorrow was hers and hers alone. No one knew the truth. They *all* believed the lie.

The doorway yawned only ten feet away, but bodies cluttered the exit. She needed to get through the throng of guests before the last broken pieces of her heart shattered into dust.

"Excuse me," she murmured, keeping her head down and angling toward the hallway.

A suffocating vise closed around her heart, radiating into her shoulders with crushing, agonizing waves at the slightest brush of contact. Her knees softened as she turned the corner and came face to face with another line of strangers. Too many people.

Who were they? They were all here for him, yet she didn't recognize a single one.

Because he wanted it that way...

The room tilted, the narrow hall shrinking as countless bystanders blended into one. Nausea churned through her empty stomach. Her veil of composure slipped, exposing vulnerabilities no one would understand. No one except the one person she couldn't speak to about this.

She swallowed down the pain as she had so many times before, but nothing came close to the agony she was up against now. This was absolutely the last time he'd ever hurt her.

She tried to bury it, pretend it never happened, which it might as well not have, being that no one else knew the truth—except *him,* the one person who deserved to *never* see her like this. The one person she wished was here. The only person who knew the real her and accepted every imperfection she hid from the rest of the world. But asking him to accept the heartbreak she suffered for another man was simply too much. She couldn't do that to him...

A sob gave way, slicing through the polite silence like a frigid wind cuts through the heat of a summer day. Heads jerked in her direction. She couldn't face their judgment, their assumptions.

The hallway seemed to lengthen with each step. She'd never make it. Her vision tilted and she leaned into the wall. She had no choice but to face this alone. Always alone.

Breathe!

Her lips parted as she sucked in a lungful of air. The moment it traveled past the lump in her throat her queasy stomach revolted.

The clashing stench of perfume and people spoiled the natural scent of the flowers. Her mouth watered. Her throat swallowed, but a jarring wooziness unleashed inside of her. Tiny beads of sweat clung to her brow, each carrying the weight of an entire ocean.

Don't you dare surrender here! You keep moving!

She staggered another step, certain everyone was now staring. Never had her secrets felt as heavy as they did in that moment. His secrets. Theirs. Now, they were all hers.

All of her polished grace was a sham, nothing but chipped layers disguising unsophisticated innocence worn thin by time. She'd never make it to the front door at this rate. It was too far.

Pivoting in the direction she'd just come, she lurched toward a discrete pocket door hidden in the wall. Faces blurred into macabre figures as she struggled to breathe, her heart jackhammering in her chest.

Her hands pressed into the panel, her mind not caring if she wasn't permitted beyond this point. She needed an escape. She needed privacy, because she was breaking in broad daylight after years of fighting for flawless composure.

Every fundamental experience had taught her how to hide—a pawn on the run, forever racing toward the elusive dignity of a queen. She had nothing left to sacrifice.

I surrender. I surrender...

As the paneled door slid open she rushed inside the private sitting room and closed the world away. Her face pressed to the wood as her breath beat out of her.

Too much pain. Too many regrets. The secrets

gutted her, slipping out in retched, raw sobs. The tears came like a harsh rain after an endless drought. Relentless.

She let go, surrendering the last of her poise to the pain. Gasping, she moaned against each brutal wave of sadness as years of silent suffering escaped in broken wails. There was no disguising it here. It was the ugly truth she'd carried for more than a decade. It was a truth she'd bear for the rest of her life.

Her shoulders curled inward as another jagged sob escaped. Something touched her shoulders and she gasped. Her hands flew to her face, hiding tracks of tears and traces of exposed anguish as a floorboard creaked, announcing the presence of another person in the private room.

Horrified to discover she wasn't alone, she hid against the door, blatantly visible, but crippled by the indignity that someone was witness to her distress. She couldn't bear to turn around.

"Isadora..."

Her spine stiffened as her name fell like a plea, a rasp of worry, hidden in the strong tenor of a masculine voice. Her head slowly lifted as his familiar, gentle tone penetrated her mortification and her lips parted.

Wet lashes blinking in surprise, she slowly pivoted, no longer hiding her tears. Her heart sparked in her chest as her gaze traveled over his designer suit, past his strong jaw, and fell upon his familiar eyes.

He's here...

She held his stare and her breath stuttered. There were no words for how deeply she loved him. His presence was everything. *He* was everything.

Brow pinched, he delicately dragged a thumb under her lashes, visibly reading her heartache and accepting it. He pulled her into his arms, burying his face in her shoulder as she lost herself in his sheltering hold.

Safe.

Chapter 1

"Perhaps the freedom of flying in the boundless sky is but a lonesome fall through nothingness."
~Emily Patras

THIRTEEN YEARS *Earlier*

"Where were you?" Isadora called from the foot of the grand staircase, stilling her younger brother's fleeting steps. She held onto resolute hope to get to the bottom of his recent rebellion.

Shirttail askew, Lucian turned with a penetrating scowl that, had she not been anticipating his defiance, would have taken her a step back. "You're not my keeper, Isadora."

Her heart stammered in her chest, his words cutting to the shabby roots running beneath their family tree like corroded veins. Tangled and rotted, an abandoned place since their mother had passed away eight years ago.

Daunting men had always overshadowed the little authority Isadora assumed, and her younger brother's independence was rapidly dwarfing hers. But she was still his guardian, and as such, it was her sole duty to protect him—even from himself.

"Don't walk away from me, Lucian."

"Then say what you have to say so I can go to bed."

Of all of the Patras children, Lucian was the most intrepid, but despite his innate audacity he was far from invincible. No amount of pain seemed to slow his instinct to rise. He loomed over and around anything that stood in his way, growing taller and faster than all the rest. And the bigger he grew the less he answered to *anyone*.

His shadow was sometimes a cold and lonely place in which to stand, but Isadora had survived worse and wasn't about to be bulldozed by an eighteen year old boy. Holding her ground, she inwardly praised herself for maintaining a steady voice as she craned her neck to meet his scowl.

"It's four in the morning, Lucian."

"Then I still have a shot at getting some sleep." Putting an abrupt stop to further scolding, he turned and continued up the stairs at a less skulking pace.

A chill filled the grand foyer as she locked her

jaw, authoritative ground slipping out from under her.

"The rule was two o'clock," she reminded. It was a generous curfew, a bargaining chip she hoped would end the exhausting pissing match they'd entered over his incessant need to push boundaries.

"*Your* rule," he growled, disappearing down the long hall.

A nerve pinched close to her heart. Her own father had marched that same path, ignoring her words as her little voice once called to him, a quiet plea for the attention she'd thought she deserved. Lucian was *literally* following in their dad's footsteps and the distance between them was growing so vast, she feared it would soon be impossible to bridge.

The tighter she tried to hold onto her younger brother the harder he resisted, but she couldn't let go. She'd once been his equal, his ordinary sister, despite the five years that separated them. But when she became a legal adult and his caregiver their relationship changed. And now, as he entered adulthood, her role was transforming once again, into something undefined that filled her with an orphaned emptiness.

Her shoulders jerked as his bedroom door slammed. If she didn't ease off they might never resolve their differences and find the closeness they once shared.

On cue, Antoinette's door creaked open and Isadora straightened her posture, setting her features into the mask of a composed and secure woman—a façade at total odds with the uncertainty warring inside of her.

Antoinette's slippered feet shushed over the oriental runner until her sprouting body came into view, eyes bright as an autumn moon with irises of a whiskey hue instead of the typical Patras black. Although Isadora would never know the true color of her sister's eyes or anyone else's, she could always tell a pretty set despite being color blind. Her little sister had bright, curious eyes that often shimmered with mischief.

After a rapid growth spurt, Toni was tall enough to be mistaken for a teen, but head-on she still held an honest show of innocence that faded with each passing day. She planted herself at the top of the stairs, delicate fuzz showing on her shins where her nightgown rode to just below her knobby knees. Wild chestnut curls spun in disarray around her pudgy cheeks pressed with sheet prints. She yawned with cub-like magnetism that softened Isa's mood.

Toni was getting so big, already in double digits, and soon she, too, would be walking away. A sharp ache cinched Isadora's heart. The problem with raising her siblings was that if she did the job well, they'd grow up to be independent and self-assured, with little need for her.

That was the goal, wasn't it? She should be happy that both Lucian and Toni possessed the self-assured Patras charm she never quite mastered. The most Isadora could do was enjoy the present and try not to get too consumed with worry for the future.

Tightening the satin tie of her robe, she forced a smile. Switching off the light, she met her sister at the top steps and held out a hand. "Come on. It's too early to get out of bed."

"But I'm hungry. What time is it?"

"Not breakfast time." And her sister was always hungry. The joys of feeding a growing child. "Back to bed."

"Can I sleep with you?"

Toni talked in her sleep. She also turned like a propeller and kicked. But there was something sacred about being wanted by one sibling when the other wanted nothing to do with her. "Sure."

Despite Toni's hunger, she was half-asleep, and lurched down the hall toward a bedroom. Isadora pulled back the duvet and her sister clambered onto the mattress with the grace of a three-legged calf.

"Your bed's so much comfier than mine," she groaned into the pillows. As Isadora slid under the covers Toni curled into her side, too young to grasp things like personal space. "Is Lucian in trouble?"

She turned, seeing her sister's eyes were closed,

but her mind fighting to stay awake—curiosity for what the "grownups" were discussing being one of Toni's guiltiest pleasures. The truth was, Lucian had more of a grown up life than Isadora.

Shutting her eyes, she drew in a breath and let it out slowly. "I don't know, Toni. Try to go back to sleep."

"He should be in trouble." Her sweet breath teased Isadora's shoulder. "He's been late every day this week."

"And you've been nosy." She kissed her forehead and shut out the bedside lamp.

"Daddy would punish him."

Isadora stared into the shadows, only briefly tripping over excuses for their father. In the end she sugarcoated nothing. "Daddy isn't here."

Their father hadn't been there in so long it was a wonder Antoinette could recall a time he was present. Though it didn't surprise her that Toni remembered their father's temper, especially when it came to their brother, who usually caught the brunt of the man's cruelty.

Exhausted, mentally and physically, Isadora shut her eyes. "Shh... Sleep."

"I wish Claudette would come back," her sister murmured, words slurring.

Claudette had been the head of their household staff, but over the years she took up the additional role of nurturer, despite their father's objections. It was a tearful day when the maid left for France. No one wanted to see her go and she didn't want to leave, but their father wrote the checks and told her she had a job in Europe and *only* Europe, so they couldn't blame her for following him.

"She'd yell at Lucian." Toni's groggy words came with little inflection.

"I don't think Lucian needs another person to yell at him."

Toni snorted. "He needs his butt whooped."

Isadora turned to face her sister. She looked unconscious, but somehow managed to keep talking. "Antoinette, you worry about you and I'll worry about Lucian. Go to sleep."

"He's not as cool as he thinks he is," she informed, getting in the final word before falling into a rhythm of softly cooed snores.

Sleep wasn't as easy for Isadora. Her mind continued to wander and worry—a well-practiced habit of hers, which came with little rest.

Lucian's college career was right around the corner, something she never personally experienced. Her brother, however, was enrolled to leave in six weeks. The three of them living in this house together had been a consistency they took for granted and she feared Toni didn't quite understand the finality of their brother going away.

Although he was still young, Isadora's gut told her once he left he'd never come back. Lucian had always been a forward moving force and going backward was against his nature.

Despite her sister's snoring, Isadora whispered, "You should try not to fight with him. Soon he won't be here and then who will you pick on?"

When Lucian's college search began, they all had questions that needed answering. Lucian's revolved around where his friend Slade Bishop was applying. Isadora's were mostly concerned with their father's promise to pay the tuition and any additional costs. Toni, although the youngest, always asked the most difficult questions.

"Isa, how come you didn't go to college?" Toni wondered aloud just the other morning, casually depositing the sensitive topic into an unassuming moment of bran flakes.

Isadora had not consumed enough coffee for tough questions and, as Toni dribbled a good bit of milk down the collar of her nightgown, Isadora bought some time by passing her a napkin. "If I went away to school who would take care of you?"

Toni shrugged. "Daddy would send people."

As replaceable as a stranger.

Her sister was too young to understand how offensive her quick solution sounded. The irony was that Toni automatically excused their father from the job. Assuming—if in a pinch—their *father* would find yet another au pair. Even their little sister was wise enough to know the man was not a suitable parent—under any circumstances, including the emergency sort.

"What's so special about college anyway? I'm not going," her sister had announced with all the finality and assuredness a naïve ten-year-old could muster.

"Some people never get to go to college, Toni. Either they can't afford the time or they can't afford the tuition. You should be grateful you have such opportunities ahead. There was once a time when women weren't even allowed to read. Some places in the world are still like that."

She hoped her sister would take advantage of the few benefits that came from being Christos Patras's offspring. While Lucian already possessed an obstinate knowledge of the world, the female family members always seemed less...essential or significant. She was determined to make sure Toni got every opportunity their father provided his only son—even if Christos put little consideration into what his daughters might someday become.

She smirked, a strange and comforting thought coming to her. Soon it would just be the two of them living in the house. Two sisters. No boy stuff dumped in corners of rooms. No sports gear or sweat stains on the furniture. Just the Patras females holding down the fort.

As much as their emancipation from the overbearing Patras men scared her, it also pleased her. In some strange way, she found the idea empowering. Her brother's approaching absence was triggering her own liberation. She couldn't help anticipating the disappearance of his overwhelming sense of authority—which was debatable authority anyway.

Isadora was older, yet she deferred to Lucian in many instances because he possessed the inarguable confidence of every other Patras man. Despite his lack of years and experience, he somehow used stature and arrogance to make up for any shortcomings. Plus, he was a control freak who always assumed his opinion was the one that mattered most.

She loved her brother very much, but he owned every room he entered, leaving little air for others to breathe. He was a prince born to be a king, determined to not just fulfill his birthright, but also annihilate any obstacles in his way.

Sometimes, while the kings of the world moved about, shifting obstacles this way and that, the smaller people sacrificed as much as pawns. She'd always been a pawn, maneuvered to serve others' needs.

But sometimes pawns managed to push past the ranks, patiently traveling one tiny square at a time. And if they made it to the other end of the board unmolested, they were promoted to queen.

With the king preoccupied by other endeavors, she might finally be able to make some advances of her own.

Chapter 2

"From the nest they must fall."
~Isadora Patras

IN THE WEEKS leading up to Lucian's departure, Isadora savored any moment her brother graced their home with his presence, though such instances were few and far between. She chose her battles carefully. No longer waiting up in the kitchen at night, but rather, worrying from her bed and only resting once the shuffle of his footsteps echoed through the house, announcing he'd returned home safe and sound.

Soon enough he'd be on his own and she didn't want to be an enemy he left behind. But she loved him and that meant worrying about him and suffering silently.

He was changing and that was changing her,

too. It had always been the three of them and every day that passed he amputated more of his part of the puzzle from their whole.

Dominant men, like her father, could not be told what to do. Lucian was no different and she sympathized with any woman who dared to love him in the future. The impenetrable armor he'd donned since becoming an adult hid every tender part of him from the outside world—including her and Toni. Though she would miss him when he left, there was nothing quite as excruciating as missing someone living in the same home.

He seemed oblivious to how his emotional withdrawal affected her. She missed her little brother, even though he was still living there. Perhaps this was some cruel trick the universe played to make it easier to push birds from the nest when it was time for them to fly on their own. Her wings had been clipped the day her father left and she feared she'd eventually be left all alone in an empty nest, too afraid to fly after her own dreams —whatever they might be. Today was Lucian's day to fly away.

As Lucian gave Shamus Callahan a brief hug goodbye, her mind touched on other goodbyes and lingered around fading memories of their mother.

Their parents should have been standing there for this moment in their son's life. Their mother always took such pride in her children's milestones. Isadora had grieved such a defining loss long ago, but moments like this, moments when one of them shined, always seemed to prick at the fraying threads that mended the gaping hole in her heart where her mother used to live.

When her brother's dark stare met hers, Isadora pasted on a brave smile. "You have everything?"

Those flat, onyx eyes rolled as he held out his arms, engulfing her with too much strength for a man his age. "Yes, Isa," he mumbled, his deep voice full of dry tolerance.

She savored the momentary truce between them, hoping this was the end of their recent scrimmage for the upper hand and they could once again occupy an even playing field.

Taking advantage of the hug, she squeezed him tight. "Make sure you eat and don't forget to get your books before they sell out."

He let go and she fought the urge to pull him back and pamper him with a hundred more maternal suggestions. He was leaving, yet she couldn't seem to picture him gone.

Since their father left and their mother's presence had faded, Isadora had taken her brother's nearness for granted. She'd once considered running away, shortly after their mother's funeral. She'd stood at the front door with a bag in her hand and the provocation to leave burning the hole in her heart a bit deeper than it already was.

As the knob turned in her hand Lucian's little voice broke the silence. "Where are you going, Isa? You're not leaving too, are you?"

She'd paused, incapable of explaining to a boy of ten how a father could be so selfish as to abandon his children only weeks after burying their mother. Maybe part of him believed their dad would come back a changed man. But Isadora knew the truth. She knew his absence would steal every opportunity that was her due.

"You'll be fine." The lie tasted bitter on her tongue. She was not a replacement for their mother, any more than a nanny.

His little brow pinched as his dark eyes—too big for his face—shimmered up at her. "But we have to stay together—the three of us. We're a family. Remember?"

She'd stared into his sad, young eyes, realizing his fear was a thousand times bigger than hers. It was then she understood she couldn't take the easy way out. She could never act like their father and turn her back on those she loved.

And Lucian wasn't running away now. He was moving on and she was both happy and heartbroken.

Part of her harbored a great deal of envy for the experience he was about to embark on. She'd been ordered to sit at the grownup table when her feet could hardly reach the floor, never being offered the chance to run away to college. She couldn't reach her future when her father's neglect sealed her to her past.

Years spent trying to make their broken family whole had certainly come at a cost, but she refused to regret what she'd forfeited. Every sacrifice had been her choice. And the reward was watching her little brother go forward in his life—no matter how much it hurt to see him leave.

Unlike the little boy who stopped *her* at the door, she wouldn't stop him now. She was a grown woman and understood goodbyes were a part of life.

She swallowed back any sense of injustice and embraced the positive. Lucian's progress was a reflection of her sacrifices and she was proud of him. Proud of all of them.

He bent to Toni's height and gave her ponytail a firm yank. "You be good, brat."

Their sister threw her arms around his shoulders and he lifted her like a ragdoll, squeezing her tight.

"Bring me back something cool," Toni instructed.

Lucian lowered her feet to the ground and nodded. "You got it."

Carrying the last of his bags to the idling SUV, he turned and gave them one final nod. A sharp pinch stabbed in her chest as she watched the door to the SUV close. Trying to see his face through the tinted glass was useless.

As the car pulled away she focused on holding all of her confused emotions inside so as not to upset her sister or make a blubbering mess of herself in front of Shamus.

Toni's fingers gripped her hand tightly as the childlike sound of her sniffles competed with the crunching gravel. The shock of her sister's upset was enough to stifle Isadora's own tears.

Forcing a smile, she faced Shamus, who held Toni's other hand. Lucian's friend forced a smile, as though every little sniffle from Toni's nose was cutting right into his sensitive heart.

"You're upsetting Shamus," Isadora teased and Toni gaped at Lucian's friend, her big brown eyes glassy and too large for her little face.

Glancing at Toni, his brow creased, his mouth twisting with mock skepticism. "You better cry like this when I leave next year, brat."

"You're only going to school down the road. It won't be the same. Lucian's going to be all the way in the city." But Toni's grip noticeably tightened.

Isadora smiled at the sweet way her sister and Shamus always teased each other. Their special bond filled moments like this with light banter rather than sorrow.

Pretending to be affronted, Shamus scoffed. "Well ... maybe I'll transfer. Luche is stealing all the attention and the last thing he needs is a bigger ego."

That penetrated her sister's false indifference. "Don't you dare!"

Shamus laughed and nudged her shoulder. "I'd never." He gave her a playful wink. "You know what today feels like?"

Toni hung on his every word. "What?"

"Ice cream. How about we take a ride into the city? You and Isa put on fancy clothes and we'll make dinner reservations at your dad's hotel, but we'll only order off the dessert menu."

The pinch surrounding Isadora's heart eased as Toni's eyes cleared, her cheeks stretching into a wide grin. "What about supper?"

Shamus lovingly knocked a knuckle against her upturned chin. "Some situations call for special exceptions. What do you say we go break the rules of good social conduct?"

"Isa, can we?" Toni bounced with enthusiastic impatience.

"Why don't you and Shamus go? Have fun. I think I'm going to rest."

"You're never any fun, Isa."

"Hush, brat. Your sister's entitled to some time to herself."

Isadora smiled at Shamus, appreciating his help. "Thank you, Jamie."

He nodded. "Come on, Antoinette. Let's go make reservations."

Staring out at the vacant drive, Isadora sighed as Shamus escorted Toni inside the house.

"How come Lucian and Isa call you Jamie

sometimes?" her sister's raspy voice asked as they climbed the porch steps.

"Because that's my name. Shamus is Irish, but the English version is Jamie or James."

"I like Shamus," she told him.

"And I prefer Antoinette to Toni."

When the house was quiet and Isadora was truly alone, her momentary ease faded. She wandered the silent halls questioning how everything still appeared the same, yet felt so different.

She ended up in her father's study, the cold ambiance a gentle mocking of the hollowness she felt on the inside. The problem with formidable men, she decided, was when they left there seemed a whole lot of emptiness in their absence.

Twenty-three years old, suffering empty nest syndrome for a son that wasn't her own, and trapped in a life she never intended to lead—her master plan never had time to truly formulate.

When she'd thought of running away eight years ago, she'd only been a confused little girl chasing a deep yearning for any sense of home. This was her home. It was all she'd ever known, but the desire for more still lingered. The yearning to feel loved and needed—necessary—was perhaps her strongest driving force and what had made her stay rather than go all those years ago.

Easing forward in her father's chair, she pulled open the top drawer of his desk. The heavy wood gave way and—predictably—an aged bottle of

Macallan rolled to the front. She lifted the scotch, cradling it in her lap, and brushed her thumb over the label, never quite able to tell if it was brown or red. Her color blindness was just another one of her characteristics her father ignored, because when certain handicaps could not be resolved with money, he refused to acknowledge their existence.

Turning the bottle, she examined the faded words. She'd held it a hundred times but never took a sip, always worrying—or perhaps hoping— her father would eventually return and want to know who drank his aged scotch.

The ornate cork pulled free with little force, interrupting the silence with a soft pop. While she resented her father's neglect for her siblings' sake, she never said much on the subject. Toni was the most indifferent to his absence. But Lucian, who recalled his cruelty well and knew exactly what sort of cold-hearted person could jettison three young children... Lucian digested their father's abandonment like bitter poison, the sort that left a lingering aftertaste that could only fade once the venom was exorcised.

Toni forgot. Isadora compartmentalized. But Lucian remembered every cruel instance, and those bitter, flammable memories fueled so much of his unyielding drive for success. All of them, including their mother, had been affected by Christos's toxicity.

Her brother intended to even the score, had

vowed to do so since he was old enough to process the abnormalities of their family life. Once he finished college, she had no doubt he'd seek the vengeance he'd always wanted. Maybe then he could find the closure they all desired.

Sitting in the shadows, she raised the aged scotch. "Good luck, Daddy. He won't stop until he's beaten you."

She drew from the mouth of the bottle, forcing back a gasp as the fiery liquid scalded her throat. Taking a long, healthy swallow of air, she laughed in the darkness.

"How does he drink this stuff?"

Perhaps she'd become a rich lush, like so many older females in similar situations after their children left, their purpose obscured by years of subservience and little chance left to forge their own identities. The thought stung and a misplaced laugh slipped from her lips.

She wasn't old. She was the age of any college graduate, minus several rites of passage and the luxury of a degree. But she had other luxuries and complaining only made her feel like a spoiled ingrate.

"Don't be a pathetic martyr." She slouched in the large leather desk chair. "One day you'll matter as much as the rest of them."

"Isadora?"

Her shoulders knotted with a spike of surprise. Her eyes widened, but no one was there. "Hello?" *How strong is this scotch?*

"Where are you?" the masculine voice called from the hall.

She dropped her hands beneath the surface of the desk, hiding the bottle in her lap. Her face heated, as she feared someone might have overheard her talking to herself like a first class lunatic.

Clearing her throat, she calmly answered, "I'm in the study."

The door creaked as Sawyer Bishop, her father's colleague and long-time family friend, gazed into the room. His eyes rested on her for only a moment, before searching the shadows.

"Are you alone? I thought I heard you talking to someone."

Her face flushed with another flood of heat as she reached for the small accent lamp poised on the corner of the desk. A dull amber glow revealed dust over the unused surface.

"No, it's just me. Antoinette went to the hotel for dinner with Shamus Callahan."

He was familiar with Lucian's other friend. Sawyer's son Slade was one third of the boys' trifecta, though Shamus was a year behind the other two.

"What are you doing sitting in the dark?" He took another step inside the dim office.

"I was just ... thinking." *And drinking.*

The end of the workweek showed in his

opened collar. A day's worth of creases wrinkled his Brooks Brothers suit. He was roughly a decade and a half younger than her father, who had delayed having children as long as possible.

Though Sawyer was several years older than her, Bishop men wore time well, making it hard to discern their exact age. Sawyer's years were well hidden behind laugh lines and eyes so clear she could discern they were of the brightest blue—pretty eyes, the sort that shimmered. The sort she liked.

He possessed a swarthy complexion and distinguished elegance that never went out of style, and his son, Slade, had inherited the same sort of devastatingly handsome presence, but disguised it behind youthful attire. Masculine beauty such as theirs was a tricky thing, it made the young man appear older and the older man appear younger.

As he approached, her eyes did a brief perusal of his tall form. Sawyer always dressed to the nines. Even now, his tailored suit and dark vest accentuated his trim build and long torso with timeless aristocracy.

He was seasoned, sleek, and possessed such charm women of all ages tended to fall all over him. Though, to her knowledge, he hadn't been in any sort of committed relationship since losing his wife, Chelsea, thirteen years ago.

Casual strides led him across the carpet, his smile full of gentle understanding. "Rough day?"

He lowered himself into the chair on the other side of the desk, his broad shoulders relaxing with ease only confident men could master without looking slovenly.

Her gaze traveled back to his eyes. "Lucian left for college today."

He nodded. "That's actually why I'm here." Reaching into the breast pocket of his designer jacket, he withdrew a check. "Your father asked me to deliver this to you." The heavy paper landed on the desk with little flourish considering the amount inked on it. "He assumed that would be enough, but said to let him know if you need more."

Several zeroes stared back at her. *Three hundred thousand dollars.* That was more than enough to fund her brother's education.

He's never coming back.

She refused to reach for the paper insult that rested between them, the proof that her father intended to buy his way out of the debt he'd labeled his children.

"Do you need ... anything else, Isadora?" Sawyer asked, deep voice soft.

There was no use pretending their situation was normal. It wasn't, and Sawyer knew that better than anyone after seeing the fallout of their father's humiliating affairs, which she believed drove their mother to an early grave.

She shut her eyes, fearful she might see pity in

his stare. It was no secret their father didn't love them enough to be there. His absence made it easy to give up and point the blame at her when anything went wrong at home.

But at the same time, his inadequacies made it imperative that *she* prove she and her siblings were deserving of love and fine without him. It was something of a daily objective.

Sawyer's question hung in the air like a sharp hook, piercing a veil worn thin with time and neglect. She needed so much, but certain things couldn't be secured with money.

Shaking her head, she gave a sardonic grin. "I suppose the next time I hear from him will be when Toni's tuition's due."

"I'm truly sorry he isn't here for you," Sawyer murmured, his watchful gaze showing genuine remorse.

She hated being the source of anyone's pity, but was too tired to hide her hurt. "He used to call first, discuss what would happen. Now, he's sending colleagues."

Though Sawyer was more than a colleague to their family, it was how their father saw him. Sawyer had been there for every birthday and major life event when their mother was alive, back when they still acknowledged such milestones. Now he was nothing more than her father's trusted partner, capable of accessing private funds and delivering certified checks—celebratory moments a thing of the past.

But Isadora never minded Sawyer's presence. Despite their lack of family gatherings, she still drew comfort from his experience and easy guidance whenever their paths crossed. In a way, she sometimes missed him, but only recognized the emotion when his familiar face appeared out of the blue on days like today. This was not the first time he'd been sent to tidy up some financial issue at her father's bidding.

"Thank you."

She was past feeling embarrassed by her father's actions. Sawyer didn't hold her accountable. As a matter of fact, he seemed to see her apart from Lucian and Toni altogether, as if she wasn't Christos's child as much as her younger siblings, when in truth, she'd been his child the longest.

Perhaps it was an age thing, being that she was the oldest. She wasn't sure when Sawyer stopped treating her like a child and started viewing her as an adult, but his recognition had a way of vindicating certain accomplishments others tended to overlook. He was always there to remind her she was doing a good job when she needed to hear it most.

Tipping his head, he gave her a knowing glance. "Do you think Lucian would have wanted him here?"

He knew her family's politics too well.

"No." Her response was succinct and indisputable.

Sawyer nodded, but she recognized disapproval in his eyes. Not for her or her siblings, but for their absentee father.

"He asked for a favor and I accepted. Next time I'll tell him he needs to—"

"It's fine."

Having Sawyer deliver money was probably better than having their father show up unannounced. They would be fine without him. She'd had an emotional day and was simply acting out. "Him being here would only disrupt things."

Sawyer's brow lowered with concern. "Are you sure? I won't offer my help anymore if it only causes more problems."

"You don't cause any problems, Sawyer. If anything you're always there to help us when we need anything. I'm sure it's better this way and I appreciate you dropping off the money."

Sighing, as if accepting he'd inadvertently walked into an ongoing family squabble, he said, "I think if you check that top drawer you'll find some fairly decent scotch. I could use a drink. How about you?"

Her gaze flashed to the empty drawer, heat burning her face. Sharp eyes as changing as the sky prompted her to slowly raise her hand, revealing the bottle. "I've already had some."

A deep chuckle crept from his throat, seeming

to ease the chill of the office and cast warmth into the dark shadows. "So you have. Do you have a glass?"

"There wasn't time," she joked.

He grinned and held out a hand. "May I?"

She hesitated only a moment before passing it over.

He eyed the label carefully, raising a brow in a show of appreciation. "I don't believe I've ever sipped twelve thousand dollar scotch from the bottle."

He tipped it back and took a slow pull. The shadow of stubble along his jaw and throat drew her attention as he swallowed. Dragging it slowly from his mouth, his tongue traced along his lower lip and he nodded.

"Still delicious."

As he slid the bottle across the desk, she glanced at his face, searching for disapproval. Seeing none, she wrapped her fingers over the glass surface, still warm from where his hand had been, and raised it in a silent toast.

This time, as the scotch slid down, there was little shock. She welcomed the slow burn and savored the rich, woodsy flavor. Sliding it back to him, she watched as he again admired the bottle.

"There are only four hundred and twenty some labels of this in existence."

He sipped slowly, easing back into the chair, and appearing completely at ease with his surroundings. She studied his hands, finding something appealing about the lack of youth in his knuckles, lightly scarred as if he hadn't always occupied a desk job. He had nice long fingers, lightly tanned with clean nails. Strong.

Her gaze lingered on his ring finger where a gold band used to rest. It had been some time since she saw that ring. His index finger twitched and her gaze jerked to his face, those sharp, raven brows arching in question.

Her heart skipped—clearly he'd caught her staring.

Searching for a distraction, she asked, "How do you know there are only four hundred and twenty bottles in existence?"

"If that." The side of his mouth lifted. "This is Lalique, bottled in 1910, designed by Rene Lalique." His inspection of the label was more nostalgic than technical. A slight smile curled his lips. "My father was a collector. I pilfered his stash often when I was a boy. Sometimes he overlooked the transgression and sometimes he didn't. Suffice it to say, the episode that followed my drinking his Macallan Lalique will be something burned into my brain until the day I die."

"You drank it?"

"All of it. And I didn't even appreciate its fineness. I was sick all night, flushing twelve grand of scotch down the drain."

She laughed. "So you didn't even keep it."

"Not for long."

"Well," she reached for the bottle. "I'll be sure to learn from your mistakes and appreciate my father's scotch, because I still intend to steal it. Restitution, if you will."

He gave her a full grin as she tipped back the bottle.

They continued drinking over the next hour, passing the emptying bottle back and forth until there was not a penny worth of liquor left. Of course, Sawyer was drinking two sips to her one, but he was a lot bigger.

The more she drank, the more her worries eased and a sense of repose claimed her. It was easy to overlook the shortcomings that usually haunted her every thought when her belly was full of hundred-year-old booze.

Removing the pearl studs from her earlobes, she dropped them beside the heavy letter opener emblazoned with their family initial. Her body seemed to sink into her father's chair as her head tilted on a soft cloud of alcohol induced contentment.

Sawyer studied her for a brief moment, but his attention no longer weighed as heavily. "It's a lot for you, isn't it?"

"What do you mean?"

"Taking care of your brother and sister."

Her lips molded into an affectionate smile. "They were too young to take care of themselves and my father can't be bothered. They deserve more than servants looking after them."

"Perhaps his heart couldn't take losing your mother."

"Perhaps."

As a widower, Sawyer would know more about that type of grief. But they both knew her father well enough to understand dismay probably wasn't the case here. Still, it was a nice idea.

"Will you continue to do it?"

"Do what? Take care of them?"

He shifted, his posture relaxing. "Lucian's an adult now. I have no doubt he'll be self-reliant. But Antoinette..."

"She has a long way to go." It didn't need saying that despite her sister's increasing age she still had a *lot* of maturing to do.

He nodded his agreement. "Do you plan to be there for her the way you were for Lucian?"

Isa nodded, not sparing the question the level of consideration others might. "Lucian only allowed me to do so much. He was already finding himself when our mother passed. Sometimes I think he should have been born first, but then I wonder if my father would have bothered to have daughters at all. You men certainly love your sons."

He smirked. "That we do. It's an arrogance that needs feeding." Steepling his fingers at his chin, he stared at her, his expression contemplative.

"What?"

He lifted a shoulder and dropped his hands. "I was just imagining... Daughters must be completely different. You hope a son will possess a fair amount of courage, confidence, and chivalry, but daughters..."

She hung on his words, waiting to hear how he'd describe daughters. "Daughters...?"

"They're fragile. Precious."

Yes, they were, but even glass could prove stronger than expected. "I wonder if Isabelle Romee would agree."

"Who's Isabelle Romee?"

She smirked. "A mother. Her daughter's name was Joan." She arched a brow. "Of Arc."

He chuckled. "Touché. Perhaps there's a reason I wasn't given daughters. I'd be a nervous wreck if I had to watch them run into war."

"Some queens have proven better rulers than kings in terms of war. And some men are more fragile than the most delicate woman."

Holding up his hands in mock surrender, he laughed. "I didn't realize you were hiding a little feminist inside. My apologies if I offended you."

"Oh, she's not little. She just appears that way next to so many large men." She reached for the bottle only to lift it and find it empty.

"Too many sons inheriting their fathers' arrogance, I suppose."

She considered his words, thought of *his* son, then realized her huge oversight. "Slade left today." Feeling like a thoughtless heel, she sat up. "Oh, Sawyer, I'm sorry. Here I am going on and on about my life when you sent your son off—"

He cut her apology short with a wave of his hand. "We men like our sons, but eighteen years with them is enough. I wished him luck, gave him some sage advice about condoms and cafeteria food, and he was as glad to be rid of me as I of him."

She laughed. "I suppose it's different for..."

"Mothers?"

"Women," she amended.

His gaze met hers and something shifted in the air. Perhaps it was the intimate knowledge of the circumstances they shared. Although her mother's memory wasn't one she hoped to replace, in another ten years she'd have accumulated more experience parenting than her actual parents could claim. But it still felt wrong calling herself a mother.

Isadora had yet to know what holding a baby in her womb felt like. The love, the worry, the secrets only a true mother could own. But perhaps someday...

"Chances are, Antoinette will regard you as her mother. You do everything a mother *and* a father typically do for their children."

"I suppose the unfortunate part of that is that she'll eventually forget our mom and I'll never get to just be her sister."

"You'll still get to be her sister. Give it time. Before you know it, she'll be a young woman, confiding in you, asking your advice, and perhaps giving you some of her own. When that friendship comes you can remind her what a great woman your mother was."

She tilted her head, his prediction stirring a deep craving for such a bond. "One can only imagine what sort of advice a girl like Toni might give in time." She laughed, trying to imagine her opinionated sister as a mature adult.

His regard suspended for a moment. "You call her Toni? I always assumed she went by Antoinette or Annie."

"My father calls her Annie. To the rest of us she's just Toni."

Silence fell, as if discussing her little sister somehow altered his train of thought. Did mentioning Toni remind him of her age as well? There was nothing inappropriate about their conversation, but maybe getting tipsy together in a dark room bordered on improper to him.

She hunted for something intriguing to say, anything to stifle the sense that they'd run out of topics to discuss. Her liquor soaked mind seemed to be dredging through a thick swamp in search of clever material. She had nothing.

He shifted and glanced at his watch. "I should go."

"Must you?"

His contemplative gaze collided with hers. There was something unnamable in his stare, something that hadn't been there before. Something she wasn't sure she wanted him to voice.

"Isa—"

"There's another bottle of scotch at the bar. If I drink it alone I could end up repeating your mistakes."

He grinned and settled himself back into the seat. "I can't let you do that, now, can I?"

Relieved, she rose to retrieve the other bottle, hoping it was indeed scotch. Part of her suspected he was drinking to spare her from alcohol poisoning. If she had finished the last bottle on her own she would've passed out—which was still an objective.

Searching the cabinet, she squinted through the shadows. "Glenfiddich. That's scotch, right?"

"A wonderful brand. What year?"

Breaking the wax seal, she opened the bottle and tipped it out of the shadows, hunting for numbers. Her eyes struggled to read the aged label in the poor lighting. There it was.

"Thirty-seven." While she was at the bar, she searched for two rocks glasses.

"Shit."

Confused by his whispered curse, she turned

and came up short. Sawyer had vacated his chair and moved right behind her. Sucking in a breath, she stared up at his bright eyes, the scent of his cologne permeating the drunken haze of her mind.

"Let me see that bottle, sweetheart."

Isadora stepped aside as he examined the bottle and cursed again. Her balance seemed off, but it hadn't been a second ago. Processing his words on a delay, she frowned. "What's the matter?"

He laughed and stared at the label, slowly shaking his head. "Son of a bitch. Your father sure is something else."

"Why?"

"This bottle, the thirty-seven, it's exquisitely rare. There are only a few left in existence. The last time someone auctioned a bottle it sold for something close to seventy-thousand dollars."

"For *one* bottle?"

"Yes. Let's hope it wasn't your father placing the bid."

She took the bottle out of his hands. Perhaps she was being petulant, or maybe the better word was drunk, but she couldn't muster a bit of concern for her father's spoiled collection. The seal was already broken anyway.

"Well, it's already opened, so there's no sense in wasting it." They had no choice but to drink it. All evidence must be destroyed. She generously filled two glasses and slid him one. "Cheers."

He eyed the scotch and then glanced at her as she patiently waited for him to meet her toast. "Isadora," he said slowly lowering his untouched glass to the bar. "Perhaps we should call it a night. It's getting late and Toni will likely be home soon—"

As if on cue, the front door opened and her sister's footsteps preceded the call of Shamus's voice. "Isa?"

She returned her glass to the bar next to his. "I only need to thank Shamus and send Toni to bed. Don't leave just yet."

He seemed ready to object, but she turned before he had the chance. Leaving the study door open a crack, she hustled down the hall and met her sister and Shamus in the foyer.

"Did you have fun?"

"We had so much fun!" Toni beamed. "Shamus ordered two banana splits made like flambé and they cooked the bananas right at the table with a blowtorch!"

"Wonderful!" She glanced at Shamus. "Do I owe you anything?"

"Knock it off. Besides, the moment Antoinette introduced herself there was no chance we were paying. We got the royal treatment."

"Thank you." Her hand brushed lovingly over his sleeve and he stilled, shooting her a peculiar look.

Easing close, laughter dancing in his eyes, he whispered, "Are you drunk, Isa?"

Her cheeks burned, though they already felt unusually warm. "I might have indulged in a nip or two."

He laughed. "I love it. Good for you." Directing their attention back to Toni, he said, "Okay, brat, I'm taking off. Why don't you head up to bed so your sister can enjoy the rest of her night off? Remember everything we talked about."

Rather than put up a fight like she usually would, Toni smiled and nodded obediently. "Goodnight, Isa." Her arms wrapped around Isadora's waist, startling her with the force of such a loving hug.

She glanced at Shamus in question, but he only winked. Her hand rested on Toni's hair. "Goodnight, baby."

Toni pivoted and lunged at Shamus, throwing her arms around him with enough force to make him grunt. "Goodnight, Shamus. Thanks for an awesome dinner!"

"Night, brat. Be good."

Toni made her way up the stairs and Isadora turned back to him. "What did you say to her?"

"Nothing you need to worry about. I just reminded her that not all sisters would give up so much for their younger siblings. I also might have promised her we could go out again if she stopped being so contrary every time you asked her to do something."

Impressed, Isadora grinned. "I'm amazed she listened to you. Toni doesn't listen to anyone."

"She's tough. I'll give you that much. But I remember how difficult I was at her age. Teenagers suck and she's going to be a challenging one. I figured, with Luche away, you could probably use a little ... assistance."

He was absolutely right, on all counts. "Well, thank you, Jamie. I really mean it."

He nodded. "Any time. I'll see you soon, I'm sure."

"Goodnight." She walked him to the door, smiling as his car pulled away.

Standing in the quiet foyer, she wondered why that moment seemed to carry more weight than so many others. Toni was quiet in her room, right where she was supposed to be. Lucian was likely unpacking the last of his belongings in his dorm— she hoped.

Switching off the front lights, she sighed, thinking she might actually get to bed before three in the morning tonight. The house was silent, she was feeling incredibly relaxed, and everything seemed just—*Sawyer!*

Spinning in the direction of the study, she hurried down the hall, hoping he hadn't slipped out the back door while she was preoccupied. Wow, she definitely had too much to drink. She almost forgot about him and went to bed! That would have been awful.

Drawing in a deep breath, she pressed into the study and was relieved to find him waiting on the settee, staring into an empty glass. Her excitement that he hadn't left was inexplicable. He was like a hidden present found under the tree, buried by crumpled paper after all the gifts were already opened.

His gaze lifted and settled on her as she lingered at the threshold, slightly short of breath.

"I'm back," she whispered.

"So you are," he said, his level stare seeming totally undistracted by anything else in the room.

Three

*"Life is a swift tumble through the clouds, too
fast to spend time searching for regrets or
chasing wrongs."*

~Lucian Patras

"SORRY ABOUT THAT," Isadora
apologized, stepping further into the room.

Sawyer's focus shifted, a troubled look flashing
in his eyes. His jacket now draped over the chair
he'd occupied earlier, but he looked as if he were
thinking of putting it back on. Maybe he was
mentally collecting his belongings before he made

another excuse to leave. She didn't want him to go —mostly because she didn't want to be alone.

"Toni's in bed," she informed, not sure why that information concerned him.

"Did they have a nice time?"

"Yes. Jamie's wonderful with her. He took her to Patras."

He nodded, but made no further comment.

Unsure what to make of the shift in energy, she collected her glass from the bar to buy time, but something was definitely different, and she didn't understand why.

"Is something wrong, Sawyer?"

His gaze followed her as she came to sit on the empty side of the settee. "When did you stop calling me Mr. Bishop?"

The soft, cajoling rumble of his voice was more soothing than probing. Voices like that could make audio instructions sound like Shakespeare.

Thinking over his question, her brow tightened. "I'm not sure. I suppose I was a teenager when you invited me to call you by your first name. Should I go back to calling you Mr. Bishop?" she teased. It seemed silly to think of him as anything other than Sawyer.

Turning his wrist, the ice in his glass shifted. "The boys ... they've been friends for a long time."

"And hopefully they will be forever."

"And I've been your father's friend for as long

as I can recall. He gave me a job when I was fresh out of college.”

“And now you run one of his companies. What is it you’re trying to say, Sawyer?”

“You’re very young, Isadora. Too young to have a boy in college and a ten-year-old in your care, but you do it with the maturity of an experienced woman.”

“Thank you, but Lucian’s my brother, not my son. And Toni… I may act like her mother, but I’m not. I take no joy in erasing our mother’s memory.”

He glanced at his empty glass, the filtered moonlight reflecting in the crystal as he placed it on the table. “I should go.”

Tipping her glass over his, she filled it with a finger of scotch. “Not before you finish your drink.”

Peering through thick, black lashes, he gave her a questioning look that made her feel immediately foolish. Why had she done that?

He twisted to face her. “What are you doing, Isadora?”

“I don’t know. I’ve had a lot to drink.” Her voice dropped to a rasp as her gaze latched onto his, holding so tight she could hardly spare a blink.

“Is that it then?”

Her lashes fluttered, breaking the spell, and she laughed nervously. Those eyes were hypnotic, especially when he looked directly into hers. She shook her head, shaking off the affect. "Is that what?"

Lifting his glass, he finished her offering in one swallow, placed the tumbler on the table, and stood. She rose as well, the camaraderie they'd shared earlier rapidly evaporating. Perhaps thirty-seven wasn't such a good year.

Tension closed in on her, its impending heaviness puncturing the inebriated haze cocooning her mind. The unfamiliar imbalance was more than the effect of alcohol. Maybe she was coming down with something.

She didn't want him to go and his proximity to the door filled her with panic and heat. *Stay*, she wanted to say, but something kept her quiet. She wanted him to make the decision without her prompting his response.

It became a game of guessing what he might do or say next and she liked the uncertainty, found it unsteadily thrilling. Her heart beat too fast as she tried to identify a time she'd ever felt so nervous in such a fulfilling way. She didn't typically favor anxiety, yet she coveted the feeling now, a dark anticipation for every motion, every word. So much to lose in such a simple decision, yet she hadn't a clue what she'd gain if he chose to stay.

"I apologize for intruding on your evening," he said, stepping around the table.

Her heart jerked. Her disappointment was a

physical jolt that convinced her something else was happening here—something she shouldn't feel.

She stepped around the other side of the coffee table and met him on the carpet, frantic to keep him there a while longer. She didn't want to be alone, but maybe he was feeling this strange energy too and figured it best to leave.

"Sawyer, what changed?"

"The fact that you don't know is a testament to your young age."

Affronted, she drew back. Perhaps she was a bad drunk, because his words hurt more than they probably should.

She wasn't an idiot and though she didn't have much experience with men like Sawyer—or any men for that matter—she wasn't a prude. Something changed between them tonight. A sort of chemistry had evolved.

She never felt this kind of attraction around him before and maybe he felt it too and that was why he was trying to escape. But she *was* drunk, so perhaps her perception was off.

Rather than further embarrass herself, she stepped aside. "I'm sorry if I did something to of-fend you."

Gah! She always said the worst things. What was she trying to get, a sympathy stay? That was not what she was after.

"You did nothing offensive. It's just ... not appropriate for me to be here—alone with you. It's late."

Embarrassed that her eagerness reeked of inexperience, she looked away. She shouldn't let him see her like this. She'd have to see him again and it was utterly humiliating to think he might assume she was some sad, desperate woman trying to seduce her father's colleague when she just wanted a little company. Oh, God, she *was* desperate.

Her gaze dropped to the carpet as a dark sense of inadequacy swallowed her. "I understand. I didn't mean to..." ...*whatever I've done.*

"Goodnight, Isadora."

She didn't look up to see if he was staring at her. She didn't need to. She could feel his stare measuring her. He hesitated as he approached the door.

"You'll call if you need anything?" he asked softly.

Never. "Of course."

With nothing more to say, he left, his leather-soled footfalls drifting almost silently as he made his way to the foyer.

Humiliated, she turned to the bar and lifted the expensive bottle. No matter how much her life resembled that of an adult, she never stopped feeling apart from the actual authority figures. A little girl with a license to leave the kiddie table for one meal before an early bedtime.

Rethinking the last couple hours and degrading herself for every unflattering impression she might have left, she wished desperately to erase the entire evening. She was not on his level and he saw her as his colleague's pathetic kid who was astoundingly short on friends.

Collecting the glasses filled with watered down ice, she decided not to return to her father's study anymore. Every time she left this room she felt like half a person—tonight more so than usual.

She dumped the ice in the sink at the wet bar and sat the glasses on the counter. "What a waste."

The door to the office creaked and she pivoted, gasping as she found him still there and staring at her from the threshold.

"My..." He shook his head, brow tense with lines of tension. "I forgot my jacket."

Her chest tightened as she blinked at him in question. His jacket was behind her, yet she lacked the will to move.

Was he really back for his jacket? Had he left it there on purpose? He watched her, keeping his distance, like she was some sort of black widow. She mentally laughed. She was about as threatening as a baby bunny.

Putting her back to the bar, she gave him room to get his belongings and go. Reaching past her, he slid the jacket off the back of the chair and stilled, close enough for her to see the contrast of silver threaded in the dark hair at his temples.

Her skin tingled as breath locked in her lungs,

his scent crawling into her. A million moments she *should* have had collided in her mind, borrowed memories from novels and cinematic romances and what she knew most girls experienced years before approaching her actual age.

His arm brushed the front of her blouse and his eyes shut on a whispered curse. Every breath she took tightened her clothing. She was winded, yet standing perfectly still.

"Tell me to go. Tell me to forget the jacket," he whispered, voice low as it scratched along her every tender nerve.

She said nothing and he let the jacket slide down the chair and onto the floor. She couldn't blink and she began to tremble subtly as he turned to fully face her, staring into her eyes.

Each inhalation lifted her breasts higher. Her lips parted, the scent of expensive scotch, rich cologne, and sin clouding her mind. She wasn't a small woman. Thin, yes, but too tall. Yet, looking up at him now, she found her height perfect, and his stature arrestingly right. Strong.

"Tell me to go, Isadora," he repeated, voice rasping in a way that prickled the back of her neck, seeming to lift the fine hairs along her collar.

There was something more than drunken secrets here. She edged closer, never one to act audaciously, but maybe this was the self-indulgent moment she'd been waiting for. Brazen seemed right.

Drawing in a shaky breath, she softly whispered, "I didn't want you to leave in the first place."

Uttering another curse, he reached for her so fast she took a startled step back, only to be blocked by the bar. His hand swept into her hair, fingers terrorizing her sensible bun, as he jerked her body to his on a gasp. His aggression was as unexpected as his intensity. The shocking press of his lips was a welcome delight. Warm. Unquestioning. Experienced.

His other hand surged low on her back, pulling her body flush to his as their heads tilted and his mouth opened against hers. Heat swirled low in her belly as her hands sought a place to rest.

A fever took hold, burning hot, as her knuckles flexed and her fingers dug into his broad shoulders. The distant thud of the bottle hitting the carpet only vaguely registered, as he spun her and backed her toward the desk.

His mouth opened wider, his tongue spearing between her lips, greedily taking as he dipped her over the surface, arching her backwards and exposing her neck. The five o'clock shadow covering his jaw scraped over her delicate skin, making her toes curl.

He lifted her and objects moved along the desk, the lamp light jostling in the shadows. Her knees drew up as a chair skidded out of the way.

He towered over her, kissing, licking, *biting*. And her body was on fire.

Objects clattered to the ground as his touch dragged up her leg, hiking her simple pencil skirt higher. The bunched material gave way, sliding as high as her hips when he fit his legs between hers.

The weight of his arousal pressed against her core. She gasped and everything stilled.

His heavy breathing mingled with hers as his stormy eyes flashed in the light shining from the desk lamp. She'd never been in such a tangle. They were so close it was difficult to determine whose parts were whose.

"Shit." He made to rise, but her grip on his shirt tightened. "Isadora," he rasped, almost pleadingly.

Hating the regret she recognized in his gaze, she almost let him go. Almost.

She could do this—*they* could do this. Who would know? They were both adults.

Lifting her head, she gently brushed her lips against his. Shockingly, it seemed enough to hold him there. His mouth tilted over hers, pulling, slowly taunting, until everything inside of her seemed to stretch like warm taffy and melt her body into his. The tension left his shoulders as his weight sank into her.

His hand followed the curve of her hip, tracing the nip of her waist and un-tucking her blouse one ripple of fabric at a time. His warm fingertips scorched the hidden skin of her belly, skimming over her ribs with practiced ease. Her body arched as the swell of her breast filled his palm and her lips parted on a sigh.

"We shouldn't do this," he whispered, his thumb tracing delicate swirls over the hardening tip of her nipple.

There was no way she was letting him leave now. The press of his arousal was leaving her panties slick and his hand was working some sort of magic under her blouse.

"Yell at me, Isadora. Tell me to stop, to take my hands off you."

"Stop fighting it, Sawyer." She loosened the top button of her blouse. And another. And then another.

He eased back as the silk parted. He looked at her as no man ever had. "Jesus. You're beautiful."

Blinking, he stood and gently pulled her with him. Leaving her shirt open she quickly straightened her skirt.

His attention drifted around the room and he grimaced. "Your bed—"

"Is upstairs. Too close to my sister's room. Here's fine."

His mouth pursed. He didn't seem pleased with the options.

Releasing her hand, he shut the door tightly and turned the antique key sitting in the lock.

Shoving the coffee table out of the way, he came back to her and glanced at the floor.

She didn't care where they were, so long as he kissed her some more. Nodding, she stepped closer to his front, eager to pick up where they'd left off.

With trembling fingers, she loosened the buttons of his vest. Though she struggled, he patiently allowed her the time she needed. Once she had the garment off his shoulders, she laughed. Another line of buttons awaited under his tie.

She'd never been so close to a man. Her breasts were throbbing, the heat coming from the strong wall of his chest the greatest sensation ever to touch her skin. Her fingers fumbled with the knot of his tie.

"Let me..."

But rather than open his shirt, he tucked her hands at her side and brushed a strand of hair from her cheek, removing the clip from her bun. His fingers sifted through the weight of her loose hair, spreading the long locks over her shoulders as he studied her face.

"You're so pretty, Isadora."

His words were disarming and strangely uncomfortable to hear. "I'm not—"

His sharp gaze silenced her. "Yes." Deft fingers slid her blouse off her shoulders, letting it fall to the floor. "You are."

She followed his gaze to the clasp at the front

of her lace bra, her heart trembling behind her ribs. He was still dressed and her breasts wore only a light layer of fabric.

"May I?"

Unsteady on her legs and throat too dry to talk, she nodded.

The lace tightened, plumping her breasts, then gave way. The garment slid down her arms, joining her shirt on the floor. Cool air closed around her, puckering her skin as he stepped back.

Shadows swallowed the stormy pupils of his irises as he stared at her—truly stared—like no man ever had. Something dark was born in that moment and she accepted that nothing, not jewels, not exotic furs nor luxurious gowns, *nothing* had ever felt as good as his stare on her skin.

With nimble dexterity, he removed his tie and unbuttoned his shirt, never taking his gaze off of her. Despite being a man in his early forties, his body was unquestionably appealing.

She drew in a shaky breath as the first patch of tanned flesh revealed a light dusting of dark hair over chiseled masculinity. The focus of his attention caused a tremble inside of her that rattled from her limbs all the way to her lips.

Swallowing hard, she took a step forward, her palm hovering just over his heart and slowly touching down. Heat. Virility. So much power rested inside of him.

His heart beat beneath her palm and she

glanced up at his face. She couldn't recall ever touching another person so intimately. "I can feel your heart racing."

He tipped her chin, brushing a gentle kiss over her lips and pulling her closer. The warmth of his hand closed over her breast, cupping, pulling, fingers gently pinching as her knees softened and she moaned against his lips.

"Your mouth is pure temptation," he whispered, the zipper at her hip loosening as her skirt slipped to the floor.

Kisses traveled to the corner of her lips, to her jaw, down the side of her throat as chills chased over every curve. Shivers skipped down her spine as he lifted her breasts, his lips closing over the tips and pulling tightly as she struggled to draw in enough air.

Her body came alive, thrumming with a desire for more. His arm banded around her, arching her backward as he lowered her to the carpet.

"Is this okay?"

The carpet was lush and cool against her back, but none of that mattered. As she looked up at him she realized how much trust lay between them. He wouldn't hurt her. On some level he cared about her, always acting so gentle and considerate of her feelings.

"This is perfect," she whispered.

It was like a dream, one she had no desire to wake from. Hair tousled, his head dipped to her throat, kissing and teasing, while his warm hands slowly caressed her curves. She had no idea how badly she needed this until it was actually happening, no idea how hungry her skin had been for any sort of affection.

A fire singed beneath her skin, sweeping through her with an intensity so strong she found herself clutching and pulling him closer. He subdued her excitement with gentle touches, tamed the burn into something slow and decadent.

The delicate silk at her hips pulled away as his fingers stroked between her thighs. Soft, wet heat waited within her folds. The first caress of his fingers over her sex had her gasping, nervous and excited for what might come.

"So soft..." He parted her tender folds and gently probed her slick flesh. Deeper and deeper he pressed until she wasn't sure if she should cry in pleasure or beg for more.

His mouth left her breasts and traveled lower. He slowly kissed down her belly. Her hands fumbled over their discarded clothing until her fingers sifted through his silken hair. She arched sharply as his tongue licked a straight line to the sensitive peak of her sex.

"*Ah*..." The pleasure was so acute she feared she might break from the inside out.

Her hands tightened, as did his lips. Fingers probing deeply, he licked and kissed as her body throbbed with awareness.

Her blood pumped, thick and hot through her veins, as if traveling toward something magnificent. Tighter, sharper, the pleasure built until control slipped away and she cried out in a rush of frenzied ecstasy.

Her body quaked under a cool dew of perspiration and desire. The whisper of his clothing hardly registered as her thoughts floated outside themselves, drifting softly back into her bones like a feather falling to a pond, sending slight ripples of sensation to all her edges in a gentle tickle.

Strong hands adjusted her limbs as Sawyer rose above her. The press of coarse hair along her thighs caused her eyes to open.

"You're ready, bella," he whispered, tenderness banked in his stark blue eyes.

Drawing in a steadying breath, she nodded, her body opening to him. His shoulders lifted as his strong arms supported his weight. In a moment of panic, her mind seized, her sex tightening before he could enter.

"What is it? Do you want to stop?"

Her heart raced. "No." She shook her head. "I'm just ... nervous."

"We can stop—"

"No, I want this." This was her moment, her opportunity to do something indulgent for herself and she couldn't imagine sharing it with anyone other than him. "I want this with you."

"Okay, bella." He leaned down, his lips

chasing up her neck, his fingers softly combing through her hair. "Relax a little."

Her body calmed, her palms resting on his broad shoulders, and her knees opening to make room for his hips. Gradually entering her with slow advances, her spine stretched to accommodate his girth.

He peppered her throat with kisses as his breathing quickened. "That's it, bella."

She blinked up at him, assured by his steady gaze borne of tenderness. Those eyes were the most adoring pair to ever set on her. They promised secrets would be kept and—perhaps only in her fanciful heart—that she might never be alone again.

He thrust deep and pulled her body against his, his mouth finding hers as he held her with loving hands. The initial sharpness of pain was curbed by the tender way he took her mouth. Perfect. And seconds later she was lost in a whirlwind of pleasure.

"You feel incredible, bella."

She loved that he already had a special name for her, one only she would know. "So do you."

It was the most intimate moment of her life. He was claiming parts of her—personal, secret parts—and nothing had ever felt as good as his possession.

His rhythm built, but he paced himself. Steady, deep motions rocked her. Their bodies clung to each other, flesh slick, her pulse fluttering until there came another moment of rapture. Her muscles tightened around him and he groaned, pressing his chest to hers, losing himself right in her arms.

She'd never seen a man so unveiled or imagined anything remotely close. Such fleeting vulnerability mixed with a flash of innocence as he finished, some unnamable glimpse of fragility that matched her own. Elusive, but there, letting her know he needed this as much as she did.

Panting, he lowered his head to her shoulder. Her hand ghosted over the back of his silky hair, cradling him.

"I've got you," she whispered, unsure where the words came from, but feeling like his equal, now more than ever.

He shivered and pressed a kiss to her neck, as he lingered inside of her. "My God, Isadora. It should be illegal for anything to feel so good."

She laughed, glad to know she'd done okay for her first time.

Slowly, he eased off of her. Her body protested his withdrawal as an unfamiliar soreness awakened inside of her.

Sawyer stilled and silently cursed. "It seems I need to take my own advice. Please tell me you're on birth control."

Of course she wasn't. She'd lectured Lucian plenty of times about being responsible, which made it all the more mortifying that she'd been so careless. Not wanting to lie, she simply said, "Don't worry."

He sighed with notable relief then looked around the room. Rising, he walked—*stark naked* —to the bar and poured water over a linen napkin. The moment he turned and caught her staring, her blush spread across her entire body.

Grinning with male arrogance, he shamelessly sauntered back to her, completely undaunted by his nudity or hers. She frowned as he nudged her knees apart.

"Let me," he said softly, pressing the cloth between her thighs. His brow pinched. "There's a little—" His frown deepened and she pressed her thighs together, but he held her knee still. His expression blanked as he met her gaze. "Jesus. Was this your first time?"

Her cheeks burned. Enough. Brushing his hand away, she closed her legs, but held his stare, unsure if he was more shocked by her age or her virtue. Either way she refused to justify something as silly as virginity. It was what it was.

"Does that bother you?"

He looked away, brow still tight. "Why didn't you say something?"

She laughed. "What would I have said?"

"That you were a *virgin.*"

There was no censure in his tone, but she sensed his immediate regret. No way would she let him take something so lovely and paint it in some shameful light.

"And then what, Sawyer? Would you have taken the authoritative position and decided for me? It makes no difference."

"It makes a *big* difference, Isadora."

"Why?" She was an adult for God's sake. At this point, her virginity was more of an embarrassment than anything else. She was glad to have it gone.

"Your first time should be special." He appeared frustrated, but his voice remained low, his tone not exactly gentle.

She sat up, refusing to let him ruin this for her. "It *was* special." Pulling her shirt to her chest, she confessed the truth. "I have no regrets."

He shook his head. "Would you tell me if you did?"

"Have I given you a reason to doubt my honesty?"

Lines of tension bracketed his mouth. "No."

They awkwardly sat in the shadows as her body cooled and shivered. "What now?"

"You're cold. Let's get dressed then we'll decide what happens next."

Though he helped her up, his eyes remained cast toward the floor, somehow filling her with uncertainty and additional disdain for her sheltered life. No matter how much she didn't want the loss of her virginity to ruin this moment, it seemed like it was going to anyway.

Chapter 4

THE EVENTS of the last hour settled over her like a cool wind creeping in after a hot summer rain. Her fingers shook as she managed to lift the zipper of her skirt. Buttoning her blouse was not as simple.

"Allow me," Sawyer's gravelly voice spoke softly behind her as the heat of his tall body seeped through the thin material covering her shoulders.

With choppy breaths, she lowered her hands and turned to face him. Sliding each little button through its hole, his gaze remained focused on the task. His fingers gathered her long hair and lifted it over one shoulder, as he pressed a kiss to her neck —apparently over his regret.

"Your pulse is racing."

Maybe she should have another drink. Her gaze skated to the bottle of scotch on the floor, thousands of dollars seeping into the priceless Oriental carpet. No, she'd definitely had enough to drink.

Taking her hand, he guided her to the small settee, righting the coffee table on his way. As they sat, she smothered the urge to fidget, and folded her palms neatly on her lap, waiting for him to make whatever silly apology he felt she was due.

"You're quiet," he announced.

"I'm not sure what people say in situations like this."

"This was your first time."

It wasn't a question, so she didn't answer.

With a delicate touch, he raised her chin until their gazes met. "Isadora?"

Why was he so hung up on this? It wasn't like she was a teenager. Most girls lost their virginity around sixteen. "I told you it was."

"But you're twenty-three."

"And while my friends were dating I was mourning my mother and waiting for my dad to step in so I could be a kid again. You know how that ended."

Those sharp aristocratic eyes stared into her

and he sighed. "There are twenty years between us —practically another lifetime, by your age."

She supposed forty-three wasn't *too* much older. His features were young and their polite friendship was several years old. Time had marked his face, leaving soft lines around his temples and mouth, but there was nothing haggard or tired in his visage. He was a good-looking man—distinguished by age, not diminished.

Sawyer was old*er,* not *old.*

Above all, she trusted him. "Your age doesn't bother me."

"Your father's been a friend of mine since I was a young man, Isadora. He trusts me to look out for you while he's ... away."

"I know."

Although her father treated him as his protégé, entrusting him with personal matters he wouldn't typically trust to anyone but himself, they weren't necessarily close friends anymore. But Sawyer relied on her father and that might be what his concerns were about.

Without her dad, the Bishops never would have become what they were today. Sawyer was now an active partner at Leningrad, one of her father's many companies. But Leningrad was Sawyer's *only* company. Was he worried about his job security?

There was more than just a business association between the Patras and Bishop names. Their families shared a trust generations old. Lucian and Slade were best friends. The Bishops were always popping up at social events. There was no reason to assume relationships like that could be jeopardized by what they'd done here tonight.

He was being paranoid. She didn't see why they were even discussing her dad. They knew each other well enough to leave her father out of this conversation.

"Why even bring my father up?" she asked. "This doesn't concern him."

"He would kill me if he knew what happened here." There wasn't fear in his voice, only absolute certainty.

Isadora found it difficult to imagine her father conjuring any level of passion on her behalf. Part of her wished he'd find out, just to see if he would react. But a bigger part, a lonely part, didn't want him or anyone to know, sure that if people found out they'd somehow spoil everything.

If their association remained a secret it had a greater chance of continuing—unpolluted by outsider's unwanted opinions. That was what she wanted. This was her chance to do something solely for herself, something no one else could touch. "So we won't tell him."

His smile was sad. "If something has to be kept a secret it's something you shouldn't have."

His gaze turned to her hands and he closed his fingers over hers. Though his touch was meant to comfort, there was an implication in the gesture she didn't like, a level of apology she wasn't ready to accept.

"We can't do this again, Isadora. It's not right."

Tightness formed in her chest as her mouth hardened. "Why?"

"Because people *will* eventually find out and I don't ever want to cause you regret. *Plus*, you're young, bella. You have your whole life ahead of you. Tying yourself to an older man isn't right. It would be wrong for me to distract you from all the things you should be doing."

Things she didn't do. Things she had no time or experience doing. "I don't mind."

"You should. You're a beautiful young woman. I'd be taking advantage of you. I can't let that happen."

"You're not. You didn't." Who was to say that they couldn't make this work? Maybe he was exactly who she'd been waiting for. "You haven't even given this a chance."

His gaze remained apologetic. "I lost my wife when Slade was only five. She was the love of my life and I don't want to love someone like that ever again. I had my time and you'll have yours—when you meet the *right* man. But I'll never be that man for you, Isadora, and you don't want me to take his place in your life."

Discarding all his talk about destiny and some

soulmate she might someday crash into out of nowhere, she only listened to his proclamations about his deceased wife. Even if she had covered her ears, the love he still held for Chelsea was evident. It was written in his eyes and in the turned down corners of his mouth.

Her chest tightened as something akin to jealousy coiled in her belly. Perhaps it was envy. What must it feel like to have such loyal love from a man like Sawyer Bishop?

She recalled a time shortly after Chelsea passed away. Slade had slept over at their house the night of the funeral, though he didn't say much. The following day, when Sawyer came to pick him up, Isadora watched from the steps. She'd been about Toni's age and unable to comprehend what could make a man look so devastated.

Love.

She'd never been in love and she didn't believe anyone had ever *loved* her. Her mother had loved her, of course, but that was different. Toni loved her—in a different way. Lucian... There was so much she didn't understand about her brother, or men for that matter. Despite always having a firm grasp on reality, love was a foreign concept. Yet she wanted it as much as any other woman.

She didn't need to take anyone's place. If her situation changed she'd adapt, but right now she wanted *him*—regardless of his warnings. Who could say if stronger emotions would develop? She was only thinking about the present. *He* was the one who brought up all this love talk.

"I don't expect you to *love* me, Sawyer."

Yes, that sounded mature, something a woman of the world might say. And, sadly, it was true. She didn't *expect* him to love her. But, oh, she *hoped* someone would eventually love her.

"But you deserve love, Isadora. Someday, you'll want your own family. I could never offer such things—not to you or anyone. This ... would be a distraction. You'd be missing out on better opportunities."

He was acting like one night had to decide the rest of their lives. How could anyone make such commitments after sleeping together once?

Maybe she did want a family of her own. She was so busy raising her brother and sister she never gave the subject much thought. But what if by the time Toni was an adult Isadora was too burnt out to do it all over again? Then they would've missed out on whatever this could have been because of some shortsighted assumption. It was simply impossible to see that far into the future.

"I'm not sure that's what I want," she confessed. And that was the truth.

Her life was too complicated right now to think that far ahead. Her plate was full and her appetite wasn't complicated. What she and Sawyer could possibly share seemed the perfect portion for her life at the moment.

"Isadora, you have to recognize that children of your own are likely in your future. There's a maternal grace about you that many women work their entire lives to achieve."

His words were flattering, but also frustrating. It seemed like she was being punished for doing the right thing. When she thought of motherhood she thought of her mother, alone, tired, always begging for her father's attention and never receiving it. A bird lost in a great big sky—alone.

Motherhood, as she saw it, was a lonesome labor of love. Sisterhood was satisfying, but her own experiences muddled that, too. She initially wanted kids, but then she unofficially adopted her siblings. And somehow that good deed was being punished by Sawyer dumping her after two hours. That had to be some sort of a record.

Her temples pounded with pressure. This was not the night to make big decisions. Her sex-addled brain was diluted in scotch and now she felt like kicking something.

The truth was, it didn't matter whether she wanted children someday or not. All the wanting in the world wouldn't make that happen for her without a man—or some decent sperm donors at least. *Always an option...*

Once again, she felt trapped, cornered by the bigger players of the world. This was always the way of things. She was living her life here in this house, doing everything a good sister would do, but it was never her turn to choose the next move. Everything seemed out of reach and she wasn't sure how or if that might change.

Toni wouldn't be an adult for eight more years. By then she'd be thirty-one. Women of her social status typically married in their early twenties. She couldn't imagine falling in love that late in life, taking the time to get married, and then the additional time it would take to start a family. She'd be forty-something by the time she got her romantic life in order.

And if she couldn't imagine falling in love in her thirties and going through all those relationship stages, it seemed perfectly rational to accept Sawyer not falling in love in his forties.

This was her best option. Yet. So far. Maybe ever.

"I don't need you to love me," she explained honestly, her hand closing over his.

She only wanted to see him again, have him the way she had tonight so he could ease some of her loneliness, but she also didn't want to beg. She was simply offering.

There was nothing wrong with a woman seeing that her physical and emotional needs were occasionally met. If they moved forward with open eyes and called their relationship exactly what it was then there would be no misunderstandings or misconceptions about the future. She was pretty sure adults did this sort of thing all the time—consensual affairs with no strings attached.

She continued to push her position. "I don't want to pretend this never happened, Sawyer. I'm glad it did. I needed this more than you probably realize, but I think you needed it just as much. Let's not cut it down before it has a chance to bloom."

"Sweetheart," he said slowly, his gaze troubled. "We can't have a normal relationship. Not a long term one or even a fleeting one. There's a lot at stake here that we have to consider. Those aren't just words. And I'm not going to change my position. Another night would be misleading."

Ignoring the sense that her worth might have just been cheapened, she focused only on the things that made her feel valuable. "I didn't ask for your future or a commitment. I'm merely suggesting that you not remove the possibility of us ... meeting again. I'm not a little girl, Sawyer, and I'm not going to make this into something it's not. "

His fingers ghosted over her jaw as he studied her, eyes appraising. "You say that now but..."

Her soft laughter was devoid of cheer. "Don't expect too much, Sawyer." How come men were never short on self-worth? "My life's here, with Toni. Sometimes I don't even have time for myself. I'm not a high maintenance person and I never expect anyone else to answer for my own actions. I've also become quite competent at relying on myself."

"I know that and I'd love to be with you again, bella, but I don't want to hurt you."

"*I'm* responsible for me."

He studied her for several silent seconds. "This is really what you want? You'd be able to live with my conditions?"

"I think it would be nice if you visited again, like this, nothing more. If my feelings on the subject change, you'll be the first to know."

As his eyes shifted she sensed his mind working, though he remained silent for a moment. "I hate having to ask you this, but—"

"I wouldn't tell anyone," she assured, saving him the discomfort of asking. "It can be our secret, no one's business but ours."

"That should bother you."

Perhaps over time it would, but there were no rules saying she couldn't walk away. All she knew was that she wanted him. Tonight he'd shown her sides of herself she'd never expected, sides that were exclusively hers and no one else's.

It was the first selfish thing she'd done for herself in—she couldn't remember a time she'd last done something only to serve *her* needs and no one else's. And with her limited experience, it was probably wise to practice with a man like Sawyer. They could explore. Then if she did move on, she wouldn't be a bumbling idiot with the next guy.

And if no one knew what they were doing, no one could judge her for experimenting with a man twice her age. But the age thing really was a non-issue.

Meeting his gaze, she gave him a confident smile. "Discretion doesn't bother me." In a way, she favored it, and in this case it suited them.

Tracing a gentle finger along her jaw, he looked into her eyes and brushed his mouth over hers. Warm fingers swept under her hair, holding her to him as he deepened the kiss.

Her body awoke with the now familiar twinges of desire, longing rekindling inside of her. He pulled her over his legs and she giggled, feeling awkward yet delicate on his lap, and giddy that he was no longer trying to push her away.

As his hand gripped her hip, massaging firmly, the press of his arousal surprised her and she broke the kiss, staring down at where their bodies touched.

"Ignore it," he said, pulling her mouth back to his.

But she couldn't ignore it. When his fingers flexed into her hips, a sensual, almost feline part of her came alive, begging to be touched, greedy for every caress. As much as she respected his desire to do the right thing, she was determined to prove she was not a little girl needing to be coddled. She was a grown woman who could decide for herself.

It didn't take much to convince him once her

hands were under his clothes, yet he never truly surrendered his control. The urgent need to touch him was bolstered by familiarity, but every time she rushed to expose his skin, he slowed her motions.

Capturing her wrists, he brought her fingers to his lips and kissed them gently. "Slow, bella. Feel."

She had absolutely no reservations about sex. And while she had no grounds for comparison, she believed Sawyer was an excellent lover.

It seemed this time he intended to make it meaningful. He lifted her and turned her to her back, cupping her face as he slowly fed his length into her, his stare penetrating any shield that lie between them. There was a level of intimacy so intense she sometimes needed to close her eyes, but Sawyer was inescapable.

He was everywhere, in the air she breathed, on her lips, against her chest, deep in her body. She loved it.

Every time he touched her she desired more, became less inhibited, and caressed his body as brazenly as he explored hers. The longer she tasted and teased the more he unveiled. And then he was the one shutting his eyes and she saw the raw, exposed intimacy for all that it was. Making love.

Watching him lose himself in that moment of completion was perhaps her favorite part. Seeing him so vulnerable and open had an empowering affect. To think, she—an inexperienced woman—could draw that response from a man like Sawyer Bishop. Yes, she liked sex very much.

"That wasn't supposed to happen again," Sawyer murmured, bare limbs tangled with hers as they slowly caught their breath.

Isadora giggled, feeling quite daring. Men thought they knew everything. He seemed pretty happy with her decision—despite his earlier objections. And regardless of what was *supposed to happen*, she was more than certain this wouldn't be the last time they made love.

She snuggled into his side and kissed his chest. "Maybe next time we can use a bed. I think you gave me rug burn."

His laugh was gruff, his lips teasing over her bare shoulder. "We definitely need to find a bed."

The side of her mouth pulled into a smirk. Yes, they would definitely be doing this again.

Chapter 5

> *"Heart, we will forget him,*
> *You and I, tonight!*
> *You must forget the warmth he gave,*
> *And I will forget the light.*
> *When you have done pray tell me,*
> *Then I, my thoughts, will dim."*

Emily Dickenson
Heart, We Will Forget Him

AS THE DAYS passed there was little word from Lucian and even less from Sawyer. The more time that went by the harder it became not to pick up the phone and ask what was going on, but she'd made it clear to Sawyer she wouldn't treat this like a traditional relationship and she needed to keep her actions as low maintenance as possible. That meant she couldn't appear needy in any way.

Unsure how affairs worked, Isadora adapted her expectations on a regular basis. It was easy to get upset when he didn't call, but no amount of longing made her phone ring or gave her the courage to contact him. So she did her best to occupy her free time with other things.

Toni had started sixth grade and they spent a lot of time shopping for the school year. If anything, her sister's temperament could be subdued with a new wardrobe. It was a decent excuse for retail therapy. Isadora only wished Toni found equal excitement in her books and school supplies.

By mid-September Isadora understood a new level of parenthood. Though Toni was young, her classmates were not. Her sister seemed to be hitting the tedious tween stage a lot faster than Lucian had.

Hoping to get to know some of these new middle school players in her sister's life, Isadora agreed to let Toni have a sleepover with three friends. She didn't anticipate the level of privacy eleven and twelve-year-olds could demand.

Isadora found herself lingering outside the den where they shut the doors. The boisterous giggles and whispered confessions had her longing for a part of her childhood she'd somehow misplaced. She'd been in eighth grade when their mother first became sick and that time of her life would forever be shrouded in grief and confusion.

After endless nagging and getting the permission of the other girls' parents, she allowed them to watch a PG-13 movie. Eventually the girls passed out like puppies on a stack of pillows and blankets on the floor. Isadora locked up the house and made her way to bed, no more familiar with her houseguests than she was when they arrived several hours earlier.

She had to be cooler than the other moms. She was a sister, not a mom. She was in her early twenties. Somehow these facts didn't translate to Toni and her friends the way Isadora had hoped.

As she lay in the darkness, her mind turned over mundane thoughts, but always pulled back to Sawyer. She wondered if she'd embellished her memories, painted a fairytale that could never match the reality.

It seemed her imagination was the only guarantee she could count on. Picturing his dark hair, she shut her eyes and pressed a lock of her own between her fingertips.

Her mind worked hard to conjure the exact scent of his cologne. Sliding her panties down her legs, she slowly drew circles on her torso, her touch traveling lower with each pictured detail of him.

Every time she touched herself like this it became a game to recall as many characteristics as possible. When her fingers finally reached between her thighs she was soaking wet.

Her body arched, driving the fantasy into darker territories that had nothing to do with her time with Sawyer. Sometimes she surprised herself with how erotic her fantasies could get. Other times she struggled to reach completion, too irritated by her lackluster reality to feel much of anything.

As her hand worked between her thighs, her teeth bit into her lower lip, stifling her moans. Stroking faster, deeper, she arched against the bedding, yearning for the exact moment she tipped into ecstasy.

"Sawyer," she rasped, sliding her fingers over tender flesh. "Yes…"

Her toes pointed and her heart raced. Tiny shivers chased over her exposed skin as a delicate tremble spread through her middle. It was a small victory, but still a victory. Knowing that she could do such things for herself was the only consolation she had in a reality where the guy never called.

Letting her limbs fall flat on the bed, she sighed and stared into the shadows. He'd better call soon or she'd never be able to look him in the eye again.

But time carried on with no sign of him. She felt foolish for harboring hope. Perhaps this was not an affair at all, but a one-night stand. Maybe the second time they had made love truly was an accident, a mistake he honestly didn't want to repeat.

The thought that she might have pushed him cheapened the memory, making it something tawdry, steeped in expensive scotch and desperation. She blamed herself for getting into this mess, but she also blamed him, because what hurt most was the shame—shame that hadn't existed until he refused to contact her.

She'd gone to her doctor and requested a prescription for birth control, relieved that her cycle hadn't been interrupted by a night that apparently meant nothing. But every morning she swallowed that silly pill she felt more ridiculous than the day before. By Halloween she was certain the birth control was unnecessary.

Sawyer had always been a quiet constant in their lives. His continued absence spoke of more than busyness. It reeked of avoidance. She should have run into him by now. She wasn't sure what was worse, the fact that she thought about him all the time or the worry that he might never think about her at all.

She occupied herself with plans for the holidays. Lucian would be returning for Thanksgiving and she decided to host a feast fit for kings. She never prepared a turkey before, but the kitchen staff was more than helpful. She suspected they would've preferred to do the job themselves, but she was determined to have a holiday like ordinary people, one made from love and recipes found online.

Isadora wasn't prepared for the changes in her brother. Though he'd only been gone a short time, she expected the same person to return. The man who walked through the door on the eve of Thanksgiving was not the boy she watched drive away last August.

Though it pained her to see him grow up so fast, it also filled her with immeasurable pride. Even his clothing seemed more mature.

Toni was thrilled to have their brother home again and it pleased Isadora very much that Lucian appeared equally thrilled to see his little sister. Not only was he attentive to Toni's prattling tales, he appeared genuinely interested in her middle school drama, teasing her that if any boys dared to kiss his baby sister he'd cut out their tongues.

This confused Toni, who had yet to discover what a tongue might have to do with kissing.

As Isadora peeled the sweet potatoes for tomorrow, Toni disappeared with the phone. Lucian turned to her and grinned. "She's growing up too fast."

"The same could be said for you."

He didn't acknowledge her indisputable observation. "Soon she'll be able to stay home by herself."

"I don't see why that's important. There's always someone here."

"Exactly."

She frowned at him. "What are you trying to say, Lucian?"

He shrugged. "Just pointing out that you aren't chained to the house. You could make time for yourself."

She rolled her eyes. "I have all the time I need."

"Really? When's the last time you went on a date?"

She laughed at the idea. "I don't date."

"I know. I'm suggesting you start."

Holding the peeler in her fist, she lowered her hand to the counter and twisted her lips. "And how am I supposed to do that? Go sit at a bar and wait for some stranger to approach? Or perhaps I could just introduce myself then have the luxury of swatting away all the gold digging letches who care nothing about me and everything about Daddy's legacy and the doors his name can open."

"I'm just saying you should get out there."

"And what about you? Are you *getting out there*?"

"I'm not short on company, but I'm too ambitious to tie myself down."

That he certainly was. "And I'm not ambitious?"

He shrugged. "Are you? What do you want? I want to see you happy."

Why did she feel like the child here? "I am happy. I appreciate you checking up on my social life, Lucian, but I assure you I'm fine with the way things are." *Sort of.*

He opened his mouth to argue, but paused when a voice called from the foyer.

"Anybody home?"

Toni's shout echoed through the house. "Shamus!"

Isadora returned to peeling potatoes as Shamus walked in with Toni at his heels. Lucian greeted him and her hands slipped when she heard another familiar voice.

Ignoring the slice she'd nicked out of her thumb, she drew in a staggering breath only to be swathed in disappointment as a younger version of Sawyer entered the kitchen.

Piercing blue eyes met hers. "Happy Thanksgiving, Isa."

Covering her frustration and giving herself a quick reality check, she smiled and wrapped a paper towel around her bleeding thumb. "Happy Thanksgiving, Slade. You too, Shamus."

"What are we making?" Shamus asked, sidling behind the island and lifting the various foil coverings off the dishes set along the counter.

She offered a description of the menu and then they fell into small talk. There was something magical about the way the three boys laughed, sharing years of inside jokes and unguarded ease with one another.

When Slade bumped Lucian's shoulder with his and gave his head a shove, she suffered a pinch of envy. Her brother rarely let people get that close to him, yet these boys managed to break down his walls.

"How's your father, Slade?" The words left her mouth before she had the chance to consider if that was a strange question for her to ask.

"He's good. I worry about him being all alone in the house now that I'm away, but he says he's glad to have me gone." There was laughter in his eyes, eyes so familiar in shape and shade.

"What are you two doing for Thanksgiving?"

"Same as we always do, heading into the city for dinner. Then I'll probably go out with the guys and he'll likely go home to watch reruns of *NCIS*."

"You should come here for dinner."

Lucian turned, his dark eyes questioning, but not really suspicious.

Trying to sound casual, she explained, "I don't see why the two of you should have to travel all the way to the city to eat in some restaurant when we have plenty of room at our table."

"Thanks. I'll run it by him and see what he says."

The conversation shifted, her presence already forgotten as they moved on to plans for the current evening. Isadora wanted to remind Slade to be sure he asked Sawyer about dinner tomorrow, but that seemed pushy and might draw suspicions. For the rest of the night she obsessed over the possibility of seeing him again.

After only a few hours of sleep, she found herself back in the kitchen, preheating the oven and readying the bird. While it was her goal to have a nice home cooked meal for her family, it now became imperative that everything be perfect.

As she bathed and dressed two things became clear. If Sawyer showed up he might not touch her. She accepted that and would make do, because the other possibility was that he wouldn't come at all and her disappointment would be enough to spoil the entire holiday.

By two o'clock the table was dressed. Toni continued to walk around the house on the phone, telling redundant stories to anyone who would listen about how immature a boy in her class was.

Lucian appeared in the dining room and gave a slow whistle as he spotted the table. "Wow, I didn't know you had this sort of domestication in you, Isa."

"Does it look all right? It's not too much?" She fussed with the napkin rings that she'd crafted out of hot glue and silk foliage.

"Yeah, it looks great. But why all the fuss? It's just us."

She stilled, a painful ache forming in her belly. "Are Slade and his father not coming?"

"I don't know. He probably forgot to ask."

"Why don't you call them?"

"I would, but Toni has the phone attached to her head."

Uncharacteristically frazzled, she went to the door and saw her sister plopped on a chair in the library on the other side of the foyer. "Toni, get off the phone. It's Thanksgiving and you've been at it all morning. Give it a rest and go get dressed for dinner."

She scoffed. "It's only two o'clock and what's wrong with what I'm wearing?"

"It's a holiday. You should look nice."

Her sister frowned and continued her conversation, making some snide comment about nagging grown-ups not understanding today's fashion.

Returning to the dining room table, Isadora brushed a hand over her brow, startled to find it slightly damp.

"Hey, Isa, take a breath," Lucian said, noting her fatigue. "Everything looks great. Sit down and relax."

But she couldn't relax. Once she'd extended the invitation to the Bishops everything seemed so much more important. She'd waited three months to hear from Sawyer without a word. And now, with the boys home from college, she had an excuse to see him again and was determined to get an explanation for his absence.

She wasn't sure what she wanted more, to see him or to hear why he hadn't called. The fading chance to have either undermined every bit of calm she'd established over the past twelve weeks.

Turning back to the library, she snapped, "Toni, hang up the phone!" She faced her brother. "I'm going upstairs for a few minutes. Find out if they're coming, because if not I have too many plates on the table."

Leaving him with a confused expression she retreated to her bedroom, shutting the door firmly behind her. Her eyes closed as she fought for equilibrium. What the heck was wrong with her? She was waspish and emotional, and behaving nothing like herself.

Sitting on her bed, she stared at the carpet, waiting for the tension in her shoulders to ease. It seemed even the deepest breath couldn't penetrate the barrier between her common sense and her anxiety.

It aggravated her that a man could make her so unbalanced. She'd been fine, accepting that he wasn't going to call until she saw Slade and found out Sawyer was doing nothing more than sitting home every night watching reruns. Now her little crush—or whatever this was—had bubbled up and erupted out of control. She had to do something about it, but she couldn't do *anything* until she was able to look him in the eye and demand an explanation.

She deserved *something*. Her aggravation only multiplied when she admitted Sawyer wasn't just any man, but a man she'd known her entire life. A man she trusted. A man who didn't have the courtesy to call!

Enough was enough. Sawyer needed to come to dinner. She needed to see him again so she could understand what the heck was going on. If he came and nothing happened then that would be the end. She would not pine her days away for a man who didn't want her. She was not her mother.

And if he didn't come... Once the boys were back at school she would drive to his house and confront him. He might be a coward, but she'd be damned if she'd scare so easily. *Ridiculous!*

Once she composed herself, she returned downstairs. Toni was wearing a dress Isadora couldn't discern the color of, but it looked nicer than what she'd had on before. Lucian was watching television.

"Did you call?" she asked, as she nosed through the bar for a complimentary bottle of wine.

"Yes. I told them four o'clock. Is that good?"

She turned, her breath suddenly reaching her lungs. "They're coming?"

Lucian nodded. "That's what you wanted, I thought."

"Yes. Yes, that's good. Four o'clock will be fine."

Over the next hour, she dressed the hors d'oeuvre platters with centerfold worthy garnish and set the sides in the spare oven to keep warm. The doorbell rang at precisely four o'clock and her mind scrambled.

Removing her apron, she checked her reflection in the window and adjusted the straps of her bra. She'd worn a dark sheath dress with a pale cardigan. Out of necessity, her hair was twisted into a chignon at her nape.

Voices carried from the foyer and her heart thundered wildly in her chest. Should she greet them? Act busy with the food preparations? Perhaps offer them a drink or pour one for herself?

Before she could decide, the door to the kitchen swung open and Lucian walked in, Slade on his heels.

"Happy Thanksgiving," she greeted, her smile a bit shaky. Was there a misunderstanding? He was supposed to ask his—

Sawyer's tall form appeared and her breath skittered out of her lungs. He was as handsome as ever in a cable knit crewneck sweater sewn of what looked like soft blue. It brought out the shade of his eyes. Yes, she was pretty sure it was blue.

"Happy Thanksgiving," he greeted, placing a bottle of wine on the counter.

The boys disappeared into the dining room where she'd set out the appetizers. She remained frozen in place, unable to utter a sound or break her stare as she looked into those intense eyes.

"I considered bringing scotch, but after last time ... everything I had on hand would have been an affront to our palates."

As he mentioned their last encounter she realized how much she'd feared he wouldn't. The knot in her chest eased and she smiled. "Thank you for the wine."

"Thanks for inviting us. It's been a long time since we had a home cooked holiday meal."

"Well," she responded excitedly. "This is my first. I was hoping to make it as traditional as possible, but we'll see."

She looked at him, a thousand questions running through her head, but suddenly she'd lost the nerve to ask a single one. *Where have you been? Why haven't you called? How could you just leave me wondering like that? Didn't you like being with me? Did I do something wrong?*

Everything inside of her seemed to jump and bounce too fast for her frame to hold still, so she opened the spare oven and reached to remove the stuffing. *"Ouch!"* The hot dish clattered against the oven rack.

Sawyer rounded the counter as she cradled her singed fingers to her chest and cursed herself for being so scattered.

"Are you all right?"

"It's fine. They've been warming for the past hour. I should have expected the dishes to still be hot."

"Let me see." He carefully extricated her fingers from the clutch of her hand and examined the tips.

He was so close she could see the grain of his beard, the coarse hairs waiting to grow along his jaw and form a shadow by evening. He had a small freckle by his right temple. Thick black lashes fringed his piercing eyes as they studied her fingertips.

Her heart beat with clumsy thumps behind her ribs as she breathed in the familiar scent of his skin, so recognizable the fragrance triggered some sort of accelerated arousal in her body. Her clothing was suddenly an irritant and she had the urge to strip as if she were on fire.

"I think you'll live," he whispered, sparing her a teasing smile. Bringing her hand to his lips, he pressed a kiss on the pads of her fingers.

She studied him, a deep urge to climb onto him and wrap her limbs around his strong hips. But there was also the urge to slap him. Looking away, she searched for an oven mitt.

But when her hand pulled, he tightened his grip. She glanced back at him questioningly, hoping to read something in his expression that might tell her what he was thinking. She held his gaze he slowly released his hold. *Coward!*

Flustered, she said, "Dinner should be ready in a few minutes. Why don't you pour yourself a glass of wine?"

"Can I get something for you?"

Yes, an explanation would help, then you can get undressed and meet me in my bed. "No, I'm fine, thank you."

He waited with the men at the table as she and Toni carried the last of the dishes to the dining room. Lucian carved the turkey with inexperienced flare and Sawyer offered a toast.

"I'm grateful to be spending the holiday with good friends. Everything looks delicious, Isadora. Thank you, again, for inviting us." When he spoke, especially the word *delicious,* his gaze seemed to devour her, though no one else appeared to notice, so maybe she was hallucinating.

The side dishes were wonderful, though the turkey turned out dryer than she'd hoped. The men helped themselves to seconds and several bottles of wine were emptied.

It occurred to her that their father hadn't called. Perhaps, being that Thanksgiving was an American holiday, it slipped his mind all the way over in Europe. The thought niggled, but didn't consume her as it once would have. If anything, she was irritated on Lucian and Toni's behalf.

"Can I sleep over at Liz's?"

Isadora's thoughts of withdrawn family evaporated. "It's Thanksgiving."

"So?"

"So I'm sure Liz is doing stuff with her family."

"Only dinner at her aunt's. She asked, and her mom said it was okay. Lucian's going out."

"Lucian's an adult," she diplomatically pointed out.

"God." Toni shoved her fork across the table. "I'm never allowed to do anything."

Before she could comment on her sister's rude manners Lucian spoke. "Antoinette. Apologize. If Isa says no then the answer's no. Don't argue."

Taken aback by her brother's mature intervention, she stared at her sister. Sawyer and Slade remained silent, waiting for the awkward family moment to pass.

"Sorry, Isa," Toni mumbled.

Her instant apology was another shock. Though it was a holiday, it was also the start of a long, much-needed weekend. "If Liz's mother said yes, then I suppose it's fine, but I have a lot to clean up. You'll have to get a ride."

"Lucian can drop me off."

"Oh, can I?" their brother asked, voice thick with sarcasm. "Fine, but you have to help Isadora with the dishes first."

"Deal."

Who *were* these people?

Once everyone seemed pleased with the terms, the easy conversation continued. As the meal concluded, Isadora found it difficult to look in Sawyer's general direction.

The men retired to the den where a football game played on the television. Toni dutifully helped her clear the table and wrap the leftovers.

"There's so much food left. We should take it somewhere."

"Where?" Toni asked, making quick work of returning the serving trays to the hutch.

Isadora shrugged. "Maybe a shelter?" She wasn't sure if leftovers were an acceptable donation to food pantries. She'd look into that for Christmas. Sawyer was somehow tied to the board at St. Christopher's. Maybe he'd know.

Once the kitchen was clean and the dishes were all put away it was dark. Lucian returned with a fresh shirt and a look of masculine intent glimmering in his dark eyes. "You ready, brat?"

"Yeah. Let me get my bag."

Toni disappeared and Isadora sighed. "Thanks for taking her."

"No problem. You have plans tonight?"

She laughed. "I'll probably read for a split second, then pass out."

"You should come out with us."

She frowned. "Where are you going?"

"A club in Folsom."

"An *underage* club?"

He rolled his eyes. "Come on, Isa. Be real."

"I don't want you drinking and driving."

"I'm not. I'm just driving to Slade's and the city, then we'll probably end up staying overnight at Patras."

She groaned, lectures of safe sex dancing in the forefront of her mind. Not that she was one to talk. "Be safe, *please*."

"I will. I promise."

Toni appeared with her bag and Lucian withdrew his keys. Slade and Sawyer appeared and the tightness she'd suffered over the past few months returned with a vengeance. He was leaving.

"Thanks again," Slade said, slipping on his coat. Sawyer echoed his gratitude, but made no move to hug or kiss her goodbye.

"You're welcome. If you aren't busy for Christmas..." Feeling stupid, she let her words drift off.

In a flurry of keys, coats and goodbyes, she watched them shuffle through the front door and stared silently as the taillights disappeared into the dark night. A vacant ache formed in her chest.

"Alone again," she whispered, shutting off the front lights.

As she replayed the night she tried to figure out what this meant. Was he done with her? There was that moment in the kitchen and a few smoldering looks across the dinner table, but nothing concrete. He didn't even casually kiss her goodbye.

Disappointed that this was probably the end and she'd worked herself up for nothing, she slid into bed. Her book rested on the nightstand with little appeal. Maybe Lucian was right. Maybe she should start going out.

She was embarrassing herself holding out hope for Sawyer—even if no one knew what she was doing. She needed to get a life. It was pretty sad that her eleven-year-old sister had a more exciting social life.

The chime of the doorbell startled her. Breath stilled in her lungs. Swallowing hard, she stared at the ceiling waiting to hear it again and a little alarmed, because no one visited at this time of night. If she was imagining doorbells she was going to the doctor tomorrow.

Another ring and she sprang out of bed, racing out of her room. Her heart so desperately wanted it to be Sawyer, but more than anything she swallowed back a hint of terror that something might have happened to Lucian or Toni. A hundred horrible scenarios raced through her head as she rushed to the front door.

Her feet carried her swiftly across the foyer as she tied her robe, but her hand hesitated on the front lock. Flipping on the porch light, she eased to her toes and checked the peephole.

All her fear washed away, replaced by some unnamable emotion teetering between relief and distrust. *Sawyer...*

Her breath caught at the sight of him and her mind snagged on unwanted scenarios—break up conversations, explanations she didn't want to hear. Flipping the deadbolt with shaky fingers, she turned the knob and pulled the door open. Intense eyes flashed in the glimmer of the porch light, as her chest seemed to fill with helium.

He gave a quick, somewhat telling grin and she sensed his uncertainty. A reoccurring mantra whispered through her mind... *We don't have to end this...*

"You're back," she said, stating the obvious.

"It occurred to me," he began softly, "that I wasn't tired. Am I interrupting your evening?"

"No." *But you might be ruining it, depending on what you're doing here.* "Come in."

Breathless, she stepped back to let him in, a thousand questions playing through her head. How nice it would be if this wasn't an end, but a beginning, that they were finally ready to face this chemistry like two adults and stop hiding in the shadows.

Whatever this was, she would be getting some explanations.

# Chapter 6

"He was my boundless dreams, my grounding thoughts, my daily themes, and my stomach's knots."
~Isadora Patras

SAWYER MOVED SLOWLY, gracefully, like a man in complete control of himself. Shutting the door, he waited a beat before facing her. It gave her enough time to piece together what likely happened.

Lucian would have dropped off Toni before picking up Slade, which meant Sawyer knew where everyone was, but more importantly, he knew she was alone and would be until morning.

"Can I take your coat?"

His gaze held hers as he shouldered off his jacket and a slow jitter of nerves fell into her stomach then swooped into her chest, kicking her heart into overdrive. "You're in your robe. I should have called."

"I wasn't sure you knew how to use a phone after three months of silence."

He flinched. "I owe you an apology."

Was he sorry he hadn't called or sorry they slept together in the first place? She waited, brow raised for him to tell her which apology she'd be getting.

"I can go if you don't want me here."

Was that an apology? She didn't think so. Rolling her eyes, she took his coat.

As she faced the closet his hands closed over the thin material at her shoulders and she sucked in a breath. Shutting the closet door, her body halted as her heart sped wildly out of control. A needy pulse filled her lower body where her emotions seemed to gather and throb.

"I'm sorry I waited so long."

Her eyes closed as she accepted his simple apology, believing he tried to rationalize what they'd done and minimize it as much as possible. He obviously failed and for that she was grateful.

"Is it too late?" he asked quietly.

Too late to fix this after months of silence or too late for a visit? In her mind he'd made it just in time either way. "I want you to stay," she whispered.

"Are you sure?" His voice was low and thick, tugging at unseen places.

She nodded, her nipples pulling tight under the satin of her nightgown.

His touch briefly firmed, massaging gently. "I've thought about you. About that night."

The tension in her back eased as she stood before him, his breath teasing the fine hairs at the back of her neck. His hold remained light, almost questioning.

"I've thought about you, too." More than she planned to admit.

"I told myself that was it, that I wouldn't do that to you again."

He said it as though he'd done something terrible. Didn't he realize he'd saved parts of her soul, tiny neglected pieces that were dying?

"But then, when I saw you tonight, I knew I needed to have you again, bella. I can't seem to resist you and no amount of time seems to dull my memory of our night together."

With shaky motions, she turned and faced him, unprepared for the stark regret bracketing his eyes.

She didn't want to be a regret. She wanted to be a comfort, a solace he reached for. Just as he satisfied her lonesome need, she wanted to satisfy his too.

The anxiety of the past three months faded, all her indignant questions no longer necessary as his words settled over her like a balm. He had only been trying to do what he believed was right.

"Sometimes," she said slowly, leaning into his hold. "There are reasons we can't get certain people out of our minds. Maybe you should stop trying to resist."

Her fingers slowly lifted and hesitated, her heart lacking the brazen assuredness to freely touch him like last time. But the impulse was there, hungering to feel him against her skin.

Gently touching down, she traced the fine lines of tension by his eyes and his lashes lowered. His nostrils flared as he leaned his cheek into her palm, pressing a kiss to her wrist.

"Why is it, one touch from your fingers feels better than every touch I've ever known?"

She didn't want to be compared to his past or discuss his love for his deceased wife. She wanted the night to only belong to them. "Take me to bed, Sawyer."

His eyes searched hers, the last of his reserve fading into lust as he curled his fingers around the back of her neck and took her mouth with un-apologetic need. Her body pressed into his as she met his desire with her own.

The tie of her robe loosened and the material whispered to the floor. Her bare arms wrapped tightly around his neck as she gave into her earlier urge to climb him. Her feet left the ground as he lifted her, cupping her bottom, his growing arousal pressing into her core.

"Where?" he whispered, dragging his full lips against hers.

"Upstairs. Fifth door on the left."

He turned to the grand staircase and stilled. With a deep breath, he chuckled then carried her toward her room. At the top of the stairs, he pressed her back into the wall and caressed her some more.

"I've never wanted anything the way I want you," he confessed, tipping her head back as he dragged drugging kisses down her throat. "I think it's because I know I shouldn't have you."

"Or maybe I just make you happy."

He groaned, the sound full of hunger and rumbling from deep within his chest. "That too." As he faced the long, expanse of hallway he laughed. "Couldn't be the second door?"

She giggled. "I like to make you work for it."

He pinched her bottom through the satin of her gown and she squeaked. "I'm an old man, bella. You'll kill me before we get there."

"Stop. You're forty-three and you're making me feel fat."

He kissed and bit her neck. "Now, you stop. You're the most willowy creature I've ever seen." He carried her through the empty hall, her mouth nibbling at his throat with each staggering step. "This door?"

Her body was so focused on him she had to consider where they were. "Yes."

He pressed into the room and carried her to the unmade bed. Easing her onto the mattress, he braced his arms on either side of her and smiled. But then his expression turned serious, as if something was wrong.

Worried he might change his mind, she softly asked, "What is it?"

His head gave a slow shake as if something unimaginable had occurred to him. "What a beautiful woman you are."

Relieved and flattered by his words, she smiled. Her fingers brushed through his dark hair, hooking in the collar of his sweater, and giving his clothing a little tug. "Take this off."

Rising to his full height, he removed the sweater and tossed it aside. Leaning over her again, he pulled at the straps of her nightgown until her breasts were bared. Her nipples pebbled tighter as his head dipped, his mouth capturing one sensitive bud between his lips.

Her mind rallied at the return of his touch. So many fantasies coming to life as she arched into him while he suckled and groped her curves. The slick material of her nightgown skated down to her hips and he tugged it to the floor.

He licked at her flesh, spreading kisses over her

abdomen and tracing circles with his tongue at her navel. She giggled at the slight tickle, her cheeks pulling into a euphoric smile.

The soft hair at his temples teased her thighs as he moved lower. There was a sense of urgency between them that heightened every sensation. The first lash of his tongue against her sex had her sighing. More of the tension from the past few months faded away, replaced with tangible satisfaction.

His large hands cupped her bottom, holding her sex to his talented mouth. She writhed beneath him, as the need to have him inside of her filled her with a burning ache.

"I need you, Sawyer."

"Not yet," he whispered, warm breath fanning against her flesh, driving her higher, closer to that precipice of pleasure. His fingers returned to her nipples, pulling and strumming gently over her most sensitive spots.

His experienced touch liberated her. She arched into him and moaned, as he worked a steady rhythm. She crested a wave of unequivocal sensation and shattered.

Her body shook as he kissed up her belly, whispering tender words of desire. "Bella ... beautiful bella..." The heat of his skin was a welcome presence, matching the fire burning in her blood.

His gaze met hers, acknowledging her consent. "I'd never hurt you, bella. You have my word."

Moved by his promise, she brushed her fingers

through his hair and smiled. Though her worries were quite real during the time that passed, he'd put many of her concerns to rest. He was here and that's what mattered.

"I know. I trust you, Sawyer."

His eyes darkened as he nudged forward. The vaguely familiar intrusion was a long awaited pleasure. She feared the manifestation of him in her mind had built to an unreachable standard, but as he filled her she understood her recollection paled in comparison to the reality.

His breath teased her skin as he pulled her closer. Her legs held him buried deep inside of her. She never wanted him to leave.

Her inhibitions were shattered by a confidence no amount of expensive scotch could mimic. She greedily took what she wanted, her nails dragging over his muscled shoulders as her lips pressed to his throat and chest, nipping and kissing. She lost herself in the fact that this gorgeous man was making love to her, a fantasy come to life and one she wanted to repeat again and again.

Slowly, his gentle handling evolved into something darker, hungrier, as he moved without any regard for her delicate inexperience. He took her, as she believed a man was meant to take a woman, hungrily, passionately, and intensely carnal.

Tremors carried from her legs to the tops of her ears as he thrust hard, and together they shivered at the delicious wash of pleasure that followed. He collapsed over her, not crushing, but comforting her with his weight. They panted in the dimness, neither of them ready to let the other go.

After a long while, he rolled to his side, pulling her with him, and tucking her lovingly against his chest as he kissed her temple. She wasn't sure how things would be after this, if he'd wait another length of time, refusing to contact her until the opportunity was thrust into his lap. Or if he'd reach out. Let her know he was thinking of her as often as she thought of him.

She was determined not to let him run away again. She wouldn't let him hide. As she lay in his arms, she collected her words, trying to piece together the best way to tell him she wouldn't be cast aside.

"I won't be able to go another three months without seeing you," he assured her before she had a chance to speak.

Thank God. "I don't want you to." She traced a finger over his arm and he pulled her closer.

"When will I be able to see you again?"

A coy smile turned her lips as she looked up at his face. "When would you like?"

A clipped laugh vibrated in his throat. "Tomorrow."

She wasn't sure if this changed things between them or if their association would continue to be a secret. All she knew was that she'd go to him if he asked. "What about Slade? My father? Everything you said before?"

His mouth tightened, the shadows hiding much of his expression. "Does it bother you to keep this a secret?"

"Not necessarily. I think it would be more bothersome to explain it to others. I don't want to make anyone uncomfortable." And she didn't want any outsiders trying to interfere.

He kissed her softly. "I care about you, Isadora. I don't want you to feel—"

Her hand gently covered his mouth, not wanting to hear an unfitting description of their relationship. "I care about you, too. Let's not label anything. For now, let's just go with it and see what happens."

"You're sure?"

She nodded. Her fingers trailed down his throat to his chest. It was difficult for her to say all she wanted him to know, but she could show him.

His body twitched, muscles bunching beneath her exploring touch and his gaze flaring with lust. She explored until she was ghosting her fingernails over the tops of his thighs. His body lengthened, his flesh darkening where blood steadily pumped beneath the surface.

Closer and closer.

Her fingers teased the dark nest of hair surrounding his arousal and her hand gently closed around him. He drew in an audible breath, his chest expanding. Unsure of any tricks women might use to do this to a man, she carefully stroked.

He seemed to like her touching him there so she assumed she was doing fine, but she wanted to do more. She wanted to be an irresistible part of his life, someone he could never keep away from again.

Leaning over, she tucked her hair behind her ear and pressed a kiss to his flat stomach. His breathing hitched as her lips neared his length.

"I might need a minute, bella."

"It doesn't look like it." She brushed her lips over him, loving the smooth feel of him there, the rich scent of sex and masculinity.

Gently, she kissed him and he sucked in a breath, his hands brushing her hair away from her face. Opening her mouth, she closed her lips over the tip and gently pulled.

His fingers tenderly gathered up her hair and guided her lower. "That's it..."

She shut her eyes and took him deeper into her mouth. His legs stretched as his free hand stroked along her spine. She wanted to make him feel as good as he made her feel—better than any other woman could.

His guttural groans bolstered her courage and she moved faster, her body responding to his reaction, desperate to have him again.

"Come here," he said, rolling until she lay beneath him.

He kissed her and then shifted her to her stomach. His hard body moved behind her as he lifted her hips and stroked at her tender folds, slick with wanting.

Hitching her closer, he aligned their bodies, thrust and filled her in one sure stroke. She rocked into the bedding as he cradled her in his arms, blanketed her with his warm body. The ebb and flow was as natural as waves kissing the banks of the coast with every plunge.

He finished inside of her, his body swathing hers in a welcome heat. She curled along his side again, tired and spent, her limbs languid under a spell of well-earned exhaustion.

Gently kissing his fingers, she whispered, "Will you stay until morning?"

His arms tightened around her. "I'll stay for a while."

Good enough.

She didn't spare any real thought to future consequences. The faint belief she might be gaining more from this than him flickered in her mind, but she wasn't merely using his body. There was something about Sawyer that went beyond the superficial, beyond the physical. She liked him.

While this affair, whatever it was, might not last forever, it was hers and hers alone. She was content in accepting she deserved someone like

Sawyer in her life and so long as he wanted to be with her, she believed they could make this work.

Seven

"The mind is its own place,
And in itself can make a heaven of hell,
A hell of heaven."

John Milton
Paradise Lost

THE NEXT MORNING, Isadora awoke alone. She'd expected as much, and told herself any sense of disenchantment was inappropriate. Her body ached in secret places, but with every twinge came a sense of happiness.

Moments from the night before played through her mind, leaving her with a steady blush that wouldn't fade. Even as she stared at the pages of her newest novel, her mind drifted to fantasies between every line, fantasies that had been her reality only hours before.

"You're quiet today."

Lifting her gaze from the novel in her hand, she glanced at Lucian. "I'm reading."

His eyes narrowed. Sometimes Lucian was too perceptive, too all knowing. Searching for a distraction, she asked, "Did you have fun last night?"

He nodded. "We actually ran into Vivian."

Vivian Callahan, Shamus's sister, was an old friend of Isadora's, but their lives were on different tracks. She'd been away at school for some time while Isadora had yet to leave her childhood home. "How is she?"

"Great. Engaged. In medical school now. She seems so far ahead of the rest of us."

"She's getting married?" Strange that the information made her feel happy *and* sad.

"Well, she wants to graduate first, but she said they're planning to get married sometime before she starts her residency."

So they were only a few years away from a wedding. "Good for her. Did you meet her fiancée?"

He nodded. "He seems all right. Not what I'd expect, but a decent enough guy."

"What's his name?"

"Ian Sheffield. Do you know him?"

She didn't know anyone. "No. What's Shamus think of him?"

"Jamie's a tough nut to crack. Says the jury's out until he gets to know him better."

"I think it's cute how protective he is of his big sister."

"Jamie's protective of too many girls. Eventually he's going to have to loosen his guard."

"Why do you say that?"

Lucian shrugged. "I can't see him single for long. Whoever he ends up with, I guarantee she'll receive all of his attention. And she had better be a damn strong woman."

She tsked, thinking he was being a little hard on his friend. "Jamie's a teddy bear."

He arched a brow and his expression shuttered. "I know a side of him you don't. Jamie's easy disposition is what people see on the surface, but there's a whole lot more going on underneath that façade."

She frowned. "Are you saying he's fake?"

"No. He's an absolute gentleman when he needs to be. But no one's a gentleman all the time."

"Well, everyone has a temper."

"Not a temper. He wouldn't lose control like that. He's ... exacting. Demanding."

"Do you mean with girls?" It wasn't like Shamus had any real career experience to reference. He seemed too easygoing to be as meticulous as Lucian made him sound.

"Not girls. *Women*. You'd be surprised how many older women want him—and they aren't looking for a teddy bear."

To each his own, she supposed. But she didn't like the implied ambiguity that someone Lucian's age might be *demanding* with women. She didn't want her brother partaking in anything disrespectful, anything that some opportunistic young girl might use against him later.

It wasn't uncommon for women to fling accusations at wealthy men—even the young ones. That sort of sexual extortion happened more than the modest members of polite society would care to admit, which was why it usually ended with a large sum of money being paid out.

The three of them—Lucian, Jamie, and Slade—should all be careful. "When it comes to women, Lucian, you have to ask."

He laughed. "I know that, Isa."

"Does Jamie?"

He gave her a strange look. "Some women like to be told."

Her brow tightened. "Very few."

How much experience could these boys possibly have? They were eighteen and nineteen years old. Regardless, she didn't like the impression she was getting.

"What's wrong with women your own age? You should be meeting girls at college."

He laughed. "Don't lecture *me*. We were

talking about Shamus. And despite being in college, I'm not interested in shallow girls who think they're sophisticated because they know what a macchiato is, stage their lives to resemble some undeserving celebrity, and try so hard to appear unique their only accomplishment is looking like everyone else. Show me an intelligent woman who's different from the rest of women my age and you'll have my full attention."

Well, at least he'd put some thought into his tastes. "I think it's good you're being selective. You're too young to settle down anyway."

Lifting the novel she placed on the cushion between them, he casually examined the blurb on the back. "I don't know if I'll ever settle down. I have a lot I want to accomplish and a relationship would only get in my way."

She scoffed. "Everyone wants to fall in love at some point."

He returned the book to the cushion. "No offense, Isa, but men don't care about those things." He gave her romance novel a little nudge.

His statement took her by surprise, not because she believed he was right, but because he was so very wrong—he had to be, or there was really no point in hoping for more in terms of her own happiness. "You sound like Daddy."

"I do not." His easy expression hardened, an emotional wall going up so fast she almost felt a physical gust of wind hit her.

He did. He was putting business before human connections, before emotional ties. "Don't delay your life for some silly vendetta, Lucian. You're better than him. You don't need to prove that to anyone. The people who love you already know how impressive you are."

His expression shuttered some more. "With all due respect, Isa, let's keep you and my private life separate."

It hurt, being shut out so succinctly. More signs of their father. She couldn't just let it go.

"Men care about love. They want to be loved as much as the rest of the world. Any man who denies it is a fool and will most likely spend his life alone and miserable."

"I don't want to hurt your feelings, Isa, but ... you're wrong. You don't have any experience beyond fictional fairytales. If you did, you'd realize we don't care about those things the way women do."

She scoffed, offended but unable to share the source of her logic. "I'm not a prude, Lucian. I know more than the stuff in books."

"Okay."

"I have experience," she argued.

"Look, I'm not going to discuss my proclivities with you and I don't want to hear about yours. You're my sister."

She scowled at him. "Like you even know what the word *proclivities* means."

He raised a brow and she decided she didn't want to know if he did or didn't. But in a way she wanted to tell him her latest secret, even though she swore she wouldn't say a word. It was probably best that Lucian didn't want to know the personal details of her life—*but she had details!*

And she knew a thing or two about men. Sawyer could be very passionate and feeling. It wasn't love, but it was something.

So long as Lucian wasn't completely dismissing possibilities, she'd accept his current feelings on love. Over time they might change. Men changed. Relationships evolved. People grew.

"Just admit—for my own piece of mind—that you know not all men are cold. There are men like Daddy and then there are men nothing like him. Guess which ones are better."

"Stop comparing me to Dad." He groused and huffed. "Fine. Some men might care about that stuff, but right now, I don't."

Right now. That made her a little more comfortable. Let him be ambitious now. It would help him in college and, down the line, help him find a job. But eventually she hoped he'd fall in love. She hoped they all would.

It suddenly occurred to her Lucian was treating her like his equal, not the enemy. She'd carried so much fear they might never talk like equals again. His new attitude toward her was a huge relief.

Shooting him a smile, she confessed, "I missed you. I'm glad you're home."

He studied her for a short moment, his mouth hooking in a half grin. "I missed you, too."

It was the first time in a long time that she believed their situation wouldn't negatively affect them in later years. If Lucian continued to let her in, little by little, they might someday exist simply as brother and sister. Friends.

A sharp sense of guilt hit her as she realized now that he seemed to be opening up and letting down his guard she was the one keeping secrets. She still wasn't sure if Sawyer was a big secret or a little one. That depended on Sawyer. If things continued, eventually Lucian would find out. He was too perceptive not to. So long as no one told their father she figured that was fine.

* * *

Sawyer called the Monday after the boys returned to school. He wanted to see her again, but in her brother's absence there seemed a spotlight on her every motion. Not that Toni was concerned with her old, boring sister's personal life—she had her own life—but it didn't go unnoticed when Isadora suddenly announced she was going out after not going anywhere in ... forever.

"Can I come with you?"

"No, it's a school night and you have homework."

Toni scoffed. "I have to study. That'll take two seconds."

"Maybe if you took more than two seconds you could get that B minus up to an A."

"Where are you going anyway?"

Isadora fussed with her shirt, not liking the way it sagged in the front. Returning to her closet she said, "Out with friends."

"What friends? You don't have any friends."

Silently counting to ten, she changed into another shirt. "I have friends."

"Who?"

She couldn't think of a single believable person, so she made one up. "Susan."

"Who's Susan?"

"You know Susan."

"No, I don't. Has she ever been to the house?"

"I'm sure you've met her." Avoiding eye contact, she sorted through her jewelry box.

"No I haven't."

Isadora shut out the light on her vanity and Toni trailed her to the kitchen where she'd left her other pearl earring by the phone.

"I think you're making up this *Susan*."

"Why would I do that, Antoinette? You're just not used to me having a life."

"True. Can I rent a movie tonight?"

"No. It's late. You need to study for your test

and shower before bed. And I don't want you on the phone after nine."

"How late do you plan to be?"

"As late as I please." She grabbed her houndstooth coat, and adjusted her scarf.

Her sister, always her second set of eyes when it came to color coordination, laughed. "That scarf's yellow. It totally clashes."

Toni's honesty wasn't always delicate, but Isadora appreciated her sister's bluntness on occasion—especially where style was concerned. If not for Toni, Isadora would be a fashion disaster.

She pulled the scarf from her neck. "I've been wearing that with this jacket all week. Can you find me something that matches?"

Toni examined the print of her coat and nosed through the closet, pulling out a soft pashmina. "Here, there's red in your coat. This'll match."

Isa twisted the material around her neck. "Thanks. Do as I said and I'll see you in the morning. If you need anything, Lucy's in charge." Lucy was their youngest maid.

"I'll just call you if I need something."

"Fine, but only if something's wrong."

"Like if the house is on fire?"

"Toni," she warned, and her sister snickered. Buttoning her coat, Isadora took a deep breath. "Okay, I guess I'm ready."

"Ready for what?"

She sighed. The conversation had escalated to

a point of tediousness she wouldn't escape until she was out the door. "Goodnight. Behave."

"Bye. Have fun with *Susan.*"

Isadora rolled her eyes and entered the eight-car garage. Hitting her key fob, the lights of her Volvo XC90 came to life and the engine purred. She slid inside, the seats warming her bottom as she waited for the car to heat.

The Bishop's estate was picturesque with modern undertones, situated on an expanse of lush land butting up against the local country club. The nearby golf course gave the impression of more acreage, making it difficult to discern where one property ended and the Bishop's began. She liked that his house was so close to hers—well, her father's.

Sometime over the past several years since her father relocated to his estate in France, she'd come to think of the home they occupied as hers. It wasn't. She knew that, but the remaining servants now answered to her. Her father merely paid the bills, which, with a house the size of theirs, was nothing to dismiss. She should be grateful he let her stay there.

She scoffed. He should be grateful she stuck around to meet the obligations he abandoned—namely, raising his children.

When she pulled onto the long drive the front door opened. Sawyer waited on a long cobblestone patio that seemed more suitable for a backyard than a front one. She'd never been inside his home. She'd only acted as her brother's chauffeur in the years before he got his license, caddying him to and from his friends' houses.

Sawyer approached and opened her door. "Hi."

She smiled, a little jittery with the sense that they were somehow breaking the rules. It was silly. They were both adults. "Hi."

"Want to come inside?"

She unbuckled her seatbelt and he took her arm, guiding her down from the raised seating. "Thank you." She adored how gentlemanly he was with her.

"I ordered dinner from the country club. I figured that would be easier than enduring my abysmal culinary skills."

Her laughter held a tinge of nervousness. "I'm sure you're as capable in the kitchen as you are in any other room."

"Your faith is flattering, but I'm afraid my skills in the kitchen versus the bedroom are worlds apart."

"Well, at least you're modest," she teased.

Men like Sawyer had a habit of doing everything well. So she couldn't very well blame him for taking credit where credit was due.

He waved a hand for her to step into the house first, but as soon as the door shut he caught her hand, this time with a touch of urgency and turned her back to the wall. His mouth found hers, the evening shadow of his jaw scratching against her chin deliciously as he kissed her.

He was so good at hiding his attraction until precisely the right moment when they had absolute privacy. Still waters sure did run deep, because once he showed his hand there was quite a bit to see. Melting into him, she sighed.

His devastating eyes peeked under full lashes as he stared at her, their lips only a breath apart. "Why don't we apply some of my better skills *in* the kitchen?"

She giggled. "I don't know. A bed makes a big difference."

"Are you saying you wouldn't enjoy it?" He nibbled her lip, pulling back slowly as tempting promises danced in his heated gaze.

"Counters might be easier than carpets. I won't know until I've tried."

Something flashed in his eyes and he chuckled. "Who knew there was this side of you?"

People always assumed she was so prim and proper because she was a Patras and a generally quiet person. To be taken seriously at school functions and conferences, she had no choice but to act the part of a respectable middle-aged woman, but that really wasn't her at all.

She loved playing around and being silly. The problem was, no one ever wanted to play with her. Everyone seemed in such a rush to grow up. She'd been forced to be an adult before she could legally vote. Her younger years were a collection of missed opportunities she doubted she'd ever get back. Any opportunity to be a little adventurous seemed an opportunity she couldn't miss.

"Did you want to?" she asked, thinking fooling around in a kitchen might be a rite of passage she should check off her list.

His tongue swirled beneath her ear and he groaned then grudgingly stepped back. "I should feed you first. I did promise dinner."

She really didn't care about eating, but he was probably right. This was nice, having the chance to sit and talk like a normal couple—sort of like an actual date. It definitely clarified things. She obviously wasn't just there for a booty call, although that had its merits, too.

His hand slid into hers and he pulled her away from the wall, further into the house. "I'll give you the grand tour."

Her blood heated and she was certain she wore a deep blush, just from being near him. He led her through his home and there was a familiar sense of him in the air. She greedily appraised every surface for clues about the sort of man he was in private.

Books, there were lots of books, and a large television in the open living room. "This is nice. Did you read all of those books?"

"No. An interior decorator chose them."

She snorted. "I don't know what's funnier, the

idea of you having a decorator or the fact that you have a gorgeous wall of books only to stare at the spines." She stepped closer to the shelves and frowned. "No wonder. Who wants to read *An In Depth History of Igneous Rocks?* Don't you enjoy fiction?"

She turned and found him leaning against the adjacent wall watching her, an amused grin on his face. "I'm more of a TV guy, but I take it you like to read."

"I *love* to read. I think it's a crime for a non-reader to have such a beautiful bookcase. I have a sort of obsession with fancy bookshelves. It's almost pornographic the way I ogle them."

He chuckled. "Maybe later I'll show you the moldings in my office," he teased. "There's a bookcase in there, too."

"So unfair. I want the name of your decorator —not for my reading list, but for shelves like this."

"That would be my carpenter. I'll get you one of his cards. Come on. Kitchen's this way."

His kitchen was impressive for a man who claimed not to cook. He'd set the table with white dishes and linen napkins. As he unpacked boxes of food, she analyzed the various surfaces—hard granite counters, cold porcelain tile... Maybe sex in a kitchen wasn't all it was cracked up to be.

"Did you have a hard time getting out of the house?"

Giving up her appraisal of the room, she took

a seat at the table. "No, but Toni had lots of questions." She smirked. "I told her your name was Susan."

He stilled in the midst of removing another carton of food from the box. "Susan?"

"Well, she wanted to know who I was meeting and I couldn't think of anyone."

"I suppose I could be Susan. Though I doubt Toni's old enough to draw any conclusions about our relationship."

"Toni's nosey and has a big mouth. I didn't want her saying anything to Lucian."

"Then it's probably wise I remain Susan for the time being."

He took a seat at the table and dished out food. The conversation came easily, being that Sawyer had a firm grasp of the main players in her life. They discussed his career, raising children, and briefly touched on her parents.

"Your mother was a patient woman," he commented, fondness hidden in his gaze.

"She'd have to be to put up with my father."

"Christos has never been an easy man."

That was an understatement. "No, he hasn't."

"How are he and Tibet?"

She shrugged, not able to offer much in the way of her father's second marriage to the woman who was once his mistress. "Happy, I suppose. We rarely hear from them."

"I'm sorry about that."

Certain burdens seemed so heavy at first, but over time, they were simply accepted. Putting them down felt like losing a piece of herself, so she preferred to lug her resentment with her everywhere she went. But she wanted to make sure Sawyer didn't see her as any sort of martyr.

"I'm not sorry," she explained. "I think the house is happier without him in it. Lucian seems to finally be letting go of his anger. I know I'm a better parent than my dad ever was, so things are just better this way."

"Your brother's definitely someone to watch. I have no doubt he'll do well for himself. Slade says he's already making connections. I wish my son would take a page out of his book."

"What connections?" She knew very little of her brother's personal life, which, according to their recent conversations, was exactly the way he preferred it.

"People in the industry, colleagues of mine and your father's. He's making a good impression, from what I hear."

She frowned. "I don't understand. He's at school. When is he meeting these people?"

"He has a busy social life. With their campus located in the heart of the city, it's expected, don't you think? Rather than wasting time at keggers, he's working the proper circuits, grabbing odd jobs as they come."

"Working? He should be studying."

"I didn't bring it up to start trouble, bella. I was merely paying a compliment."

Her brother had a habit of watching the stock market too closely. Chances were he was investing a great deal of the money she'd sent him—via their father—into various shares. "I suppose if he's keeping his grades up I can't comment."

His fingers brushed over hers. "You can always comment. Whether others listen is anybody's guess. But I'll listen."

And that was why she enjoyed him so much. Sawyer always paid attention to her words and never dismissed her feelings, especially when it came to family life, which was all she really had at the moment.

"How's Slade doing this semester?"

"B's. Let's just hope they transfer."

"Transfer? Where's he going?"

His lips parted, his words hesitating a split second. "I thought you knew. He's transferring to Lucian's school in the spring. Next year they plan on splitting an apartment."

"Lucian didn't tell me any of this."

Although it made sense. Lucian had wanted to attend the same school as Slade. Sawyer's son seemed to visit her brother every weekend. But still, he should have let her know he planned to move out of the dorms. "I swear, sometimes I wonder who's actually in charge."

He caught her hand and gave it a comforting

squeeze. "He's an adult, Isa. Let go of the reins. I'm pretty confident your brother will do just fine."

After dinner they moved to the couch and he put on a movie. She wasn't interested in watching television, but she liked the opportunity to snuggle close and touch him freely. Each stolen caress heightened her desire to have him.

Sawyer's hand rested on her thigh like a weight of temptation. She hardly paid attention to the television, her full focus on willing that hand to move higher. When his fingers curled against her knee, making slow whirls over the material of her pants, one would have thought she was being fondled in the most intimate of places.

Her feet slowly dropped to the floor and her knees eased apart. He spared her a sidelong glance and smiled, his focus returning to the screen. It took eons for his hand to work its way back up her thigh and by the time he was only a few inches from her sex she was soaked.

Her heart pounded with wanting, but his composure seemed unshakable. Biting down on her lip, she glanced at his profile, his focus still on the movie. She casually rested her hand over his, lacing her fingers in the space between his knuck-les. He spared her another smile, but seemed obliv-ious to the havoc his hand was causing.

Drawing in a deep breath, she sucked in her stomach and pulled his hand to the center of her thighs. His head turned and he looked at her, eyes assessing.

Still nibbling her lip, she held his gaze and flicked open the button of her pants. Without breaking eye contact, she guided his hand inside of her panties and watched as his pupils expanded.

His finger slid through her arousal, slipping between her folds and drawing a sigh from her lips. He pressed a long finger as deep as it would fit and she eased her body into the couch cushions, parting her thighs more.

No longer watching the television, he pulled back and thrust his finger deep again, startling her with the intensity of his penetration.

His eyes darkened as his lashes lowered. "Is this what you want?"

Her breath labored as she held his challenging stare, refusing to shy away from her body's desires. "Yes."

He filled her with another finger, stretching her and teasing a sensitive spot deep inside. "You're soaked."

Her hands moved to the cushion of the couch, showing him she wouldn't stop him from touching her. His gaze traveled over her body, and he turned to fully face her, slowly pumping his fingers into her sex.

Soft keening moans passed her lips as he worked his hand between her wet flesh and damp panties. The longer he touched her the more restless she became. Her hands couldn't keep still. She cupped her breast through her shirt and arched into his touch. That seemed to entice him. He withdrew his fingers, shifted so he was kneeling in front of her and yanked off her pants, stripping her from the waist down.

"Spread your legs."

She complied and his mouth dropped to her sex, his fingers stabbing deep as he drove her into a rapid fit of pleasure. Every time they were together it was better than the last. He made her feel like a woman, sexy and desirable.

She loved when they made love. But more than anything, she loved the way his attention felt, unsure what neglected part of her psyche he was mending, but knowing it needed everything he provided.

Before long his clothing was tossed aside and he was driving into her with hard thrusts. The movie played, an insignificant backdrop to their sighs of pleasure. He exceeded her growing expectations and in the end she was deeply satisfied and deliciously sore.

The movie came to a close and they held one another through the credits, the soundtrack a soft backdrop to her fanciful thoughts as they rested. All too soon, she found herself dressing. He walked her to her car and kissed her goodnight. "Can I see you again next Monday?"

She tried not to overreact at the idea of not

seeing him for a solid seven days. "Sure. And maybe we could see each before then, too."

His smile was too gentle to reach his eyes. He tucked a strand of hair behind her ear. "I don't want to monopolize your time, bella."

"You're not. I have plenty to spare."

His eyes creased. "You should be going out with friends your own age. I don't want you to wait around for moments when we can be alone."

But her friends were all in college or had moved away to start new jobs. The few that remained in the area were planning futures and falling in love or already in love and starting families. Every month she received another *Save the Date* card in the mail. All she seemed to do was wait from one wedding to the next. And every time she forked over another sizable wedding gift she wondered if it was her attendance those old acquaintances were after or a Patras check.

Now she feared her relationship with Sawyer would be another waiting game she'd have to endure. "Sawyer, are we only going to see each other once a week?"

His gaze skated away from her face for a split second. "Bella, I haven't been with anyone in a long time. Is it too much to ask that we ease into this?"

She supposed taking it slow was okay. "What about other women?" The thought of him touching someone else the way he touched her made her stomach turn. "I'd like it if we were monogamous."

"I have no issue with monogamy. You're the woman I want."

Relieved, she smiled. "So, no one else."

He hesitated. "There may be certain functions, social things that require I bring a guest. In situations like that I usually attend with a colleague who has something to gain from networking the event."

She frowned. "Are you talking about fundraisers and things like that?"

"Yes. Social obligations. Benefits that better a cause by the number of guests that attend. It's frowned upon to go to such things alone."

She supposed it would be fine if he was only bringing colleagues. "As long as we're monogamous, I suppose that's fine."

"If there's ever a time…" His words drifted off. "I won't hold you back, Isadora. We can be exclusive, but if you met someone … I'd understand."

The chances of her meeting anyone were unlikely. Her life was pretty consumed by Toni's schedule. "We'll cross that bridge when, and if, we come to it."

"Fair enough. So I'll see you Monday?"

Knowing he'd already met her biggest demands, she didn't want to sound unsatisfied. Monday wasn't too far away. She could manage that. It was still early and he wanted to ease into things. She could be patient.

"I'll see you Monday."

"I look forward to it." He shut her car door and remained at the front door as she pulled away.

The sadness that filled her with every lengthening mile seemed natural. Most lovers probably suffered such longing when they separated, not to mention how greedy she was for the physical part of their relationship.

As the weeks followed, she and Sawyer continued to meet on Mondays and Toni slowly accepted that her friendship with Susan was a private and important one. Sawyer did his thing throughout the week and she ... well, she did hers.

With the holidays approaching there was always something to occupy her time. Wednesdays were her only free evenings, but even then, after she dropped Toni off at her dance class, Isadora attended yoga at the gym down the street.

While she'd worried seeing Sawyer one day a week might be difficult, she honestly couldn't spare much more time for him. Her life was busy, if not with her own obligations. Toni was an energetic kid and that meant plenty of school meetings, countless social calls, after school clubs, and even the occasional sewing for recital costumes and such.

But there was a void. The pace of her life wasn't dictated by *her* desires, but the desires of those in her life. Sawyer seemed the only thing in her world that was solely hers and even he was limited.

Lucian had received several college brochures in the mail and they were still piled in the library. Every time she entered that room, a cold and dark area that emanated hints of her father's time in the house, the brochures taunted her.

Occasionally, she'd page through a few, imagining certain classes and considering signing up for one or two. But it never seemed the right time.

What would a couple classes prove anyway? If she ever wanted to earn an actual degree it would take years. Someone had to be there to pick Toni up from school, take her to her activities, and help her with algebra.

In the end, she tossed the brochures into the trash, preferring not to be taunted in her own home. By the time her schedule opened up the course calendars would all be different anyway. As a consolation, she used her spare time to find less demanding activities that brought her joy—gardening research, crafts, studying foreign cultures—hobbies she could call her own.

The Bishops declined her invitation to join them for Christmas, which was conveyed through Lucian since Mondays were more difficult when the boys were home on winter break. She and her siblings had the unspeakable pleasure of hosting their father and Tibet.

Though their father hadn't been home in years, he suffered no awkwardness at dominating every square inch of the house. Lucian was outraged to learn that Tibet would be sleeping in what was once their mother and father's bed, so he stayed with the Callahan's over winter break.

The few times her brother visited the house a fight erupted, he and their father butting heads until one eventually backed down. It was no surprise the one to usually walk away was Lucian.

Isadora hated the tension that existed between the two of them, finding it sweltering. Lucian had given her a new laptop for Christmas and she wasn't sure why she needed one. But being that her Monday nights were temporarily free, she found herself toying around with the state-of-the-art device and getting frustrated that she lacked the simplest skills in terms of technology. She did figure out how to manage the word processing program and that seemed just her speed.

Avoiding her father, she spent most of the holiday in her room writing a short story. It was nothing she would ever show anyone, just a silly tale of a girl who wanted to make something of her life and fall in love. The frippery passed the time. In the end, she saved it. But hid the story in a file marked PRIVATE then thought better of it and changed the file name to RECIPES—that seemed less tempting to wandering eyes.

Typing out her fantasies did nothing to make

them turn into reality. She missed Sawyer and if her father and Tibet didn't go back to France soon, she was going to lose her mind.

"I can't wait for them to leave," she confessed to Sawyer one evening as they spoke on the phone. "I need to get out of this house. Can't we go somewhere?" Another drawback to having her father around was that it made Sawyer reluctant to see her.

"People will talk, bella, and we don't want anything getting back to Christos. Imagine how unpleasant his stay would be then. How long is he in town?"

"I didn't ask. I don't know my place when he's here. He tells Lucian how to think and Toni how to dress. The servants are quiet and everyone's tense."

"*You* should get out."

"I could come there," she offered, desperate for an escape.

His voice held regret. "Slade's home. He's in and out so often I never know what his schedule is."

"Oh."

"Why don't you go out with your brother? Have a drink and blow off some steam."

"Lucian shouldn't be anywhere they're serving alcohol."

"But you know he is, bella. Don't carry responsibilities that aren't yours. Just go have some fun. Be young for once."

She frowned, not sure if she knew how to do that. "I—"

"Hold on, Slade's coming down the steps." The phone muffled and she recognized Slade's voice in the background. "How long will you be?" Sawyer asked.

Slade's answer was garbled. As she waited, hope flickered. Maybe Slade would go out for the night and she could sneak over to Sawyer's—

Sawyer's voice interrupted her train of thought. "An associate. I'll see you later tonight." The phone shifted. "Sorry about that."

"Am I the associate?" she teased.

He chuckled. "Yes, I believe I'll call you *Susan*."

Her humor turned hollow, the joke not as funny as it should have been—something lost in the irony of another woman's name.

Why was it okay to have a *Susan* but not an *Isadora*? She knew the answer, of course. His association with her father and the friendship between Lucian and his son complicated things. It wasn't just Sawyer who worried about their families judging them and interfering. She had concerns as well. Then there was the issue of their age difference, which might scandalize members of polite society. Whatever would they do!

Her phone beeped. "Now it's my call waiting. Can I put you on hold?"

"Sure."

She flipped to the other line. "Hello?"

"Isa, I'm going out tonight. You should come."

She hesitated, surprised by her brother's invitation and his coincidental timing. "Where are you going?"

Lucian was leaving in a day or two and this might be the last chance she had to see him before spring. She'd hardly spent any time with him since their father's arrival.

"A little jazz bar in Folsom. It's a quieter crowd. Good people. You'd like it."

Rather than lecture him on the wrongs of drinking underage, she thought of Sawyer's advice about acting *her* age. "When are you leaving?"

"I can pick you up in an hour. You in?"

She smiled, the idea becoming more appealing to her the deeper it sank in. "Okay."

"Great." He sounded surprised, but pleased. "I'll see you in a little bit."

She flipped back to Sawyer. "Apparently I'm going to try my hand at that twenty-three thing. That was Lucian. He's taking me to a jazz bar." When he didn't respond she checked to make sure she hadn't lost him. "Sawyer?"

"I'm here... Good. That's good."

For as much as he encouraged her to get out and do things people in their twenties did, he didn't seem as thrilled when she actually took his advice.

"I'm sure we won't do anything crazy. Lucian said it would be a quiet atmosphere. Is Slade meeting him, do you know?"

"No, Slade has a date."

"Oh."

Maybe Shamus would be there. She didn't like imagining her brother drifting off to talk with some young woman at a private table and leaving her stranded at the bar alone. She wanted to go out, but not without a wingman.

"You'll enjoy yourself, bella." His words were encouraging, but his voice held reservations. He didn't sound like his usual self.

It had been five weeks since they'd started sleeping together on a regular basis and sometimes he'd dropped hints about her possibly meeting other people—male people. But she believed he was growing used to her and part of him would be disappointed if she met someone more ... permanent.

Lacking the energy to decipher his feelings at the moment, she focused on her first priority—getting out of her house.

"I better get going."

They made their goodbyes and she avoided her father and Tibet as she made her way up the stairs to change.

As she waited for Lucian, she entertained the

idea of confiding in her brother, asking his opinion of Sawyer, but in the end she decided to keep her promise and keep their relationship a secret.

Lucian might have helpful advice, but he might also find the whole thing disturbing. She wasn't prepared to face that sort of judgment or chance what she and Sawyer had. Right now, this was enough.

Chapter 8

"A lonesome dove soars alone."
~Claudette Dubois

THE RIDE to the city was smooth and luxurious in her brother's new Mercedes Maybach, but the closer they drew to the metropolitan area the more Isadora's nerves jangled. Her mind continued to deconstruct Sawyer's subtle hints that she not hold back where her social life was concerned.

She needed a distraction. "How are you paying for this car?"

Lucian glanced at her then back to the road. "It's a lease."

"You couldn't find something less conspicuous?"

He smirked. "Why would I want to? This car tells people I'm coming."

People often thought women were the vainer sex, but those people clearly didn't know any Patras men.

She wanted to ask him about the "connections" he was making outside of school and how that sort of networking might affect his classes. She wanted to know why he didn't tell her Slade was transferring or about the apartment they were planning to rent.

But she couldn't ask any of those questions, because all that information came from Sawyer. She pursed her lips, frustrated by the tedious drawbacks of living a secret life.

"Relax, Isa. It's a bar, not an execution," Lucian commented, glancing at her again.

She flicked a speck of lint off her pants. "I'm not used to going out." Her explanation was solid, but not what was truly weighing on her mind.

"Toni said you've been going out every week—with some friend, Susan. Do I know her?"

"No, and you're not going to. She's not your type."

He laughed. "I wouldn't hit on your friends. There are certain rules about mixing pleasure with family acquaintances. It complicates things."

Exactly the reason she shouldn't be sleeping

with her father's associate and Lucian's friend's dad.

"I know."

"Still," he commented, his gaze on the road. "If you wanted Susan to meet us here, I'd be fine with that. I promise I won't hit on her."

"You sound thirty," she teased, amused by his arrogance that didn't match his actual age.

"Not a kid anymore."

"I know." Neither was she, but sometimes she still felt as clueless as one.

When they reached the bar she was pleased to find it was much like Lucian described. A small band occupied a stage, playing in accordance with the charming ambiance. A soft amber glow spilled over each table from antique gaslights and she found the atmosphere soothing.

"Are you meeting friends here?" she asked as he glanced around on their walk toward the bar.

"No, we're making friends."

She excelled at the opposite.

They settled on two stools situated far enough away from the live music to talk comfortably, yet close enough to the central area where future friends might gather.

Lucian ordered a drink and looked to her expectantly.

"Um, I'll just have a soda."

He rolled his eyes. "Bring her an amaretto sour please."

"What's that? And doesn't anyone card you?"

He laughed. "No. I look them right in the eye as if daring them to question me. Hasn't failed me yet. And you need a drink."

"I don't *need* a drink," she muttered. But when the bartender delivered the cocktail she was pleasantly surprised by the tart flavor. "This is actually tasty."

The crowd shuffled and several women approached Lucian, though he never really paid much attention to any one female in particular. She believed he'd told her the truth when he said he was selective.

But despite his specific taste, he had a way of making people feel like the center of the universe. There was something magnetic about him—a gift she hadn't inherited.

When one woman he'd been chatting with excused herself, Isadora leaned close and whispered, "She's too old for you."

He grinned. "She doesn't care."

"You should."

"Why?"

Leaning closer, she hissed, "You're nineteen."

"So?"

"Lucian—"

"Isadora," he mimicked. "Age is just a number."

True. And who was she to talk? Her thoughts

were obsessed with someone twenty years her senior.

It was interesting watching Lucian. No one ever questioned him, and older gentlemen tended to defer to him. He certainly had an alluring presence.

"That guy's checking you out."

She turned and flushed, her gaze colliding with a man sitting on the other side of the bar, clearly staring at her. "No, he's not."

"Don't be naïve, Isadora. He is. You should go talk to him."

"No, I don't want to."

"Why not?"

"I just don't. I'll embarrass myself."

He laughed. "No, you won't. Go say hello." He nudged her and she nearly lost her seat.

Clutching the stool, she scowled at him. "Lucian, *no*."

Her brother frowned. "I don't get you. How come you won't talk to anyone? Don't you get lonely?" His voice was laced with concern.

"Of course I get lonely, but I highly doubt I'll find the answer to my problems at a jazz club."

"You have a better shot finding the solution here than locked up in that house."

"I'm not locked up."

"Is this ... is this about Susan?"

"What?" Breaking into a nervous sweat, she

fussed with her hair, which was fine. "What does Susan have to do with anything?"

He shrugged. "I'm just saying, if you and she are ... *more* than friends, I wouldn't have an issue with that."

Her face heated and her mouth slackened. "I'm not gay, Lucian. I like men."

"Then go meet one."

Rolling her eyes, she growled, "You're impossible."

"Come on, Isa. I know between now and the next time I'm home you'll do nothing more than *maybe* go out to dinner or whatever you do with the mysterious Susan. Having girlfriends isn't the same as getting a man's attention. I worry about you. I don't want you to sacrifice too much by taking on all the things Dad left undone."

"I'm perfectly fine doing what I've been doing. I don't mind taking care of you and Toni."

"Well, I can take care of myself now, so maybe you should reallocate your energy. You act like you're forty."

"Forty's not that old," she snapped, her voice far too defensive.

"Christ." He took sip of his drink, his patience waning. "I'm going to talk to that redhead over there."

She panicked and caught his arm. "You're leaving me?"

He stilled, giving her a confused yet assessing

glance. "I'm just going over there for a few minutes. I don't want that guy to assume I'm with you. I'll be ten feet away. I'll never take my eyes off you. I promise."

"Lucian." Her grip tightened.

"Step out of your comfort zone, Isadora. You might like the way it feels."

Seeing she was no match for her brother, she released his sleeve and fidgeted with her cocktail napkin. The bartender refreshed her drink, swapping it out with a new one she hadn't ordered.

"This is from the gentleman at the end of the bar."

Confused, she stared at the drink and then glanced at the man Lucian had pointed out. He lifted his beer in a sort of casual, silent solute.

Was this something people did? She'd only been inside a handful of bars in her life. Was involving the bartender some type of modern mating ritual? Unsure how to respond to such a gesture, she lifted the glass and nodded, hoping she wasn't subliminally agreeing to anything.

He smiled and her gaze lowered back to the bar.

She sipped her cocktail and covertly chanced glances at him, hopefully without appearing interested—but she was curious and somewhat flattered. There were no outward flaws that she noticed.

His hair was light, lighter than Sawyer's, and

his complexion was nice. He wore a blazer over a T-shirt, somehow managing to master the art of casual sophistication.

Taking another look to better see his features, she peeked around the curtain of her dark hair and sucked in a breath. *Where'd he go?*

"I figured I'd come over and say hello. I'm Jack."

She swallowed a gasp of surprise. "I—I'm Isadora."

"I've never seen you here before, but I've seen the guy you came with. Is he a friend of yours?"

"My brother, actually."

"Oh, so you're a Patras."

Here we go. "Yes."

"Mind if I sit?"

"Help yourself."

He slipped into the seat Lucian had vacated, his arm close enough to brush hers. "Do you like jazz?"

"I like most genres, but I'm no connoisseur."

"I come here for the ambiance. I love the architecture of the building." His gaze dropped to her hand. "Are you married?"

"No. You?"

"No, but I was engaged once. She wanted to put her career first."

He said that like it was a bad thing. "You didn't want to wait for her?"

"I did for a while, but then I realized she'd always put her job before me and that's not the sort of marriage I want. Do you work?"

"I..."

She hated being asked that question. Anyone else her age would have a job or be in school. She did neither, for the simple fact that she had other obligations, obligations she certainly wasn't going to disclose to a stranger at a bar.

When people found out she didn't work, they usually concluded that, as Christos Patras's daughter, she was living the heiress life. Nothing was further from the truth. She had a job—raising her siblings—but it wasn't the sort of work others typically recognized as ambitious.

Either way, it was too personal and complicated to explain to a stranger at a bar. "No, I don't work."

He nodded, but asked for no further explanation. Apparently Patrases didn't need to explain. But part of her wanted to. She was not some coddled princess who needed *Daddy* to survive. She was practical, damn it! And she'd manage to survive with or without her father.

"This band's pretty good, don't you think?"

The impersonal conversation was starting to irritate her. What was the point?

"Sure." Where was her brother? She casually craned her neck.

"What do you like to do in your free time?"

It all seemed so artificial. "I like to read." *Make love on Mondays.* "Garden. Sometimes I cook."

"Don't you have servants that do that?"

Jesus. Her skin grew uncomfortably warm. This was exactly why she hated introducing herself as a Patras.

"My father does. I prefer to run my own home." That was partly true. They had Lucy and sometimes they—*Why are you justifying yourself?*

"What's your dad like?"

She glanced over her shoulder and Lucian caught her panicked stare. "I think my brother's looking for me. Could you give me a second?"

"Sure."

"Excuse me." She slid off the stool, leaving her glass half-empty, and went to Lucian's side.

Lucian grinned with the ease of a man totally comfortable in his own skin. "This is my sister. Isadora, this is Genevieve."

"Hello," Isa smiled tightly. "Lucian, can I speak to you for a second?"

"I'll only be a moment," he informed his pretty companion. "What's wrong?"

"Can we leave? It was a mistake for me to come here."

He scowled, not at her, but at the man waiting by the bar. "Why?"

"I just don't fit in. This is awkward."

"Sure, you do. Let me introduce you to some people over here."

She gripped his sleeve, this time leaving no

room for escape. "No, Lucian. I came to spend time with you, not to be fixed up. Please... Can you just take me home?"

His dark eyes studied her, his expression wounded. "How about if we go somewhere else? I didn't mean to cast you off. We can still hang out."

"No, you've met someone. I don't want to take you away from her."

"I don't care, Isa. I wasn't looking for anything serious anyway. Come on. Let's get out of here and go somewhere else."

She weighed his words, trying to figure out if it was really so easy for him to meet women that he'd walk away from the opportunity of spending a night with a beautiful woman like Genevieve. "Are you sure?"

"Positive. Let's go."

They left the jazz club and wound up at a little restaurant with a bar that was more her pace. No one sent her drinks or curious glances. It turned out her brother was the perfect barricade between her and all other males, as no one seemed brave enough to question his protective presence at her side once she became the center of his attention.

He'd stopped drinking early in the night since he was driving, but he encouraged her to enjoy herself. Once the pressure was off she did just that.

As she loosened up they revisited the topic of Jack. "You shouldn't be afraid to let people know who you are," Lucian told her.

"It's different for women. Our name might open doors for you, but for me and Toni it looks like a passageway for climbers trying to find an easy way to the top."

"Only if you date pricks. You're smarter than that, Isa."

Was she? Maybe that was why she enjoyed Sawyer. He didn't need her name or her money. He just needed her. But how long he'd need her was anyone's guess.

"Do you think I'll ever get married?"

"Yes."

"That was fast. Don't you want to think about it?"

He laughed. "What's to think about? I know you. I guess I always pictured you with a bunch of kids and..."

"And what?" She was intrigued to hear how he pictured her future.

"I don't know. I see you with someone different. Down to earth. The sort of guy who would build a tree house with a hammer and nails and isn't afraid to play in the grass with your kids. But he doesn't do that stuff out of obligation. He does it because he loves his family. And you're happy because you love him and you're both totally devoted to each other."

Something expanded in her chest as she pictured everything he described. "That sounds lovely."

Lucian knew her better than she realized, because that short portrayal fit the perfect picture of happiness in her mind.

"I have no idea where you find someone like that, though." He sipped his water.

"Me neither." And Sawyer was *not* that man.

When he drove her home she felt warm and closer to her brother than she had in years. "Lucian, can I tell you a secret?"

"Anything."

She believed Lucian was a man of his word and someone she could trust, but her loyalty to Sawyer held her confession back. She wanted to be a woman of her word, someone people could trust. But so long as she kept her secrets inside, she worried she wasn't being a woman at all. She was lying like a paranoid child who lacked the integrity to answer for her own actions.

What if she confided in Lucian and her confession bothered him? Knowing the sort of man he pictured her with made her almost certain he wouldn't understand her choice in Sawyer.

Chickening out, she said, "I can't wait for Daddy to go back to Paris."

He laughed. "That's not a secret. And you're not alone. Don't worry. He's leaving Wednesday."

"He is?"

"Yeah."

"How do you know that?"

"I checked with his staff."

"Oh. I didn't think to do that." She also didn't think they, as Christos's children, had the right, but apparently Lucian didn't care.

His gaze remained focused on the road. "Eventually they'll all work for me, Isa."

"I know." She wasn't interested in inheriting her father's businesses. Those decisions were a long way off anyway. "As much as I dread him in the same house as us, I still don't like to think about his demise. He's still our father."

Lucian made a grunt that almost sounded like disagreement. "I'm not talking about his death. I'm talking about the not so distant future. I always keep my word."

Her shoulders knotted with tension. It had been a long time since her brother mentioned his vendetta.

When their father openly began dating his mistress, breaking their mother's heart, Lucian vowed to teach him a lesson. He swore, one day he'd show their father how it felt to lose the things he loved most.

It was an improbable promise made out of anger in innocence—one Isadora hoped he'd forget over time. But Lucian never forgot. And it was foolish of her to assume that just because he hadn't brought it up in a while that anything had changed.

Their father would make a nasty adversary— even against his own children. "You shouldn't worry about his dealings, Lucian. I'm sure you'll make your own fortune."

"I will," he agreed without a trace of doubt. "But I made a promise and, unlike him, I intend to keep my word." His hands tightened on the wheel and he shifted them, flexing almost imperceptibly. "He humiliated her."

There was no need to clarify that *her* was their mother.

A chill cut through her clothes. Their mother had devoted so much of her energy to a man who never loved her back. Isa believed a broken heart killed their mother as much as cancer.

Was she following her mother's footsteps?

No, she immediately rejected the thought. Sawyer wasn't cruel like her father and Isa knew better than to expect him to love her. She knew what she had gotten into.

They pulled up to the estate, but she was reluctant to leave the heated car. "Will you come back before you leave for school?"

"I don't think so. I'll call Toni, maybe take her to lunch tomorrow, but I can't be under the same roof as Christos."

"I hate how dysfunctional our family is."

"Every family's dysfunctional on some level. *You* balance us out."

His praise filled her with deep satisfaction, overshadowing her sadness. "You really believe that?"

He faced her with an incredulous look. "Yeah. You've done everything Mom used to do and then some. You don't give yourself enough credit."

She squeezed his arm through his coat sleeve. "Thank you."

"I should be the one thanking you."

She was so proud of him, so impressed with the man he'd become, she allowed her maternal grip to loosen and, for the first time in years, she didn't panic as she let go. "College is changing you, Lucian."

He didn't comment.

They stared at the front of the house and Isadora sighed. "I guess I have to go in there. It's strange how it feels like my house until he returns. Then it's like I have nothing, like I'm a guest in my own home."

"You know you could move, get a smaller place for you and Toni. The change might do you good."

"As crazy as it sounds, I love this house. I know it's too big for us and not mine, but ... I feel like this is where Mommy is, where her spirit lives."

"I get it. I've actually been thinking about the country house, but I'm waiting until I have the money to buy it outright."

The country house was where their mother was buried, where they used to spend their springs. "Daddy will never sell it."

"He will if the price is right. Despite all his posturing, everything has a price."

It hurt to know their father would give up the home where their mother rested, to know Lucian already realized that fact. "You're too young to be so cynical, Lucian."

"So are you."

She laughed. Maybe they all were. "I love you."

"I love you, too." He surprised her with his easy response. "I'll call you tomorrow about taking Toni out before I leave."

She hugged him goodbye and took her time making it into the house. When she reached the second floor her sister's door creaked open. "Isa?"

She went to her. "Why aren't you asleep?"

"Please don't leave me here alone with them again."

"What happened?"

"They're horrible. Tibet only speaks French—but I know she's fluent in English—and Daddy insists I speak her language, because she's *our guest*. Then she has the nerve to correct my pronunciation. And Daddy keeps making comments about my weight."

Isadora's teeth locked. That was the sort of thoughtless parenting he excelled at. His cruel comments were just words to him, but to his children they became badges of shame permanently tattooed on their character.

"I'm sorry, baby. Don't listen to them. There's

nothing wrong with your body. They're leaving soon anyway and tomorrow Lucian's taking you out."

Her mood immediately brightened. "He is?"

"Yes. Before you know it, everything will be back to normal."

"When are they leaving?"

"Wednesday."

"Thank God." Toni's body sagged against the door with relief.

"Thank God," Isadora echoed.

Wednesday couldn't come fast enough.

/ # Chapter 9

"A life is meant to be lived, not placed upon a shelf."~Shamus Callahan

LIFE TOOK ON A NEW PACE, a sort of rapid momentum that never quite waned. Winters unfurled into springs, followed by sweltering summers, and everyone seemed to be on the right path, heading toward different goals.

Although Isadora still didn't have the time to be a full time student, she moved around her schedule and made room in her life to take some classes here and there. She'd taken a pottery class and created some dreadful art pieces. Tap dancing, which turned out to be a humiliation she couldn't bring herself to share with others, but a decent workout. And then she moved on to Italian, which was just challenging enough.

She promised herself if she mastered the language she'd treat herself to a long vacation on the Amalfi coast one day. Perhaps Sawyer would go with her and they could openly be a couple there.

Lucian, to no one's surprise, did exactly as he said. As soon as the market turned in his favor, he pulled half of his investments and made an offer on their family's country home. Their father had the good sense to turn him down, appearing to have a conscience for a split second, but when Lucian came at him with a better offer the following winter he crumbled.

Toni was too preoccupied with her own life to care that the family she hardly remembered was tearing at the seams. She seemed satisfied enough just to know they had another home to visit, one with a heated pool in a beautiful countryside, where she claimed her brother would host her sweet sixteen—which was still three years away. But according to Toni, such parties took as much time to plan as a wedding.

Her sister seemed in such a rush to age. Isadora tried to explain that nothing fun happened once you were an adult, but her sage advice fell on deaf ears.

Sawyer had become a constant in Isadora's life. They still met on Mondays, and very rarely in between. Sometime around their two-year anniversary Isadora admitted—only to herself—that she was in love with him.

He never made any promises about their future, and as time passed Isadora's need to know where things were leading faded. They were clearly committed to each other, and whether he labeled it or not, they were in a relationship.

Sawyer was more than her lover. He was her closest friend, her confidant, and her happiness.

By the time Lucian entered his junior year of college, he started making comments about how tedious his education was becoming. She feared he wouldn't finish his degree, but on the same hand, she feared encouraging him to stick it out was a waste of time. Lucian did what he wanted.

There was no doubt her brother had arrived, a man bursting with ambition and wise beyond his years. She supposed certain traits were simply genetic.

It was impossible not to envy him, his confidence, his courage to demand satisfaction from every corner of the world as if it was his due. He was a distant storm that fascinated her and although he was younger, she admired him greatly. His determination to make something of himself often encouraged her to do the same.

The invitation to Vivian Callahan's wedding came the following spring. The event was scheduled for that August and Toni was thrilled that she'd garnered a place on the guest list, claiming this was some implication that she was one of the grown-ups.

According to her sister, no ordinary dress would do. Their summer consisted of multiple shopping sprees and many disagreements.

"But I like this dress," Toni argued one afternoon in the Neiman Marcus dressing room.

"Toni, you can't wear that. Daddy's going to be there and he'll have my head if he sees you dressed like that."

"Why?" she scoffed, clearly outraged. "I like the way I look."

Perhaps a little too much.

For all the curves Isadora lacked, her sister certainly made up for the both of them. On the cusp of fourteen, she was built like a seventeen-year-old pinup model.

"I said no. Take it off."

"Damn it, Isa. Why can't I get it? You're not the one paying for it."

"Hey, don't you swear at me. Either try on something else or we're leaving with nothing."

Her sister glared at her for a long moment, but Isadora didn't bend. With a huff, Toni turned and marched into the dressing room, muttering under her breath.

"Everyone else gets to buy whatever the hell they want with Daddy's money, but I don't get a choice in anything. I hate being the baby."

"Antoinette."

"Fine," she grumbled. "I'm almost sixteen you know."

"Let's get through fourteen and fifteen first, hmm?" Yes, they all knew she was growing up, but no one else credited teenage milestones with the significance her sister presumed.

They settled on a classy "pink" dress that exposed her shoulders, but hid superfluous cleavage.

"What about you?" Toni asked, as they searched for shoes.

"Oh, I'll just wear one of the dresses in my closet."

Toni rolled her eyes. "Buy something new, Isa. It's a wedding. Your future husband might be there."

"A wedding isn't a sophomore mixer, Toni. It's supposed to be about the bride and groom."

"I'm happy for Vivian," she said. "But that doesn't mean that I'm going to miss out on a chance to dance with *my* future husband."

"Lord give me strength," Isadora muttered, pinching the bridge of her nose. "You *are* aware that most of the guests will be adults? Vivian invited you as a courtesy to us. I don't think many kids will be there."

"You're wrong. She invited me as a courtesy to Shamus. He promised to dance with me."

Isadora frowned. "Toni... You know Jamie's just a friend, right? He's too old for you."

"He's only seven years older than me."

"And you're only thirteen. It's illegal. I don't want to hear anything more about it. It's totally inappropriate."

A twinge of hypocrisy gave her pause, but what she had with Sawyer was certainly not comparable to her thirteen-year-old sister having a crush on her brother's twenty-year-old friend. She wanted to make sure Toni understood why her feelings were not okay.

"If a twenty-year-old came near you in that way he'd go to jail, Antoinette."

She snorted, not measuring Isadora's warning with any sort real concern. "So would Lucian, because you know he'd kill the guy. Trust me, Isa. I know what's appropriate and what's not. But I'm going to dance with Shamus at his sister's wedding and I don't need you making a big deal about it."

She decided she'd have a word with Lucian about their sister's little crush and let him make sure his friend wasn't unintentionally encouraging her feelings in any way.

Toni talked her into buying a gown that—by the time they were on their way home—Isadora regretted purchasing. The back was cut so low the slightest draft would tickle parts of her best left hidden. But Toni, with her impetuous persistence, insisted she *needed* this dress.

It was deep violet, which was as good as black to Isa, and cut rather simply in the front. But the back... That was going to make her uncomfortable all night. She'd likely wind up wearing one of the plain gowns in her closet.

She mentioned the Shamus situation to Lucian, who assured her his friend was not interested in *some kid*. He'd even gone as far as asking Shamus, which, in turn, mortified the poor man and embarrassed all of them for even thinking such absurdities needed clarification.

In the end, Isadora was relieved, but Toni was furious when her brother teased her about her crush.

"How could you tell him? I trusted you! God, I can't talk to you about anything!" He sister stormed off to her bedroom.

Isadora contemplated the value of friendship with her sister and hoped moments like that didn't damage their chances of getting along in the future.

Their father would return to Folsom for the wedding, but announced he'd be staying at his hotel rather than at the family estate—something they were all grateful to hear. Knowing he'd be in attendance at the reception meant Isadora couldn't expect a moment alone with Sawyer, so she made the most out of their time before her father returned to town.

Lying next to Sawyer in his bed, she trailed her fingers over his chest. "You know what I was thinking?"

"What?"

"I think we should take a trip to Italy. I haven't been there since I was little and I'm getting pretty fluent at Italian. We could take a vacation, rent a vista overlooking the Mediterranean, make love with the windows wide open in the warm sea air. No one would bother us there."

He smiled and caught her hand. "That sounds lovely. But people would notice we both went at the same time."

"Only if we told them. You could say you're going to Spain. Who would know?"

Her stomach pinched with familiar longing. She was growing tired of hiding their relationship, certain if people knew they'd been dating for so long they'd understand outside opinions were insignificant at this point.

"But you would tell Lucian and Toni you were going to Italy?"

She shrugged. "You could just tell Slade the truth." Maybe starting with Slade was the first step. Then over time they could broach the subject with her family.

He sighed. "Isadora, things are peaceful. No one bothers us the way things are. And if the news got back to your father..."

Her father missed nothing and he was the last person she wanted involved in her personal life. Things had gotten very nasty between him and Lucian in the past year. She wasn't sure if learning of his daughter's ongoing affair with his trusted partner might push him over the edge. She certainly didn't want any severe consequences to affect Sawyer's job.

"It was just a thought."

"And a nice one." He lifted her hand and kissed the backs of her fingers. "I'm not saying no, but I don't know if this is the right time. I promise I'll take you one day—when the time's right."

Satisfied that he'd made the promise, she let her other concerns go for now. Eventually they'd find normal and all of this sneaking around would end.

Lucian had somehow acquired a private driver for the wedding. The chauffeur, not much older than herself, was named Dugan and had a very intimidating presence. But despite his gigantic height and unshakable expression, he seemed like a nice man. The limo, one from their father's fleet, had been washed and readied for the evening.

Dugan wasn't the only unexpected guest. Just as Isadora fastened the clasp on her earring, her bedroom door burst open.

"Oh my god, Isa, you're never going to believe this!" Toni exploded, shutting the door at her back.

"You scared the crap out of me! What's wrong?"

"Lucian brought a *date*."

She frowned at her sister. "So?"

"Not just a date. A *girlfriend*. She said she's

been dying to meet us, and her and Lucian have been seeing each other for over a month!"

Isadora's mouth opened. "*Our* brother?"

"Yes!"

Her lips slowly curved into a smile and she quickly collected her clutch. "What's does she look like?"

"Super pretty. Blonde—not natural, but flawless. Skinny. Tall."

Her heart raced with anticipation to meet this woman who had spent a considerable period of time with her brother. "He didn't tell me he was in a relationship."

The idea thrilled her. Lucian needed a steady woman in his life. Someone who could ground him and make him see there was more to life than financial advancement spurred by their vindictive father.

But the second she set eyes on his date—Monique—she knew she wasn't the right woman for her brother. She couldn't decide what was off about her. She was stunning to say the least, but not right for Lucian.

After only five minutes in the woman's presence Isadora picked up on a shallowness that could make anyone unattractive. While Monique showed great interest in Lucian's attire, cars, and assets, there was a lack of any deep interest in Lucian himself. It struck Isadora as odd that *this* was the woman he chose to settle in with after years of proclaiming he didn't have time for anything serious.

The ceremony was lovely and the reception was a lavish affair. Shamus's sister—the newly titled Dr. Vivian Sheffield—was a stunning bride. She'd certainly grown into a striking woman. The fact that she was also smart made her the whole package. Isadora hoped this Sheffield man was everything Vivian deserved.

While there was a familiar flicker of envy in watching another friend get married, Isadora harbored no resentment. It was Vivian's time. Isadora's time would come. Eventually she'd have her happy ending just like the rest of her friends.

They were seated adjacent from their father and Tibet's table, which she also suspected was where Sawyer would sit. What she hadn't anticipated was his *plus one*—or the fact that he'd *bring* a date, knowing full well she'd be in attendance.

Unfortunately, life lessons sometimes had a way of creating natural consequences that needed little translation. Painful truths were indeed excruciating.

Sawyer's *date* appeared in her mid-forties. Her clothing spoke of a secure bank account and her jewelry was tasteful. None of that mattered, however, because Isadora hated her on the spot.

The moment her gaze crossed with his, Isadora started to shake. How could he humiliate her like this with no warning? This was not a benefit for some charity. It was a wedding for a mutual friend.

When Slade sat himself beside Monique at their table, Isadora casually gathered information. "Is your father dating?"

Slade's eyes, much like Sawyer's, danced with humor. "Hardly. You should have seen what I had to go through to convince him to bring a date tonight."

So this was partially Slade's doing. That helped ease a bit of her outrage. Although, if they'd just come out of the closet, no one would be trying to fix either of them up.

Very aware that she was frowning, she distracted herself by staring around the room, but her jaw wouldn't unlock and her scowl wouldn't relax.

Although no one else knew Sawyer had humiliated her with his date, her response to the situation was not flattering and people at the table were starting to give her questioning looks. Escaping to the bar, she ordered a glass of chardonnay and prayed it was a good year.

"You okay?" Lucian asked, surprising her at the bar and ordering a cocktail of his own.

"Fine."

"You look like you're going to be sick. Do you want to get some air?"

She hesitated, glancing to Sawyer's table where his date held court with all the men. "Yes, okay."

Lucian walked her outside and they took a path into a garden lined with stone benches. "Is it Dad? Did he say something to upset you?"

"No, I'm just bad with crowds."

He frowned, likely wondering when that had happened. Providing a distraction, he said, "Vivian's a beautiful bride."

"She is. Classy. There's always been something timeless about her."

He nodded.

She wished Lucian would find someone like that—beautiful without realizing how much. Maybe that was what was wrong with his girlfriend, she seemed too in love with herself to form any real affection for anyone else.

"How long have you been dating Monique?"

He chuckled. "I wouldn't call it dating."

"What would you call it?" That was the impression the woman gave Toni.

He shrugged. "Passing time."

"Does she know that?"

"I don't know."

"Maybe you should tell her."

"I will at the right time."

Why were men such procrastinators in matters of the heart? Other guests drifted onto the path, commenting on the beautiful landscape and remarking about the happy couple.

He finished his cocktail. "You ready to go back inside?"

No. "Sure."

When they returned, Monique was dancing with Slade. Isadora glanced at Lucian who appeared to take little issue with his friend and his date sharing a moment during a slow song.

They weren't dancing like people who just met.

"She knows Slade?"

He nodded. "They're friendly."

Apparently so, going by the way his friend held her in his arms. She glanced back at Lucian. Didn't he see what she was seeing? There seemed a shared intimate knowledge between the two. Very intimate.

She bit her tongue, deciding it wasn't her business to comment. Lucian wasn't a fool and he would realize if anything inappropriate were going on.

Toni scowled at them as they returned to the empty table. "You left me alone."

"You weren't alone when we left," Lucian commented.

"Well, everyone else left me." Toni's glare turned to the head table.

"It's a wedding, brat. Try not to look so miserable," Lucian teased, nudging her shoulder.

Brothers weren't always good at noticing subtleties, but Isadora noted the way her sister's eyes shimmered a bit more than usual and the way her arms wrapped around her ribcage as if holding herself together. Isadora followed her gaze and immediately understood.

Shamus's date was a beautiful bombshell. Dark hair pinned high on her head, accentuating her long neck and trim build. There was no arguing with exquisiteness.

Empathizing, she scooted her chair closer to Toni's and whispered, "It's sort of an unwritten rule that those *in* the wedding party should bring dates. I bet half the groomsmen don't even know their guests' middle names."

Her sister blinked up at her and her eyes cleared, a fragile smile trembling to her lips. "Thank you, Isa."

She smiled and patted her knee. "You're prettier than her anyway. But he's *still* too old for you." She scanned the room. "That boy over there looks about your age. He's cute."

Toni followed her gaze and made a face of absolute revulsion. "Ew! Gross, Isa. That's Brice McCleary. He's a total dickwad."

"Language."

"Can't curb the truth."

Isa laughed and leaned close to her sister's ear. "Then learn to whisper."

After dinner the dance floor filled and Toni's mood lightened. Her concern for her sister overshadowed her own turmoil. Which, in a way, helped Isa mask her own pain so not to exacerbate Toni's.

Taking her own advice, she pasted on a smile and pretended not to care about things she had no control over at the moment. Later, in private, she would care very much.

Certain men, unfamiliar men she had no interest in knowing, occasionally glanced Isadora's way, but she used those moments to talk with her sister, appearing too preoccupied to be disturbed.

Monique was what Toni called "an attention whore". But Lucian hardly gave into his date's nagging, which bordered on relentless. Slade didn't seem to mind playing stand-in, acting as Monique's dance partner most of the evening and Isa was starting to see why Lucian didn't care.

"I think it's about time I took my daughter for a spin around the dance floor."

Isadora looked up as her father stood across from her table, his hand held out expectantly. Startled and pleasantly flattered, she smiled and placed her napkin on the vacant seat next to her—

"Annie?"

Toni tensed and Isadora suffered a sharp pang of envy, angry she still, after all these years, fell prey to his vapid attention. She should be happy to see him acknowledging Toni, who'd gone the longest without a father figure. But being overlooked still stung.

She nudged her sister. "Go on."

Keeping her expression blank, Toni stood and took their father's hand. As they moved into the crowd, Lucian turned to Isadora, but she ignored his assessing stare, hating to be the source of anyone's pity.

"Do you want to dance, Isa?"

She shut her eyes and forced herself not to laugh. If Lucian danced with her after his date had begged him all night to no avail, the other woman would surely throw a fit.

"No, thank you. I'm fine."

She stared at Toni and their father, hoping to see some sort of bonding, but his focus was elsewhere and Toni looked as if she were about to have a root canal.

"Care to dance?" Her body tightened as Sawyer's voice carried over the crooning vocals of Louis Armstrong.

As she stared up at him, she casually noted her brother's obliviousness. Still, what the hell was he doing?

"I don't think—"

"One dance. This is one of my favorite songs."

She glanced at his table, wondering where his date had gone. "Okay."

She rose and he took her arm like an uncle might take his niece's. The intimacy they usually shared in private was completely masked by his impeccable propriety.

"What are you doing?" she asked though a tight smile.

"Dancing with the most beautiful woman in the room."

"Sawyer—"

"It's just a dance, bella. Try to enjoy it."

"People will—"

"People will hardly notice. Your father's dancing with Toni and you were sitting alone—*a crime*. I'm merely being a gentleman."

He took her hand and pulled her into step, leading her gracefully across the floor. It was the first time they ever danced together, the first time they ever did anything remotely intimate in front of others, yet it wasn't intimate at all. It was hiding in plain sight and she hated it.

Her frustration from earlier returned and despite knowing she should wait until they were alone to discuss his actions, she couldn't help herself. "Who's your date?"

He grimaced. "A colleague. She's on the board at the shelter with me."

"She's pretty."

"Do you think?"

"I do. What's her name?" Her voice pitched with blasé inflection, fully patronizing him.

"Paula. Where's your date?"

"Slight miscommunication."

"Bella, you know we couldn't be ourselves here. Your father's sharing my table."

That point was made clear the moment he held her arm like a valet driver would assist a stranger. "I don't want to talk about it. The least you could have done was told me you were bringing a guest."

He waited a moment, then whispered, "You're right. I'm sorry. Slade insisted I bring someone and I assumed you'd do the same."

"Why would I do that, Sawyer?"

He frowned at her like she was speaking gibberish. "Isadora, I'm always encouraging you to keep your options open."

How open could they be when they'd been in a monogamous relationship for years?

"I'm not discussing this here. I didn't bring a date, because I didn't want to. End of story. But in the future, a little advance notice on your end would be nice." But she couldn't let it go. "So much for exclusivity."

"She's just a friend, bella. I told you there would be situations when social conduct dictates how I attend certain functions."

"Fundraisers and things that raise money for causes based on head counts. This is a wedding."

"I already apologized. I can't change anything now."

"Then let's drop it," she snapped, regretting she'd brought it up at all.

"Fine."

"Fine."

The song played and he led her easily with the

tempo. "You really are the most beautiful woman here tonight. The bride likely hates you."

That got a chuckle out of her. "She does not. Vivian's my friend."

"Sometimes friends hate each other. Jealousy can do nasty things to a person."

"Are you suggesting I'm jealous?"

"No, I know you're smarter than that. You wouldn't waste jealousy on a meaningless association. You know where my interests lie."

She hated that she needed to hear that, but his assurance eased some of her tension. "We could sneak away for a moment."

"Not here."

His quick rejection struck her with the preciseness of a bayonet.

He studied her for a long moment as they glided beside other dancers. "You're disappointed, but I think you know better. Everyone knows us here. We would get caught."

Oh, the horror.

He sighed. "I'd understand if you danced with other men."

"I said, we're not having that discussion here." Her jaw locked and she blinked rapidly.

"I'm not the only man watching you tonight. Look around. You could have your choice of any bachelor in the room."

"I've made my choice."

"Make another. At least dance with someone."

"Sawyer—"

"Please," he whispered. "I deserve it."

Her vision blurred and she tried to hide the rush of tears prickling her eyes. A dance was all she was able to get from him tonight, so dancing apparently meant a lot more to her than it meant to him. "You're ruining this song."

"You've spent the entire evening talking to Toni and using her as a buffer every time men approach your table. I've been watching you. What's the harm in talking to other people?"

The song ended and a much faster one began. He released her hand and she glared at him. Surrounded by strangers, there was no proper way to say all she wanted to say without making a scene.

She loved him, and she truly believed he loved her on some level, too. Yet here he was, trying to pawn her off on the other male guests.

Maybe he was trying to ease his own guilt. It made no difference. His persistence and pretended indifference infuriated her, insulted her on so many levels.

Dancers crowded around them, laughing and smiling while her heart trembled in her chest. "What do you want from me, Sawyer?"

"I worry you've made this so much more—"

"*We* made it more," she snapped, refusing to accept that he couldn't take accountability for his part.

How could he say such things here, in public,

where she couldn't react? Why now? Because she didn't bring some meaningless date with her? What would that prove? This was more than his date. There was something else going on, a distance she hadn't felt a few days ago.

Her jaw quivered. "Are you breaking up with me?" *At a wedding?*

"Our relationship isn't like that. You've always been free to do as you please. I want you to explore your options."

"I'm not some caged creature and I don't need permission to socialize. Maybe I'm enjoying my sister's company. Stop trying to change things."

"Because she's safe and familiar, just like I'm familiar. Every safety net has holes, bella. You're letting opportunities slip through the cracks, because you're too afraid to step outside of your comfort zone."

His expression was so casual, as if they were only two distant acquaintances playing catch up at a wedding, but his words... His words sliced through her until she was shuddering inside and struggling to remain still.

"Why are you saying this now? Here?"

"Because you've completely closed yourself off to everyone. And seeing you like that, when I know everything you have to offer... It's infuriating. Especially when I feel partially responsible."

"So this is about your guilt," she snapped.

"No, it's about you using everyone around

you as an excuse. It's Toni. It's Lucian. It's your father's absence. I refuse to be one more excuse for why you aren't living."

She. Was. Shaking.

Her hands balled into fists, the urge to slap him making her dizzy. "Are you finished?"

"Yes, we should probably return to our tables—"

"Just a minute," she caught his arm. "Despite your wisdom, there are some things I know that you don't. For instance, I know I'm more than a Monday night booty call to you. I know you have feelings for me. But I also know you'll never admit them. You're so worried I'm not living. Well, I am!

"I've felt more alive in the past three years than I have in my entire life. There are two people in this relationship—and it *is* a relationship—so you don't get to make decisions without giving me a say. I don't tell you how to live, so don't assume you have any right to decide for me."

His expression was blank as he stared at her. Voice level, he said, "You're making a scene. People are watching us."

Was he even listening? Looking up at him, knowing another song was about to end and they needed to get off the dance floor before people really got suspicious, she drew in a deep breath.

"I love you, Sawyer. I'm tired of lying. If we have to hide what we have, that's one thing, but

I'm not going to hide my feelings from *you*. What's the point?"

He looked down, away from her face and shut his eyes, slowly shaking his head. Of all the responses she expected, she wasn't prepared to see his obvious regret. "We don't have the time it takes to have this discussion here."

Unbelievable. All of that and he still didn't get it. "You see, Sawyer, to most couples it doesn't require a lengthy discussion. They're just three simple words."

His gaze narrowed as he leaned closer. "Those words are *anything* but simple! If you knew what real love was you'd know those words are the most complicated in the entire English language."

She drew back as if he'd slapped her. *If you knew what real love was...*

Her skin prickled as a chill chased down her limbs. Her breathing labored as she fought to keep her composure. A lifetime of lessons in decorum trembled as she lost sight of proper etiquette and lost control to her emotions.

"Fuck you, Sawyer!" She spun away from him and shoved her way through the throng of dancers.

Stalking past the tables of smiling guests she bee-lined right to the bar, her body shaking so intensely it was difficult to stand in her heels.

"May I have a shot please?"

The bartender looked at her expectantly. "A shot of...?"

"A fucking shot! Anything! Vodka. Tequila. Whatever's closest!"

Chapter 10

*"Heaven has no rage like love to hatred
turned,
Nor hell a fury like a woman scorned."*

William Congreve
The Mourning Bride

"YES, MA'AM," the bartender responded with deliberate politeness.

A clear shot slid in front of Isadora and she brought it to her lips with a trembling hand, throwing it back.

"Thank you," she rasped.

She reached for her purse only to find it missing. "I left my bag at the table. I promise I'll be right back."

"Sure," he commented, voice thick with skepticism.

She pushed through the crowd and found her clutch resting on her seat. Cracking it open, she removed a fifty. She shouldn't have snapped at the poor bartender. He didn't deserve her anger.

"Where were you?"

Her head snapped up at Toni's question. "I... I was having a drink. I need to go run this over to the bartender."

"Why is your face all red?"

Her hand fluttered to her warm cheek. "Is it?"

"Yeah. Lucian, isn't Isa's face red?"

She shushed her sister. "I have to go."

"Where are you going?" her sister called as her brother's assessing gaze marked her quick escape.

She walked away without offering an explanation. She was twenty-six years old. Lucian answered to no one, and he was five years her junior. She was tired of being treated like a child when she was the eldest.

She slid the fifty across the bar. "I'm sorry I snapped at you."

The bartender's brow lifted. "It's cool. Let me break that for you."

"Keep it. But I'll take another shot."

He eagerly poured. Turning, she tossed it back and scanned the room.

Where? *Where* were all these supposed admirers? She scoffed, not seeing a single person looking at—*Well, hello. Aren't you handsome?*

Holding her clutch at her hip, she sauntered across the ballroom toward a man with sandy brown hair, dressed in a striking Prada three-piece suit. The music pulsed loudly as she reached the edge of the dance floor, nearest to the speakers.

The man laughed, conversing with another attractive gentleman. She pasted on a smile, eased by the alcohol throbbing through her veins, and drew in a breath to back her words.

"Hello, gentlemen. Either of you care to dance?" She wasn't being choosey.

Their conversation cut off as they both stared at her. Oh boy, maybe Sawyer was wrong. Maybe he really was the only one who thought she actually—

"Absolutely," three-piece said, shoving his cocktail at his friend's chest and taking her hand. "I'm Tyrian."

"Hi, Tyrian. I'm Isadora."

"You have a pretty name."

"Thanks. Are you a friend of the bride's or the groom's?"

He escorted her onto the dance floor. "I went to school with the groom. You?"

"Bride's."

Enough small talk. They worked their way

into the throng of dancers and Isadora mimicked what another woman was doing, unsure how to actually dance fast without appearing to have a seizure.

Tyrian was a wonderful partner. He stayed close and never broke eye contact. He had a nice smile and straight teeth. Everything was going great until the music changed and couples partnered off for a slow song.

His lashes lowered as his motions slowed. "Shall we?"

Catching her breath, she nodded.

It was a classic Elvis ballad and she knew it well. It struck her as ironic, that when she danced with Sawyer, a man she'd seen naked countless times and sinned with frequently, he'd barely held more than her hand, no telling signs of intimacy beyond a platonic hold of her fingers. Tyrian, however, made his intentions clear as he pulled her body close.

He possessively cupped a hand to her exposed back and Isadora, again, regretted letting Toni talk her into wearing a dress outside of her comfort zone—which she was getting a little sick and tired of people accusing her of staying inside. She took risks.

She tried new things—tap, pottery, Italian, fucking her dad's colleague... Just because she wasn't some sort of adrenaline junkie or reckless and irresponsible didn't mean she lived a sheltered life.

As they swayed, she noted Tyrian lacked the skill and self-possession Sawyer owned, but he was also no slouch. Her gaze scanned the tables, a slight panic taking hold when she saw Toni's seat empty. Searching for her sister's dark hair, she breathed a sigh of relief when she spotted her only a few feet away—dancing with Shamus.

Her heart warmed as Shamus led her little sister around the floor casually, much like the platonic way Sawyer had led Isadora. It was indeed nonsexual, the way he laughed and smiled at whatever Toni was saying to him.

Unfortunately, Toni's gaze reflected absolute adoration. Certain things just needed time to fade. Perhaps that was a lesson Isadora needed to learn as well.

Tyrian's hand moved in smooth circles over her spine. "Are you doing anything after this?"

"I'll be going home with my brother and sister. We came together."

"I'd like to see you again. Do you live in the city?"

"Just outside, about a thirty minute drive."

"I'm in the historic district. Maybe this week I could take you to dinner, somewhere quiet where we could talk."

Her father was speaking to Tibet at an almost empty table. It occurred to her how much Lucian, despite his efforts, echoed the bad habits of the man they all worked so hard not to hate.

Like their dad, her brother was sitting on his ass, while his date gazed longingly at all the other couples dancing. It was likely the last slow song of the evening.

What was it with men? They all seemed intent on disappointing the one woman they were meant to please. It couldn't be all men. Maybe she was surrounding herself with the *wrong* men, so ambivalent in regard to romance. Perhaps not all men were like that.

As they made another revolution, her gaze fell on familiar eyes and her heart jolted. Sawyer stared at her, and not in a discreet way. He looked ... jealous. But he'd been the one to suggest she dance with someone else.

Anger resurged and her focus returned to Tyrian. "Is there a place you wanted to meet?"

"How about I call you this week and we can set something up."

"Sure," she said, numbly, as Sawyer continued to stare.

How did it make him feel to actually see another man's hands on her? His expression blanked, turning to something unreadable, yet he watched her with an intensity that said he was feeling some sort of unsavory emotion. That was his own damn fault.

His harbored guilt should not deprive her of

opportunities—opportunities to be with whomever she wanted, including *him*. She never once complained or asked for more than he was willing to give. Why couldn't he just accept what they had?

The song was nearing the end. Sawyer nodded and forced a fake smile that didn't reach his eyes. Then he stood and handed his date her purse. Together, the picture of absolute middle-aged dullness, they turned to her father and made their goodbyes.

She wanted to go home. Her anger made such a fast transition to sadness, she lost track of her surroundings and her eyes prickled. It was time to leave.

"Thank you for the dance. I think my brother's looking for me."

"Can I have your number?" Tyrian asked, halting her escape.

She paused, having already forgotten about agreeing to a date. Ugh, why had she done that?

He handed her his phone and she robotically typed in her number, her attention pulling to the door as Sawyer exited the hall. She would decide when Tyrian called if she'd answer or not. A lot of her decision depended on the man who just left with another woman.

The limo ride home was quiet. Monique rested her head on Lucian's shoulder and Toni slept. Isadora watched the city of Folsom rush by in an ashen blur.

Her mind returned to Sawyer, over and over again, and stuck there as she lay down to sleep that night. She wanted to call his house to prove he'd gone home alone. But her dignity forbade it. If they couldn't trust each other, they had nothing. Maybe they had nothing anyway.

He doesn't love you...

The thought sliced through her, making her physically flinch. A tear slowly rolled from the inner corner of her eye to the bridge of her nose as she rested her cheek against the pillow.

He loved her. He had to by now. If he didn't, what the hell were they doing? If he couldn't bring himself to say the words, fine, but to flat out deny it...

She rolled onto her back and scowled at the ceiling. It was one thing for him to have issues with love, but how dare he act like she was too naïve to identify such emotions. She'd never actually been angry with him until he accused her of not knowing what real love was.

She wasn't an idiot who needed people to tell her how to feel. She meant what she said, not just about loving him but also about a relationship involving two people. They were going to hash this out one way or another—the two of them.

When she fell asleep, her dreams were sketchy. Images swirled, and she was the passenger of a carousel, whipping around the center of a ball-room, as all her friends and family watched. Her father kept giving Toni *her* things—the keys to her Volvo, the figurine he'd gifted her on her tenth birthday, and worst of all, the pearl earrings her mother had left her.

It wasn't fair. Toni had been left Momma's *sapphire* earrings. The pearls were *hers*.

Nothing made sense and as the dream spun, Lucian grew bigger and bigger while Sawyer seemed to shrink away, like a man walking backward in a narrow tunnel until he was only the size of a flea.

She awoke in a sweat the next morning, tired and cranky. Her hair deflated from its up-do, leaving some parts lifeless and others stiff. Her dress hung like a forgotten memory over the chair in her bedroom. She definitely needed coffee.

Slipping into her robe, she went downstairs. Someone was awake and in the den. She wasn't sure if Lucian came back after taking Monique home, or if he spent the night at his girlfriend's. But she was happy to find the coffee made.

Pouring a cup, she went to the den. Lucian sat, still in his tux but wrinkled and sans tie. His posture was tense and his gaze was riveted to the television.

"Good morning," she grumbled, taking a seat next to him.

He barely nodded.

She glanced at the television—some sort of breaking news.

A man was being escorted in his robe across a manicured lawn. A woman cried and a teenage boy appeared startled as news reporters swarmed a private residential property.

"What happened?"

Lucian sipped his coffee and pointed to the television. "Crispin Hughes was arrested. He's going to jail."

"In a bathrobe?"

Crispin Hughes was a heavy hitter in Folsom. It was a toss-up which name was worth more, Patras or Hughes. People joked and said Crispin Hughes and Christos Patras were gods, the two Christs of Folsom. In her mind, they operated closer to hell than heaven.

Of course that made Hughes a rival and her father liked to keep his enemies close, so she was familiar with the name.

"Daddy will be happy."

Lucian grunted and she wasn't sure if that was agreement or disagreement. She read the crawl at the bottom of the screen, a laundry list of charges against Hughes ticking by.

"Was he embezzling from all those companies?"

"Not sure. Definitely some insider-trading going on. And they're saying he's been at it for years. They've already confiscated all his computers and bank records."

She frowned as they angled the camera back to the boy and his mother. "Why do they keep doing that? That poor woman probably had nothing to do with his underhanded dealings and that kid can't be more than fifteen. They look devastated. The media should leave them out of it."

"Paparazzi. They're vultures. Nothing better to them than a wealthy family brought to its knees." He sat back, but kept his eyes on the screen.

"That's shameful." She continued to stare, appalled, as FBI agents entered and exited the family's private home, carrying more than just computers.

She thought of their personal belongings being ransacked for the sins of their father, a man they hardly knew, a man who couldn't be bothered to call on the holidays. A sense of insecurity struck with startling discomfort.

She glanced around the den, feeling like she was in someone else's house, which she was, but this was their home. If anything happened to it, she and Toni would have nowhere to go. Well, they had trusts and would figure it out, but her lack of control in such a situation filled her with anxiety.

"Do you think I should buy this house from Daddy, Lucian?"

"Yes. Either that or buy a different one. The less you're indebted to him the better off you'll be."

She thought of how large the house actually was. It was too much for just her and Toni. It wasn't practical. "I'll never be able to afford this property."

He glanced at her and back to the TV. After a long moment, he said, "If you want this house, Isa, I can help you. Not right this minute, but give me a year or two. You could dip into your savings, get a thirty-year mortgage, and we'd make it work. It's not going to always be just you and Toni living here. Eventually you'll have a husband and a family of your own."

She wanted to laugh but her chest constricted. The house would be miserable with just her living there. It was meant for a family. She should probably be more realistic and think about moving into a smaller place after Toni graduated. She didn't need all this room. Sawyer didn't want children...

Her hand fluttered to her stomach, a nauseating ache forming in the pit of her belly. Even if she and Sawyer worked through whatever their problems were, what kind of security did they really have? What was she to him? A lover? A girlfriend? Would they ever consider moving in together?

And what if when Toni graduated Isadora

didn't want to get married and jump into domestic living. It would be her first chance to actually do something with herself. She could finally get an education and maybe even a job.

She thought back to a man she'd met at a bar years ago with Lucian. He'd dumped his fiancée for putting her career before him. Isadora didn't want to make a choice like that. She wanted to be something, do something she loved, but she also wanted to *be* loved.

Lucian shook his head and muttered, "That kid's life is about to get so screwed up. I wonder if he hates his father as much as I hate ours."

Isadora tsked, feeling bad for the young Hughes boy.

"This is going to change things," Lucian muttered, eyes distracted.

She frowned. "What do you mean?"

"Taking Hughes out of the picture will open up some opportunities for those still climbing." He stood, setting his empty coffee mug on the end table. "I have to make some calls."

She looked at the clock. "It's seven-thirty on a Sunday."

He ignored her, searching his pockets as he stepped toward the door.

"Lucian," she snapped, getting his attention.

"What?"

"It's Sunday morning. What kind of man

makes business deals off another man's misfortune?"

"It's how the game's played, Isa. When you see an opening, you take it."

She scoffed in disgust. "Everything isn't a chess match, Lucian! They aren't game pieces. They're real people whose lives are about to be ruined."

"Well, I didn't ruin their lives. I'm only moving accordingly, as the pieces fall." He left the room and she took the remote, switching the channel.

Even if life was one big chess match, the world was short on shining knights. Everyone wanted to be a stupid, selfish king.

Chapter 11

> "Don't waste your love on somebody who doesn't value it."
> **William Shakespeare**
> *Romeo and Juliet*

"YOU DIDN'T EVEN CALL YESTERDAY," Isadora snapped, standing in Sawyer's kitchen the following Monday.

Avoiding eye contact, he nosed through the fridge like a man searching for an escape hatch. "I didn't know what to say."

Her arms folded over her chest as her eyes narrowed. "Yes, we've already established certain words are too difficult for you."

He sighed and shut the refrigerator door.

When he finally looked at her his eyes wore lines of stress, pinched at the corners and full of regret.

Crossing the kitchen, he placed his hands on her shoulders, placating her a small degree. "What is it you want me to say, bella?"

She pursed her lips. He knew exactly what she needed to hear.

Releasing her shoulders with a long exhalation, he dropped his arms. "You know I care very deeply for you."

But she didn't know if that was enough. The question remained, was that his problem or hers? Right now it seemed to belong to both of them.

"I've always been upfront with you, bella. I've never wanted to mislead you. Ever."

"I know that."

But she didn't expect to fall in love with him. She hadn't prepared for all of these feelings or the sense of inadequacy that came when such feelings weren't openly reciprocated. Was she that difficult to love?

His fingers massaged the tension lines from his brow. "Then why are we arguing?"

A sense of hopelessness enveloped her and she slid into a kitchen chair, feeling utterly defeated. What good were sentimental words when they had to be badgered out of someone?

"When you saw me dancing with that man, didn't it tell you anything? I saw you watching me. You had this look of anguish—"

"If you want me to say I'm above jealousy, I can't. I know I'm not. That's part of the problem."

"Why does there have to be a problem?"

He sat across from her and took her hands, squeezing tightly. "You said you're tired of lying, and you don't want to hide anything from me. I don't want that either. I've always wanted absolute honesty between us, regardless of what the rest of the world knows. But I will not let you put all the blame on my shoulders for the falsehoods that separate us, Isadora."

Other than not confessing her love right away, she couldn't think of anything else she'd concealed from him. "I don't know what you're talking about."

"That's because you're not just lying to me. You're fooling yourself."

"How?"

He gave a sad smile. "Tell me you want children someday. Let me hear you admit it."

She frowned. "What does that have to do with—"

"Please. I need to hear you admit the truth out loud."

"I..." Was that the truth? "I don't know."

"Yes, you do."

"No, Sawyer, I don't." Her voice turned pleading, conveying her honest difficulty when it came to such life altering decisions. "I enjoy children, but not all women get to have a family."

"Let's live in a world where you get whatever you want for a moment. Do you want a family?"

She shut her eyes, knowing the truth in her heart and knowing that path didn't include him. It included a mysterious man she'd yet to meet—might never meet. "I don't need—"

"What do you *want*, Isadora? This isn't about necessity or settling. I'm asking you a simple question and there's a simple answer."

"I want you." Her voice was small, the expectation of him being a part of her everyday life woven into her bones.

"Sweetheart, Slade's the only child I'll ever have in this lifetime."

"Because you can't have anymore?" There were other options.

"Because I'm done. I want to travel and retire, knowing all my obligations have been met."

A wash of fantasies seemed to fade away. Little girl dreams made of dollies and tea parties bled off the canvas of her mind so a new dream could take shape, one that included him, and better matched her reality. There was less disappointment when she worked with what she had rather than hoping for things she might never possess.

Her surrender covered her like a cool blanket, unfamiliar but with the promise that it would warm over time. "Then I don't want children."

His chair shoved back from the table and he stood, startling her. Tension flowed from his body in waves as he paced away.

When he faced her again, his eyes were cold and accusing. "Don't come into *my* house and lie to me. If you want to have an honest conversation, have the courage to tell the truth, Isadora," he snapped.

Taken aback by his abrupt mood change and sharp tone, she blinked up at him. "I'm not lying!"

"Yes, you are! Not just to me, but to yourself!"

"I'm trying to compromise—"

"*Enough compromising!* Everything in your life has been a tradeoff! You're forever putting others before yourself. Isn't there a single selfish bone in your body?"

"Why are you so angry?" she shouted, matching his volume.

"Because I don't want you to settle, goddamn it! Don't you get it? I'm trying to do the right thing here. Eventually, you need to start thinking about your future, planning for it, but you make it impossible for me to be a gentleman about it. Do I have to be cruel to get you to understand?"

Where was all of this coming from? "I'm not trying to be ignorant and I don't want to fight with you."

"Then help me get through to you. What we have is *over*. It has to end or you'll never find what you actually want in life. You're losing time and I'm stealing it from you."

Adrenaline crashed and spiked high, shooting a sharp knife of shock through her system. Over?

"What are you saying?" she rasped.

He pinched the bridge of his nose and shook his head. This was not how this conversation was meant to go. Couples disagreed, even those carrying on in secret.

Arguments could be constructive at times, clear the air for better communication, but he was just giving up. They were supposed to have a fight, not throw everything away.

Her chin trembled as she sat before him, her vision blurring with unshed tears. He was throwing *her* away. Her mouth opened, a plea resting on her tongue, but she snapped her lips shut, swallowing it back.

She was turning into her mother. Just as Lucian couldn't avoid mimicking their father, she was repeating her mother's worst mistakes, and getting a taste of the pain her mother lived with every day of her miserable married life.

A gaping hole stretched in her chest as if put there by unexpected cannon fire. This morning she woke up believing he'd always want her. Now … she didn't know what to believe.

Lowering her gaze to the table, she whispered, "I suppose it's cruel no matter what."

"I don't want to hurt you, Isadora—"

"Then don't."

"I'm doing this because I care about you."

Well, he certainly had a nasty way of showing it. He'd never been anything but delicate with her and to have him suddenly screaming that they were *over* was a pain she couldn't quite process.

"May I have a tissue, please?"

He disappeared into the den and returned with a box. She pulled a couple of sheets out and mopped up her tears. He returned to the chair next to her and gently turned her face.

The tissues left her hands and he took over blotting her cheeks, voice returning to its usual gentleness. "Don't cry, bella. Please, don't cry. Not because of me."

She sniffled and looked into his familiar eyes. The pain expanded, unfurling lengthy fears she couldn't stomach.

"I don't know how to live without you, Sawyer. I need you in my life. We can't be over."

"I'll *always* be in your life, Isadora. But we can't go on this way."

She sucked in an uneven breath as more tears fell. He acted like they were miserable when she knew they were happy. Why did they have to change anything? She couldn't stop the desperate loop of questions running through her head, her only instinct to convince him this was a mistake.

Her heart quaked with a sense of helplessness. Why? She didn't want this. Her chest physically ached because he was literally breaking it into pieces.

She pressed her hand to her heart in an attempt to ease the pressure. "This hurts."

His brow pinched and he pulled her onto his lap. "Come here."

His arms wrapped around her, holding her tightly. Safe. His arms had always been the safest place she could escape to when she needed a place to run.

"This was never supposed to be permanent, bella."

That was a lie. It was never supposed to be serious. No one said it couldn't last.

Maybe if he stepped back he'd see what they had wasn't so bad. What they shared worked. It made sense for the both of them. Why try to correct something that wasn't broken? Or maybe he saw something she didn't.

"Did I do something wrong?" She could fix it.

"No, sweetheart, no." Easing back, he turned her chin so he could look into her eyes. "Do you know, you're my closest friend in the whole world? I would trust you with my life, Isadora. This is going to be hard on both of us, but we cannot keep pretending what we have is any sort of substitute for what you truly deserve.

"You've already sacrificed too much in your life. I never want you to make a sacrifice for me. It feels like your loss, but really, I'm the one losing.

You are an incredible woman and you *are* going to find the right man, someone who can give you everything you want, even the things you don't realize you will want over time."

She turned her face away. "We're both losing."

"This is the only way you'll ever move on. I never wanted to take advantage of you and if we continued like this, you'll eventually give up every chance at a better future by default. I'm not worth it. Take my word on that."

She swallowed tightly, pain constricting her throat. "I think you are."

"Don't compromise your happiness, bella. Not for me or anyone else."

She couldn't believe this was happening. Every time she looked into his eyes she was assaulted by his resolve, his determination to stand his ground, and her heart shattered. She understood his reasoning, worse, she understood this was a way of expressing his love for her, but the pain was hers.

Fearful of the next step, she leaned forward and cupped her hands to either side of his face, pressing her lips to his as she wept. He tensed and the ache in her chest grew.

"Kiss me, Sawyer. You kiss me or I will never be able to put myself together again."

His arms closed around her as his shoulders relaxed and he slowly kissed her back.

"I love you," she confessed in a broken whisper against his lips. "You can take all of this away from me, but you can't touch what I feel. You can't change it. This is ours, but *that* is mine. Time and distance won't diminish what I feel."

His arms tightened and his lips aggressively captured hers in a kiss that seemed misplaced in the midst of such a devastating conversation. His hands were possessive, his desire evident.

There was a brief moment he tried to pull back but in the end, even he lacked the will. His inner battle was palpable and, as much as she wanted him to keep kissing and touching her, she couldn't bear the thought of being something he *fought* to avoid.

She was not a sin, a secret, or a vice. She was an innocent woman who had somehow been mislabeled as a source of her lover's shame. The realization finished off the last of her heart, tearing the frayed threads into useless scraps.

Forcing herself to pull back, she looked into his eyes, which were glassy and pink rimmed. Love. He loved her, but would never admit it. Her gaze broke away.

She didn't need the words, but she might never stop wanting them. The longer their relationship went on, the more excruciating his silence would become.

What was the point of living if you were determined to quit the one thing that brought you joy? A long silence expanded between them, their different views announced with every quiet second until she was incapable of looking him in the eye. Too much pain hidden his. Too much resentment likely showing in hers.

Accepting it was time for her to go, a strangled sound smothered in her throat. All she had to do was stand up and go, but she couldn't find the strength.

Her rattled dignity screamed at her to make some sort of dramatic exit, chin held high, maybe slam a door or two. Leave him before he could truly leave her.

But she couldn't move. Parting would truly mark the end of them.

"I'm afraid to go," she rasped.

"We'll still see each other on occasion. And you can call if you need anything. You know I'll always be there for you, bella. If there's ever an emergency or something you can't do on your own..."

She could do anything alone. Though having someone at her side made even the most unpleasant tasks tolerable, she didn't need anyone but herself to survive.

Exhausted and dreading the days that would follow, knowing she wouldn't let herself reach out to him unless there biwas truly an emergency only he could fix, she knew she wouldn't contact him. She could not bear seeing him if she couldn't actually have him.

It was time. Using her hands to sustain her balance, she stood on shaky legs, every inch of distance seeming to scrape another layer off her tender heart. "I have to go."

Collecting her things filled her with the strange anxiety of forgetting something. It was as if her soul knew she was leaving a piece of her behind, the piece of her heart Sawyer would always own.

Once she had the few items she kept there—a book, her slippers—he walked her to the door. She looked up at him, noting the way his mouth curved down and his laugh lines extended his frown.

He handed her the box of her belongings and she hugged them to her chest. Did she just *leave* now?

He sighed. "Come here, sweetheart."

Her face pinched as she shoved the box aside and leaned into his arms. His lips resting on her temple. She needed this last embrace.

One. Last. Time.

He buried his face in her hair and squeezed her tight. His voice was soft as he whispered in her ear, "One day you'll fall in love with the right man and you'll know what I'm talking about. It will be so powerful, so epic, this will seem like a child's sketch next to a Monet."

Everything inside of her argued that wasn't true. She could only see herself with him or alone. No one could ever take his place.

Their relationship, with all its faults, was right for them. Right for her. Until now.

She didn't say a word. Holding her composure by an unraveling thread, she slowly let him go. This was it, whether he realized that or not. She would not let herself contact him again and she doubted he'd call her.

"Goodbye, Sawyer." The thinnest shred of dignity guided her out the door.

I'll always love you...

Chapter 12

"A sacrifice not shed, is an invitation to pin, a
weakness waiting to happen."
~Christos Patras

IT TOOK a solid week before Isadora could accept the truth. The Monday following the breakup was one of the most insufferable nights of her life, the inescapable proof that they were over forced her to confront how much she wished they were still together, despite her knowledge that she deserved a man who wanted her.

No. Sawyer did want her, but he couldn't come to terms with his desires.

He pushed her away *because* he loved her enough to want something better for her future, something bigger than what he could offer. As much as that unspoken truth should have comforted her, it didn't. He was a coward.

Watching her mother grovel for her father, even after his countless affairs, had scarred Isadora. Her mother's blatant lack of self-respect caused Isadora to vow long ago never to let a man humiliate her in such a way.

Had her mother walked away when her father first discarded their marriage, vows, and affection, she might have found true happiness, someone who deserved her loyal heart. But she stayed, a thorn bird intent on bludgeoning its vulnerable heart in want of the impossible.

Isadora could not—*would not*—give her heart to someone who didn't want it. Yet, for all her pride, she couldn't stop herself from loving Sawyer.

In the weeks that followed she suffered a steady argument with herself, debating his logic against her inner desire to go back to him. But she couldn't go back. She would not sacrifice her dignity for a man who refused to give his heart.

It took every bit of self-possession not to call him or go to his house. Seducing him into bed wouldn't be much of a challenge, but it also wasn't a solution. The solution was finding someone willing to give her everything she deserved.

She and Sawyer never lacked chemistry. But

going back to him after being so resolutely pushed away would get them nowhere. He told her to go after the life she desired—and damn him for knowing her so well. But she also desired *him* and those feelings didn't fade easily.

Their definitions of happiness were drastically different and she believed that was due to timing. Had she been born earlier, caught him at a different stage of life, they could have made each other perfectly happy, had a family, gotten married. But there was no changing reality.

She loved a man who refused to love her back, because he believed he couldn't fulfill her needs.

It was a wretched awareness and one she wished she could shut off. She certainly didn't want to suffer anything close to this heartache again. Which made the probability of her finding someone else, trusting someone else with her heart, absolutely implausible.

Love simply hurt too much. And if she fell in love again, the fall might very well kill her.

He was her confidant, her adviser, her sounding board and closest friend. He *listened* to her, knew her inside and out. Without him, she had no one to unburden herself to and she had so much inside that needed to get out—pain that he created.

Sawyer versus a family. Love and truth or familiarity and secrets? Affirmation versus silence. Resentment or affection? Black or white? Settle or fight? She was being torn in half and couldn't focus on anything, because every option came with a drastic drawback.

The simple task of packing Toni's lunch overwhelmed her. She'd stopped going to her Italian class, because her mind was in such turmoil, warring against her heart, she could barely listen when anyone spoke.

Even books couldn't offer an escape, so she spent days wandering around the house, drifting from room to room, waiting for something to catch her interest, but nothing ever did.

Holding a secret this size was a terrifying thing.

She questioned her sanity, worried if their relationship was ever real. The longer she went without him, the more it seemed like just a dream.

In a desperate attempt to hold her memory intact, she passed several days writing their story down. But recollecting the good times made her equally as sad as the bad times. It was all tainted, over, and foolish of her to hold onto a fantasy that would never amount to anything real.

She locked their story in a file hidden deep in the documents of her laptop and made the impossible decision to never read it again. It was over and there was no promise of a happy ending.

Depression was swallowing her more and more with every passing week and no matter how she tried not to let it win, she seemed no match for the despondency. Not only did she not like her situation, she despised her weakness.

Getting over her broken heart was necessary. But she honestly didn't know if she was strong enough.

As she lay on the couch one evening, staring at the television, not registering what she watched, her phone rang. It was probably Toni wanting to get picked up which meant she had to start dinner soon. Maybe they'd just order takeout again.

Guilt nudged the other ugly emotions aside, as shame corroded her thinking. Eventually, she'd have to get back to normal, but she couldn't figure out how.

Lost. She felt so lost and no one even cared that she was missing. The phone rang again and she sighed.

I just want to be left alone in my misery. "Hello?"

"Isa? Were you sleeping?"

Wrong sibling. "No, just lying down."

As much as she wanted to escape the pain, every intrusion was an annoyance. She needed to wallow in peace. God, her thinking had turned into a landmine of hypocrisy.

"Are you sick?" Lucian asked, voice concerned.

"No. I'm fine."

"You don't sound fine."

"Well, I am." Talking could be so tedious. "Did you need something?"

"Where's Toni?"

She frowned. He and Toni didn't have much of a phone relationship. "Out. Why?"

"Out where?"

"I don't know, Lucian, out with her friends from school." Her tone came out more tart and impatient than she would have liked.

Silence. "I'm sorry I bothered you. Tell Toni to call me when she gets home."

There was something strange in his voice and she didn't like how paranoid his request made her feel. "Why do you need to talk to Toni?"

"Do I need a reason to talk to my little sister?"

"Lucian, quit playing games."

"Isa, *what* is wrong? And don't tell me nothing."

She scoffed. "You just want to get information out of Toni."

"So what?" he snapped. "Something's obviously going on with you. If you don't want me to talk to her about it then you talk to me. I can tell you're in a mood."

"That's right. Something's going on with *me*, Lucian. Not with Toni. Not with you." Why did men think they could fix everything? Like a penis was some sort of magic wand women lacked. "Just leave me alone."

"Why are you acting so bitchy?" he barked. "Are you mad at me?"

Bitchy? He has some nerve!

"Everything isn't about *you!* I think I'm entitled to a bad day. You've had plenty! Just leave me the hell alone!"

The line went dead, before she could retract her words. Staring down at the phone she caught her breath. She was being a bitch—and to the wrong man. "Oh my God."

She dialed him back and it went to voicemail so she dialed again. She never spoke to him like that—*they* didn't speak to each other that way. At least not since he was a moody teen. God help her, she was acting like a child.

Her behavior was out of control, unacceptable, and she couldn't bear the thought of either of her siblings being upset with her. She dialed a third time.

"*What?*"

She flinched at his greeting. "I'm sorry."

Silence.

"I didn't mean to snap at you. I'm... I can't talk about it." She caught a tear at the corner of her eye. "But you can't fix it anyway. No one can."

"Isa, you can talk to me about anything. We're family."

We're a family, remember?

Her heart pinched, recalling his words from over a decade ago, hearing the plea of a little lamb now disguised in wolf's clothing. He would always be her caring little brother, no matter how intimidating he pretended to be as a man.

She wished she could confide in him. "Not about this, Lucian." Perhaps that was what hurt most. Her eyes slowly leaked. "I'm sorry."

"What's *this*? Did something happen?"

She was so exhausted, her ceaseless thoughts keeping her up all night. Lucian didn't easily let things go, mostly because he took it upon himself to keep her and Toni safe. He was very protective of those he loved, but even he couldn't fix a broken heart. "It's about a guy..."

"A guy?"

"I can't talk about it with you. I'm just going through something right now. I'm sure I'll be fine once I've processed." No idea how long that would take.

His voice was frighteningly calm. "Did this guy do something to you, Isa?"

"I can't—"

"Did someone fucking hurt you? I want the truth and I want a name—"

"Lucian, it's not that sort of situation."

"You aren't hurt then?"

She lowered her head, her pain a steady ache in her bones. Some wounds hurt more than physical bruises.

She shut her eyes as the tears gathered. "I'm heartbroken."

He let out a slow breath and when he spoke again his voice was gentle. "I'm coming over. I'm in the city anyway. You're going to talk and I'll listen."

Her face pinched as she silently wept. There would be no stopping him, but even he wasn't strong enough to pull the truth out of her. It was then she finally understood so much of her pain was humiliation. She'd wasted three years of her life chasing a fantasy.

Lucian arrived—with pizza—about forty-five minutes after they hung up. As thoughtful as it was that he came all this way, she still couldn't confide in him.

What good would it do for him to know his best friend's father put her in this situation? Sawyer wasn't even fully to blame. She'd known what she was getting into. He told her his feelings on love and relationships the first night they'd slept together.

But Lucian proved to be a good distraction anyway. They watched a movie, ate, and he even made her laugh a few times, telling stories about some of his college friends.

When Toni needed a ride home, he volunteered to go get her. After their sister went to bed Isadora was hardly able to keep her eyes open.

"Who was he, Isa?" Lucian asked, his focus appearing to be on the television.

Leaning into the arm of the sofa, she closed her eyes. "I can't tell you."

"Why?"

She peeked through her lashes, appraising the tense set of his jaw and the tightness of his fist resting on his knee.

"Because you have that crazy look in your eyes and I don't want you to hurt him."

"He hurt you."

"I let myself get hurt. I was stupid."

He glared at her. "Don't call yourself that. He's the one who let you get away."

She silently chuckled. "You're very sweet when you want to be, Lucian."

"I'm not saying it to be sweet. I'm saying it because it's true. That guy must be a total moron if he didn't see what a catch you are. He did you a favor. You'll be better off with someone who appreciates you."

She laughed without humor. "He'd agree with you there."

"What does that mean?"

"Don't worry about it. Thank you for coming over tonight." Her eyes were getting too heavy to keep open.

Feeling herself nod off, she sucked in a breath and groggily jerked awake only to find Lucian draping a blanket over her.

His mouth curved in a tender smile as he brushed a hand over her hair. "Get some sleep. I'll call you tomorrow."

She shut her eyes, his care blanketing her more than anything else. "Love you..."

"Love you, too."

Thirteen

"Any little girl can wear a tiara and call herself a queen. Becoming a queen is more than jewels. It's a behavior that takes a lifetime to master."

~Antoinette Patras

THE FOLLOWING DAY, Isadora made a difficult, but empowering decision.

She wasn't going to be sad anymore.

Sawyer might be wrong about some shining knight sweeping in and offering her the perfect future, but what if he was right? Regardless, she wasn't going to live out her days waiting for someone else to come along and rescue her.

She was responsible for her own happiness and that attitude needed to start now, because she couldn't stomach the weak-willed person she was becoming.

She was going to be a strong, independent woman—with or without a man by her side.

First step in finding one's independence was learning to lean on oneself. She made an executive decision that would force her to take on more responsibilities—and called her brother.

"I think Lucy should start working at the country house for you. It's vacant and could probably use some attention."

"It's vacant, because I'm never there, Isa. I don't need a maid."

"I don't want to lay her off, Lucian."

"Why would you?"

"Because she's no longer necessary here. I'll keep Louis on as a driver *as needed*, but Lucy only does chores I should be doing, or Toni, for that matter. It'll do her good to have to vacuum her own bedroom or run a load of laundry now and then."

He laughed. "And you actually expect her to do those things?"

"Yes. I'll be doing them as well. There's no reason why we can't take care of ourselves."

She was tired of trusting others with her well-being. And she didn't want her sister repeating her mistakes by relying on other people to make her happy.

"You do realize how ridiculous that sounds, don't you?"

"It's ridiculous that the other day Toni actually asked me why some people don't have cars. She has no concept of how privileged she is and I refuse to let her grow into some pampered heiress."

"She *is* an heiress."

"Well..." She couldn't argue with the truth.

Why was it fine for Lucian to be so independently driven, yet when she wanted the same for her and her sister he called it ridiculous? That was exactly the sort of mindset she wanted to change in this family.

"Do you want Lucy or not?"

"Fine. Tell Lucy to take a ride over to the house and make a list of what she'll need to get settled. Have her email it to me."

And so it began. Her decision to take charge of things around the house was the first step in her *Become More Independent Plan*.

She was accountable for her. That meant figuring out how to be self-sufficient.

There were some bumps. The first time the vacuum clogged she lost her shit, smacking the contraption with a hanger when she couldn't get it to work. But she didn't give up. She had a drink, dismantled the thing, and eventually got it working again. It didn't matter that it now made a hideous shrieking sound when it ran. She fixed it.

Toni was outraged by her new list of responsibilities, to say the least. She started wearing clothes she hadn't tried on in years, expecting that once she wore through her wardrobe Isadora would take her shopping for more clothing. Either that or they'd call Lucy back to wash and iron the soiled garments.

Isadora did no such thing.

Isadora didn't have an ultimate goal in mind, but every day she looked for clues about herself and focused on new objectives that built back her pride. Twenty-six years old and she was finally growing up. She was moving on to better things—happier things. If there was something she didn't like about herself, she worked to improve it.

If she was going to be the sort of women who didn't have a man in her life—a strong probability—she needed to acquire more skills. Things were always breaking around the house and, without the servants, she either had to teach herself to fix items or hire contractors, which brought her to another issue.

Financial stability was something she grew up with, but didn't know how to cultivate. It was a point of embarrassment that Isadora wasn't sure how much money she actually *had* within her grasp. Bonds, stocks, and a trust fund that paid out like pensions, it was all very comforting, but nothing she could take credit for earning.

She wasn't wasteful, but she certainly wasn't frugal. That was going to change.

She put herself on a strict budget and banked the majority of her monthly allowance from her trusts in a private account earmarked for her future. One day she intended to own this house and know that *no one*, not even her father, could threaten her sense of security.

By fall, she had tightened her wallet so much she actually saved a handsome sum. She wanted to celebrate, so for Toni's birthday she treated her sister to a day in the city.

They made reservations at the Patras Hotel restaurant and were given the royal treatment. Yet she had the satisfaction of only spending what *she* could afford. Demanding a bill confused the hotel staff, but she was sticking to her principles. This was her gift to Toni, not their father's.

Isadora enjoyed their time so much, she decided to reserve a penthouse suite and stay the night, scheduling a day at the spa for both of them the next morning.

Lying in the overstuffed hotel bed wearing Patras bathrobes and pigging out on ice cream sundaes while watching cheesy romantic comedies, Isadora savored the fact that her sister was growing up and they could now enjoy some of the same things.

"You should have let Daddy to treat us to dinner and dessert," Toni commented, sucking the fudge off her spoon.

Isadora studied her sister, wondering how long it would take for her to understand sometimes pride was more valuable than money. "I can afford to treat you without his help." Patras was not cheap, but it was a bittersweet sort of expense.

"Doesn't spending that sort of money go against your whole mid-life crisis thing you have going on?"

Isadora scoffed and gave her sister a playful shove. "Brat! I'm not having a *crisis* and you have to be middle-aged to have a mid-life anything."

"Then what *are* you doing? The other day I saw you reading a book about plumbing."

"The trap in the sink was clogged!"

"So call a plumber, Isa. Reading a book about outer space doesn't make someone an astronaut. The minute you start trying to fix things they're going to *really* break."

"It was a clogged drain, not rocket science, Toni. Plumbers are expensive."

"Oh, my god." She held up her hand as if she'd heard enough. "Reality check, Isadora *Patras.* You can afford a plumber!"

"It's not about the money. It's about taking care of myself, about dignity Daddy pride. So, if you could stop acting like I'm some sort of freak for trying to fix our kitchen sink I'd appreciate it."

Her sister's expression softened and she studied her for a quiet moment then nodded. "Sorry. I didn't mean to make fun of you." Then she smirked. "But don't expect me to strap on a tool belt."

Pulling Toni back to the center of the bed, Isa pursed her lips. "I won't. I couldn't fix the stupid drain anyway. We don't own pliers and the slip nut thingie was on too tight."

Toni laughed until she snorted. "Did you call a plumber?"

"He's coming out on Tuesday," Isa mumbled.

She put her empty ice cream dish on the table and shut off the bedside lamp, snuggling deeper under the covers. Toni did the same.

A new movie started and they fell into a comfortable silence. Isadora was just starting to doze off when something brushed her fingers.

Toni's hand closed around hers under the covers and squeezed. "Thanks for today, Isa. It was a perfect birthday."

Glancing at her sister, she tried to find her voice. Her gratitude was a gift in itself. "You're welcome."

It was the first time Isadora allowed herself to honestly believe they might someday be best friends. The world was a big, often lonely, place. As independent as she hoped to eventually be, she never wanted any of her siblings to stop depending on each other.

Lacing her fingers with Toni's, she squeezed back. "Get some sleep. We have to get up early for our appointment in the morning."

The next day, Isadora awoke with the intention of getting a manicure and a massage at the salon, but Toni convinced her to get a haircut, too. It was a big change since she'd kept the same boring length for the last decade.

Nine inches of her waves were gone, replaced with a long bob that brushed her shoulders. The new cut gave her a more sophisticated look, according to the stylist. In the end, she was beyond pleased.

"We should buy you a new wardrobe," Toni said, as they stepped onto the tasseled runner exiting the hotel.

"I don't need new clothes."

"Oh, come on, Isa. Your clothes are *old*. Every new look deserves a few new outfits. Unless you're afraid someone might mistake you for a twenty-six year old."

She gave her sister a sidelong glance. "You're quite the little smart ass today."

"Is that a yes?"

Isadora sighed. "I'm trying to be more prudent with my spending."

Toni chuckled, but bit her lips so as not to comment. Isadora could see how ridiculous her sister found her words. Maybe she was being a little extreme.

"Fine," Isa agreed. "But we're not going crazy."

Toni clapped with excitement. "This is going to be so much fun!"

They visited multiple boutiques on the main line of Folsom and acquired so many packages she wasn't sure they'd fit in the car. So much for not going crazy, but Toni could be a persistent little bugger.

After shopping, they ended their retail excursion with a late lunch at a small café outside of the historic district. Isadora was laughing as her sister did an unflattering impression of her gym teacher when a vaguely familiar voice interrupted them.

"Isadora?"

She turned but didn't recognize the handsome man hovering beside their table.

Seeing she couldn't place him, he smiled. "Tyrian, from Ian and Vivian's wedding. We danced together."

"Oh, Tyrian! I'm so sorry. It's been a long day... My brain..." She also might have remembered him if he'd *called*.

"I was hoping I'd eventually run into you. The number you put in my phone is out of service."

She frowned. "What? How could that be?"

He pulled out his phone and pressed a few buttons. Flashing her the screen, she read her name and heard the recording that played when a phone number didn't work.

"Oh, my gosh. I probably typed it in wrong." It hadn't been the best night and she'd been in a rush to leave.

He smiled, appearing to accept that it was an honest mistake. "How have you been?"

"I've been ... good. And yourself?" She was definitely doing better than she'd been a few weeks ago.

"No complaints." He glanced at Toni and Isadora remembered her manners.

"This is my sister, Antoinette. Antoinette, this is Tyrian. He's a friend of Vivian's husband's."

"Hi," her sister chirped, smiling widely.

"Nice to meet you." He turned back to Isadora. "I'm still hoping for the chance to buy you dinner. Are you free this week?"

Her cheeks pulled tight, his charm warming her soul. "My schedule's pretty flexible. When would you like to go?"

"How about next weekend?"

She ignored Toni's gawking. "That would work. Why don't you call me and we'll figure out the details?"

"Definitely, but I'll need a working number."

She flushed as he handed her his phone. Sure enough there was a five where there should have been a seven. She fixed it and passed the phone back to him.

"I'm sorry about that."

"I'll let you get back to your lunch. I'll call you

soon." He turned to Toni. "It was nice meeting you."

As he walked away her sister continued to stare, her mouth agape with a wide smile, eyes unblinking. "Who. Was. *That*?"

Just then Isa's phone rang. She dug it out of her bag but didn't recognize the number. "Hello?"

"Just checking," Tyrian said.

She glanced out the window and there he was, calling her from the sidewalk. She smiled like an idiot. It was sort of adorable. "Now I've got your number, too."

He had a smile that triggered something jittery inside of her, something nice. Eyes on her, he winked and a small dimple formed in his cheek. "I'll call you tonight."

"Okay." Feeling Toni's gaze she ended the call and typed his name into her contacts. "Stop staring at me."

"That was like something out of a movie! He's, like, super hot, Isa. Are you really going to go out with him?"

She shrugged, her face burning up. "If he calls."

"He already did! He's totally into you!"

"You think?"

Stuff like this didn't happen to her. She covered her face with her palms and hid an uncharacteristic smile as she stifled the urge to squeak like a teenage girl.

When she had herself under control, she peeked through her fingers at Toni. "You really think he's into me?"

"Um, *yeah*."

Isa glanced out the window again, but he was gone. Her cheeks pulled into another smile and she looked at her sister and giggled. "I have a date this weekend. An actual date!"

The rest of their lunch was spent mentally reviewing their purchases and deciding what she should wear on said date.

Tyrian called and showed great initiative. He orchestrated everything down to the reservations. All she had to do was be ready on Saturday by seven.

It was strange having a man pick her up at home in front of Toni, but the more they bonded over the experience the more Isa realized how much hiding parts of her personal life had cost their relationship. Her sister took great pleasure in helping her get ready and even did her makeup, though Isadora refused to wear the bright lipstick she selected.

"It looks pink."

"It's more of a frosty nude, Isa. It's sexy."

She stared at the lipstick, hating that certain colors didn't register with her eyes. Her world was awash in faded blues and browns, but she rarely thought about her vision, having been colorblind since birth. The only time it really bothered her was when she was trying to look nice.

In moments like this, she had no choice but to trust Toni's judgment. "You swear it's not too much?"

"I swear." Toni painted a thin coat on her lips and smiled. "You look gorgeous."

When Tyrian's car pulled up Toni fluttered around like a nervous wreck.

"You do realize he's *my* date," Isadora reminded dryly.

"I know, but he's *so* cute. How are you so calm?"

She rolled her eyes. Toni was nervous enough for the both of them. "I shouldn't be late. Behave yourself."

* * *

Tyrian was lovely company. He conversed easily, employed chivalrous manners any girl would appreciate, and he smelled good.

They talked about the upcoming election with little tension, even though they were voting for different candidates. He was very diplomatic, never quite announcing which side of any position he favored, but making it clear he was well informed on several topics. They discussed their families and played a game of seven degrees of separation to see which friends they might have in common.

His father was in the oil business, most of their company stationed down in Texas. It was refreshing, knowing his family had money. Not because she was superficial, but because it made her father's fortune less obtrusive.

At the end of the night, he walked her to the door and kissed her on the cheek. When she told Toni nothing happened, her sister seemed disappointed.

"No," Isadora disagreed. "A kiss on the cheek is classy. It says he likes me enough not to rush things and ruin the chance at a second date."

At least that was what she wanted her teenage sister to believe. Isadora honestly didn't know what a cheek peck meant in adult dating terms.

"Is there going to be a second date?"

"I don't know. I guess that depends on him." She already decided that if he wanted to take her out again, she'd go on another date. But only if *he* wanted to. She refused to push him.

But there was a second date. And a third. And a tenth.

Over the next two months Tyrian became a steady part of her life. She had yet to feel any real butterflies like she experienced from the start of her and Sawyer's intimate relationship, but she and Sawyer also slept together an hour after they discovered their chemistry. Maybe butterflies with Tyrian would come once they reached that stage.

On their way to a new restaurant in Folsom they drove past Leningrad, one of her father's many companies. Seeing the building where Sawyer spent a majority of his days brought about a slew of emotions she'd been camouflaging with convenient distractions for the past several months. But she refused to give into her curiosity, wondering where he was or how he'd been passing his time.

Those sorts of thoughts still hurt. *Still*.

She believed Tyrian was more than just a distraction. He was fun, entertaining, and often made her laugh. He was more like a sedative, dulling the ache in her heart and helping her pass time while she healed. But nothing, not even her new relationship, allowed her to escape the pain altogether.

Pulling her gaze from Leningrad, she turned to her date and focused on the present. "I heard great things about this restaurant."

He smiled as he navigated the evening traffic. "Me too."

"Do you think there will be a wait?" The restaurant opened only a few days ago and the chef was a big crowd-pleaser according to reviews.

"We have reservations, so we should get right in."

When they arrived at the restaurant there was

a line snaking onto the pavement. Patrons were dressed in business formal attire and a valet service was working double time to keep up. Rather than wait in line, Tyrian escorted her to the hostess station.

A man was complaining to the maître d' so they waited a few paces back for the hostess to return.

"Our reservations were for an hour ago. Why make reservations if you can't honor them?" the patron argued.

"Sir, I do apologize for the wait. You're next to be seated."

Uh-oh. They might be waiting longer than expected.

The man appeared utterly flustered. "It's our anniversary. I made these reservations last week."

The maître d' looked over the man's shoulder and spotted them, abruptly forgetting about the unsatisfied patron in front of him. "Ah, Ms. Patras. We weren't expecting you tonight."

She wanted to crawl into a hole and disappear as the couple celebrating their anniversary noted the host's preferential attitude. Nudging Tyrian forward, she let him relay the details of their reservation.

Tyrian gave his name and Isadora's gaze skated back to the disgruntled man who was now making excuses to his wife. The woman wore what appeared to be a new dress. Her hair was done in a twist that looked fresh from a salon.

Menus in hand, the hostess returned and the maître d' instructed Isa and Tyrian to follow her into the dining room. Isadora hesitated and sent Tyrian a pleading look.

"It's their wedding anniversary," she whispered.

He glanced at the couple and back to her, appearing to read her mind. "Are you sure?"

She nodded and he turned to the couple. "Please, take our table. You're celebrating."

The man and woman wore matching expressions of surprise.

"Sir," the maître d' protested, but Isadora ignored him, captivated by her date's show of generosity.

The couple thanked them profusely and she and Tyrian wished them a happy anniversary.

As Tyrian escorted her back to the valet, he asked, "How do you feel about burgers and shakes?"

Enchanted, she slipped her arm into his and stepped onto the pavement. "That sounds perfect."

They wound up at a little outdoor spot sipping shakes and eating greasy burgers. A mess of crumpled napkins piled between them as they picked at their fries.

"I like to dip mine in my milkshake," Tyrian said, slipping the plastic lid off his cup.

"I do that too!"

He laughed. "I'm also a fan of pretzels in ice cream."

"Mmm. I'll have to try that."

In that moment she admitted to herself that she liked Tyrian as more than just a friend. Maybe instant butterflies weren't the only way people felt affection. Maybe some connections developed at a slower pace and came with other signals.

With every date their kisses grew more frantic and the need to do more increased until they were practically clawing at each other's clothing in the front seat of his car. Isadora missed fooling around and Tyrian was a good kisser, but sometimes when she shut her eyes she accidentally pictured someone else's face.

Pulling apart, Tyrian eyed her with evident desire. "How would you feel about spending tomorrow night at my place?"

His question was expected, but it still managed to take her off guard. Despite her ramped up libido, her stomach plummeted.

Were they already there? At *that* point? Her mind immediately went to Sawyer. Agreeing to spend the night with Tyrian felt like sweeping a big eraser over her past, something she wasn't sure she was ready to do.

Was Sawyer sleeping with someone else?

Don't go there.

It had been months and Sawyer hadn't contacted her while she'd tried to move on with her life. But she often worried he might be lonely in that huge house all by himself. She inwardly sighed and looked down into her lap. Forcing herself to move forward was supposed to ease the pain. So why did this decision hurt?

She was no longer wallowing over the things she couldn't have. She was too busy to feel badly about her situation. But when life got quiet, the ache in her heart knocked her down hard. And every time she had to pick herself back up she was reminded how much he'd hurt her and tampered with her trusting nature, causing issues in other parts of her life.

But sometimes, when she was with Tyrian, she forgot to think about Sawyer at all. That always made her feel victorious and guilty at the same time.

She was doing things with her life, becoming more independent every day. Yet she'd never felt so artificial.

The sex appeal was there, but only as a biological response. The desire to date was real, but only to subdue her loneliness. She wasn't sure if anything she was experiencing actually had to do with Tyrian. Yet it seemed to have *everything* to do with Sawyer and the mess he'd left.

Glancing at Tyrian she tallied his good qualities. There were a lot. He was a great guy, a true gentleman, and most importantly, he seemed genuinely open to possibly falling in love.

When she thought of his drawbacks there was only one. He wasn't Sawyer.

She didn't love Tyrian, but she also hadn't loved Sawyer from the start. Love took time and maybe she wasn't giving it or Tyrian a chance. She wanted someone to love her, someone who would never hurt her.

Was that even possible?

The familiar pang that dulled but never waned swept through her as her fingers tightened into a fist. She doubted that the ache would ever disappear, so there was no point in prolonging the inevitable.

She glanced again at Tyrian. Did she trust him? Yes. Would he be a good lover? Probably. Did she want to have sex? Desperately, but what if it was different and not in a good way?

"Isa?"

Most women her age had multiple experiences with numerous men. Was it really such a big deal to take a risk and try something new? Recollections of her brother and Sawyer encouraging her to step out of her comfort zone raced through her mind. She was on the cusp of something—maybe a great something—but she needed a little push.

She forced herself to say the words. "I can call my brother to see if he can stay with Toni tomorrow night." That at least gave her twenty-four hours to come to terms with her decision.

Tyrian kissed her, his hunger and excitement evident, but her private misgivings made it impossible to revel in her own anticipation.

Several times throughout the following day she considered faking the flu and canceling, but she never worked up the nerve to make the call. Like everything else in her romantic life, sleeping with Tyrian set her head and heart in opposing positions. Her brain told her sex with someone new would be good for her, but her heart whimpered every time she tried to picture making love to anyone but Sawyer.

Before she knew it, she was dressing for her date and Lucian had arrived to stay with Toni. Although her sister was old enough to watch herself, Isadora didn't want her staying home alone all night and she had no idea if she'd be back before morning.

It was happening. Something was definitely swirling in her stomach, but she was pretty sure they weren't butterflies. Several times while getting ready she had to pause and take a deep breath.

"Am I going to meet him?" Lucian asked, as he scooped ice cream into bowls in the kitchen.

"That depends on your behavior," Isa teased, finding her brother a great distraction from her nerves. "You're always threatening the boys Toni likes."

"That's because they want to do things to my sister."

She arched a brow. "And I called you over so I could go out and play checkers? Why do you think you're here, Lucian?"

"So you *want* me to kill him?"

She laughed. "You're too easy." She closed her purse and went to the front window to check if Tyrian had arrived while Lucian trailed behind, his expensive shoes making only the slightest sound in their entryway.

"You like this guy."

It was a strange assessment, one she couldn't deny or fully agree with.

"It's still early."

Headlights turned onto their property and her heart tripped out of beat.

"This isn't the same guy from before, is it?"

She let the curtains fall. "No. That's over."

It was important to say it out loud, but excruciating to hear.

She said goodnight to Toni and met Tyrian in the driveway. Lucian followed her outside and shook his hand, but saved the cross-examination for another time.

Isadora never had an active father in her life, but in that moment she felt like she did. Somehow embarrassed that her little brother was assessing a man she intended to sleep with, she said a quick goodnight and politely urged Tyrian into the car.

When they arrived at his place Tyrian cooked a homemade meal, which helped relieve some of her tension. Dinner was casual and they both appeared at ease. She was quite impressed with his culinary skills.

"Everything was delicious. Thank you."

"I have to admit, I called my mom about a hundred times asking questions."

"That's sweet." He was so close to his parents. The next step in their relationship was probably for her to meet them.

Trying to imagine how that might go made her feel like an absolute phony. She so badly wanted to be in a committed serious relationship, but her heart never seemed to follow the right pace. She hoped delay *that* introduction as long as possible. Maybe in time, as they crossed certain benchmarks, meeting his family wouldn't feel so intimidating.

After dinner they sat in the living room and talked, which eventually led to kissing. Regardless of her reservations, a tender tugging formed in her belly and she found herself leaning closer in an invitation for more. It had been so long since she'd had sex, her body was perhaps making the greatest argument of all.

"Do you want to go upstairs?" he whispered, his lips playing over her throat and teasing a sensitive spot at her collarbone.

Giving a slight nod of agreement, she adjusted

her clothes and he helped her off the couch. But as she stood her body quickly cooled. Her legs seemed made of cement as she trudged up the stairs, making it harder to move the closer they came to his bedroom.

By the time they reached his room her heart was winning and her brain's arguments to push forward had quieted into soft whispers racing through her confused mind. Meanwhile, her body was so tense, she couldn't figure out if her heart was racing with anticipation or fear.

She was going to back out. She came here, convinced herself this was right, and now she was going to completely embarrass the both of them by changing her mind.

No! If she wanted to heal she had to keep moving. Her heart was one thing, but she was not frigid. She was momentarily spooked, but downstairs her body had been having all the proper biological responses. And her brain, before this very moment, had decided this was right. She was just getting cold feet. Brain plus body had to outnumber heart.

You're doing this! Once it's done it won't feel so unfamiliar. You're getting yourself worked up for nothing!

Stepping to opposite sides of the bed, she thought in terms of movement, breaking every task down into manageable increments. Clothes would need to come off and she would need to lie down.

Start with your shirt...

She needed to shove past this mental blockade and force her hands to cooperate. Her mind flashed to the night she'd first met Tyrian. Sawyer had inadvertently orchestrated that, insisting she dance with another man.

Sawyer is gone. It's over. He doesn't want you anymore. This is what he wanted for you.

Something other than fear broke through the wall. Anger.

You have to move on. This is the next step. You need to get over him.

Her anger morphed into understanding. Sawyer was right. He was her safety net, her familiar home, but she'd never experience anything worthwhile if she couldn't jump into the unknown.

You might enjoy it. Just let it happen.

Her shoulders unknotted as she considered how pleasurable it might be. First times were always a touch awkward, weren't they?

Can you see yourself having children with this man?

A mental wall slammed down, thereby shoving her out of her thoughts and plummeting her into the present. Time to stop thinking and start doing.

With an unsteady hand, she unbuttoned the

front of her blouse, her fingers working robotically from top to bottom as her eyes focused on the bed. Drawing in a deep breath, she forced herself to meet his gaze, but could only hold it for a split second, so she slid off her jeans.

Breathing unsteadily, she stood before him in her bra and panties. Her gaze traveled over the bedding as she watched him undress through her lashes. Still unable to make eye contact, she slid under the covers and he did the same.

Her heart rattled like a tin can dragging down a country road. She could hardly move a muscle for fear that she might run out of the room like a lunatic. The light went off and her panic skyrocketed. His body eased closer, and at the first brush of his hand over her hip her mind took a vacation, traveling outside of herself where she watched the moment like an outsider looking in.

Unlike Sawyer, Tyrian touched her in an almost mathematical sense, as if her body was a formula he needed to solve. His touch moved from her breasts to her sides to her hips, and back to her breasts again, as if this would somehow equate to sex. It was as clinical and as unemotional as a doctor exam, the sort during which you stare at a pharmaceutical ad so your mind can get through without screaming.

He didn't caress her the way Sawyer did, yet he'd done enough for her body to form a biological response. Rolling to his side, he reached into a drawer and tore open a foil packet.

She'd never had sex with a condom, but was glad for it in this instance. The idea of having nothing between them was far too intimate.

He fit himself between her legs, his nearness overwhelming and her knees trembling. A tightness formed in her chest, swelling up to her throat as her eyes prickled.

"You're tight. Try to relax, babe."

His voice was gentle, as was his touch. Her mind teetered between willing her body to open and telling him to get off. Before she made up her mind, he pressed forward and there was no going back.

She'd agreed to this. At some point she'd convinced herself this was necessary. Yet, as he pumped his hips between her thighs, breathed over her skin, touched her breasts, and took his pleasure, she felt like something sacred was being ripped away.

Sawyer had been her first and her only. He was her first partner, her first relationship, her first love. With every thrust she felt his memory slipping away. Staring over Tyrian's shoulder into the dark, a slow tear trickled to her hair.

Tyrian never realized she cried, but he was intuitive enough to recognize that their first time wasn't what it should have been. In the end, he held her back to his front and whispered hopeful words regarding their next time. There wouldn't be a next time.

Although he was gentle and did everything a woman could expect, it was the most painfully intimate experience of her life—one she had no intention of repeating. Physically, she wanted an intimate connection, but that sort of emotional intimacy could not be forced. She'd forced herself to do this and it was simply too soon. She wasn't ready.

Tyrian was not the man for her. Or more accurately, she was not the woman for him. He deserved someone who could offer him one hundred percent, but sleeping together proved that her heart still belonged to someone else.

It was simply too excruciating to re-cross certain lines and she wasn't ready—no matter how much she wanted to be. Her logic didn't matter. Her libido didn't matter. All that mattered was her heart, and that might be more broken than she wanted to admit.

Distracting herself with the motions of moving on had healed nothing. More time wasted.

When Tyrian called, she made excuses not to see him, but after a few days he asked her point blank if something was wrong.

"We're moving a little too fast for me." It was the most honest excuse she could give him.

She didn't think other adult couples waited fifteen dates to sleep together, but she didn't know what else to tell him. Tyrian made a valiant effort to convince her not to give up on them, but she was done. She was done with trying to find a replacement for the one man, the *only* man, she wanted.

If it happened it happened, but she wasn't going to waste any more time searching for a soulmate when everything inside her believed she was destined to be alone.

Summer approached and that meant fewer obligations with Toni once school let out. She was stuck in the past, but time continued to move on. In a little over a year her sister would be driving and Isadora would be even less necessary than she was today.

The idea that she might soon be obsolete in some way terrified her. She *needed* to feel necessary, but every person she loved was outgrowing her help.

Late May, unable to sleep, she went to the kitchen to make a cup of chamomile tea. Sitting in the library, she stared at her surroundings, wondering how she felt at home in a house that wasn't hers. The furniture, the old books, the drapes ... they were all forgotten pieces of her parents' prior life. She was as forgotten as the chair she sat in while she sipped her tea.

Her gaze rested on the ornate chess set for a long while, recalling how her father would badger

Lucian on a regular basis, challenging him, never once letting the little boy win a match.

Kings, queens, bishops, knights... Onyx and ivory little figures set in perfect rows. She pitied the pawns, with their low stature and unimpressive detail. But she envied the royal figures for the ease in which they moved, never hesitating to change the game.

Why was it taking her so long to change her life? She'd become more independent. She'd saved money. But her larger goals still seemed a million miles away. More powerful players inserting obstacles she wasn't sure she could pass.

She was a pawn.

Her life only moved when it served others. Her one duty was to protect her brother and sister, a pawn meant to shield a king and queen. Insignificant. Sacrificial.

The bishops were able to cut across the playing field in one swift move, jerking the game back and forth. Every piece had some sort of privilege, but not the pawns.

Pawns lived a lifetime of slow aggression, one isolated square at a time. Everyone knew the pawns were the first to be knocked out of the game, the sacrificial lambs with such little value they were rarely missed once they were gone.

Players rarely considered the sacrifice of the pawn.

There were, however, ways for pawns to get

promoted. If they were brave enough to push past the bishops and other pieces blocking their way, they could make it to the other side. If a pawn succeeded, it then became a queen.

She was tired of being a pawn, tired of making sacrifices for everyone but herself. But she honestly didn't know if she was meant for more.

Her hand reached out, slowly sliding an ivory pawn out of line. She stared at the piece for so long the room illuminated with predawn light.

Turning the board, she slid an onyx pawn forward. The white pawn advanced again. And then the bishop slithered out of hiding, landing in the neighboring square.

It was her move, but she wasn't sure how to proceed, because like her actual life, she always seemed to be competing against herself. If she traveled forward, she could leave the bishop behind. Perhaps it would get knocked out of the game completely—lost forever.

Her alter ego, the fed up darker side of her soul, challenged her every move, determining which direction the onyx pieces should move and setting obstacles in her path. She was partial to the ivory figures, but the white pieces only seemed practiced at playing defense. Perhaps it was time she did something aggressive and switched to offense. Maybe that was the way to change the game.

Her fingers hesitated over the board, her eyes seeing no sensible way to take the bishop or move the ivory pawn. It was a mind game, one she was playing against herself. The white pieces were hers and the dark figures were every obstacle holding her back.

Leaving the game, she went to the desk and opened her laptop. Signing online, she filled in the search bar, her history predicting what she sought before she finished typing the first word.

The local university's website opened and she clicked on the admissions page. Her mouse toggled through the menu until she was staring at the online enrollment form. Her personal information slowly appeared on the screen. It was time to make a move. Drawing in a deep breath, she hit send.

"No more excuses," she whispered. She was done being a pawn.

As she walked past the chessboard on her way out of the library, she paused. Without thinking of the consequences, she moved the queen into the center and took out the bishop. No more games.

Chapter 14

"Love cannot be controlled
Either let it control you or it will destroy you."
~Tibet Roux-Patras

COLLEGE WAS PERHAPS one of the most fulfilling decisions of Isadora's life. Her few Italian credits from the community college transferred and she was moving toward a four-year degree in human resources.

Starting in the summer seemed a wise choice. It gave her time to adapt and there weren't as many students on campus that time of year, so finding her way around was less overwhelming.

She loved the library, where she spent most of her time. There were so many books and cozy corners to read. There was even a little coffee shop on the first floor. She used the building to study, because at home there were too many distractions, too many things pulling her back into old habits.

By the time the fall semester started she had found her groove and enhanced her course load. She was a few years older than most of her classmates, but never the oldest person in a class. Regardless, no one treated her like she didn't belong.

Her proctors and the students spoke to her as an equal, which did amazing things for her confidence. It was a beautiful and ordinary feeling, and when she got her first C, she felt so normal she celebrated. There wasn't a doubt in her mind that *this* was where she was meant to be.

After seeing Lucian graduate, she knew she wanted to do the same. She might never have the success her brother seemed destined for, but she wanted a degree—possibly more than one. Her goal was to become so qualified she would never doubt her worth again.

She loved learning and, once Toni started driving, Isadora was able to increase her course load again and open her roster to night classes. Though she started late, her ability to take winter and summer courses allowed her to earn her bachelor's degree in three short years.

College had become the perfect substitute for free time, which accumulated the more independent Toni became. While her sister still required her presence on occasion, when she didn't need her, Isadora no longer bore the same adrift feelings she suffered when Lucian had approached adulthood. This time she was handling life's natural sequence of events much better, because she had a sense of her future ahead.

She was always cramming or researching. There was no time to feel lonely. It was incredibly fulfilling. Time flew and in what felt like a blink of an eye, it was over.

Never in a million years did she expect to go to college, earn a degree, and graduate before she celebrated her thirtieth birthday. They were the most exciting three years of her life. And no one could take her accomplishments away from her.

Her pride in her own achievements was overshadowed, however, when her little sister finally graduated high school. Twelve years of conferences and school events were now just a memory. It was a day Isadora had once feared more than anything else, but her own experiences had prepared her for the next step. For all of them it seemed a chapter was coming to a close.

As Isadora watched Toni turn her tassel and blow them a kiss, Lucian squeezed her hand. Her fingers folded around her brother's and she swallowed tightly.

Lucian glanced at her and smiled. "You're responsible for that."

Isadora wiped her eyes and let the moment

wash over her. When the final commencement speech was made and the students threw their caps in the air, Isadora stood and emphatically applauded her sister's milestone.

Toni found them in the crowd, her radiant smile priceless, her eyes beaming with pride. As she raced to Isadora she cheered, "I did it!"

"I'm so proud of you." Isa pulled her into a hug, equally proud of the achievement.

They celebrated with an elaborate dinner at Patras, including the three of them, Monique, Shamus, and Slade. It was a one-sided sort of awkward seeing Sawyer's son, but Slade had been a part of their lives for far too long to exclude him from family moments.

"Congratulations, brat," Shamus said, pressing a kiss to Toni's cheek and handing her a card. Pulling a hand from behind his back he revealed a stunning bouquet of flowers.

Her sister glanced up at him with a smile only Shamus seemed able to earn. "Thank you."

"Next is ruling the world, right?"

Toni's lips pursed as a dimple formed in her rosy cheeks. "I might break a few hearts first. Ruling the world can be so time consuming."

Shamus's smile slipped, until he realized she was kidding. "Just make sure no one breaks yours."

Isadora sipped her wine. Lord help them all if her sister ever got her way and actually went after her childhood crush. Now that Toni was a legal adult there was really nothing stopping her.

Nothing but Lucian.

There came a moment, sometime after the main course and before the dessert, that Isadora watched her brother and sister laughing together, teasing one another and looking like the picture of happiness. She wanted to mark that moment in time and travel back to it over and over again.

That brief glimpse of life was sweet and good. No emptiness could be found and no heartache could intrude. They were ... satisfied.

As a graduation present to both of them, she and Toni spent two weeks in Rome that summer. It wasn't the trip to Italy Isadora envisioned years ago, but what she always said she'd do if she ever mastered the language. They visited the Coliseum, the Pantheon, threw coins in the Trevi Fountain, and even took a train to France to pay their father a short visit.

"I don't understand why we have to waste a day on him," Toni complained. "When I got in a car accident last fall, he couldn't be bothered. For the time it takes to get to his house, we could have gone to Capri for the weekend."

Isadora sighed. "We can't come to Europe and not visit him, Toni."

"He comes to The States and doesn't visit us."

Isa raised a brow. "Are you sad about that?"

She crossed her arms and glared out the train window. "No."

"Look at it this way, he'll probably give you something for graduation."

That seemed to help. Although it was a pathetic reason to tolerate their father, someone they should look forward to visiting.

The most exciting moment of their visit to France was seeing Claudette. The older maid greeted them with bracing hugs and tears of affection. But even Claudette couldn't shield them from the abrasive flaws of their father's character.

"What do you plan to do with yourself now, Isadora?" His tone implied she'd been wasting her life away up until that moment.

"I'm not sure. Get a job, I suppose."

His brow twitched. "You're a Patras. If you insist on having a career then people should work for you, not the other way around."

"I don't want to be a CEO, Daddy. I just want to contribute to something."

Toni kept her eyes on her plate, likely trying to be as invisible as possible so she didn't get interrogated next.

"You better find an ambitious man if you don't plan on making your own success. Christ knows if your brother keeps it up, I'll have nothing but debt to leave you when I'm gone."

Ignoring the barb at Lucian's recent acquisition of the United States Patras Hotel, she tried not to take offense. She'd worked damn hard to accomplish all she had and she would not allow him to devalue her efforts.

"I don't need a man to feel successful," she informed him, glad to hear the truth behind her own words.

"This isn't about feelings. It's about reality. You either make something of yourself or you don't. The world doesn't need another secretary and *feeling* successful isn't the same as *being* successful. Didn't college teach you that?"

Her sister glared at him and Isadora reached under the table, placing a calming hand on her knee, but it didn't stop Toni's temper. "Isa has a degree. She's qualified for more than clerical work. She'll be fine."

"A glorified event planner," their father grumbled. "Human Resources isn't what I'd call ambitious. An eighty thousand dollar education blown on a middle class career choice. First step in success is knowing what's profitable."

There was no point in arguing with someone who clearly viewed the world differently. Human Resources was a perfectly respectable field. She didn't need his approval to realize that.

The rest of their visit followed much the same tone and when they were on the train back to Italy she and Toni decided it would be best to get drunk.

Toni was laughing hysterically, coming up

with majors that might irritate their father. "I might get a degree in philosophy just to push him over the edge."

"With a minor in liberal arts," Isadora added.

Laughing and making light of their father's impossible standards helped mask a bit of the pain inflicted during their short visit. Though she didn't need his approval, his lack of recognition was insulting.

She'd covered for him for fifteen years and he never once thanked her. This would likely be her last visit to France.

When they returned to The States, Lucian had Dugan pick them up from the airport. Since graduating, her brother had less and less time for family, something that concerned Isadora.

Mid-August, when they had a college sendoff dinner at the house for Toni, Isadora cornered Lucian in the den.

"I want to ask you a favor."

He arched a brow. "What do you need?"

Pulling him to a chair so she had his full attention, she sat across from him and took a deep breath. "A long time ago you said you'd help me buy this house from Daddy."

"It's a lot of house, Isa."

"It's my home. I want to get a mortgage and—"

"Just buy it outright. I'll lend you the money

and you can avoid getting slaughtered by interest fees."

"No. *I* want to buy it and I don't want to use my savings for more than the down payment. I've done the math and I think I can afford it within a few years."

"Dad should just give it to you. It's the least he owes you."

"That's not what I want either. I want you to give me a job, Lucian."

He laughed. "Really?"

"Yes. I'd like something in Human Resources, but I'll take anything you can offer."

He studied her and smiled as if she'd surprised him. "You got it."

Not expecting him to agree so easily, her guard went up. "Just like that?"

"Just like that. I'm starting a new company, one that's totally unassociated with Dad. I need someone to help me with the hiring and I trust your judgment. Consider yourself the new head of Human Resources."

She laughed, thinking if this was how he interviewed potential hires, he definitely needed someone to help him weed out the riffraff. "When can I start?"

"Monday."

Giddy and a bit nervous, she threw her arms around him in an exuberant hug. "Thank you!"

He grunted and eased her back. As he stood,

he said, "I have some appointments Monday morning, but my assistant, Seth, will be there. Shamus will be stopping by, too. He's a silent partner in the company. We're meeting with Slade and Sawyer Bishop around noon to go over candidates for the open positions. I'd like you to sit in on the meeting."

She tried to school her expression, her excitement syphoning out of her at hurricane speeds. "The B—Bishops are a part of this?"

"No, but I'm also looking into buying out Dad's share of Leningrad. Eventually Slade will be taking over his father's spot as well. It's in their best interest to help me headhunt new employees. In time, we might merge into one corporation. Sawyer's open-minded enough to know it's a strong possibility."

She heard his words, but none of them registered. All she could do was think of Sawyer.

It had been almost four years since they last spoke or saw each other and she wasn't sure how to emotionally prepare for seeing him again. Not only would she be seeing him, they'd be meeting in front of other people.

She nodded and dazedly followed Lucian to the front door. Sawyer. She would be seeing Sawyer.

The next night, she hardly slept despite being exhausted from moving Toni into her new dorm. Her mind was a rioting mess of worries ranging from what shade stockings to wear to whether or not she would be able to make eye contact with her new colleagues. When she drove to the address Lucian gave her she was such a mess she had to circle the block six times.

The lobby was still under construction in the new high rise and the elevators weren't yet inspected, so she had several flights of stairs to climb. It didn't help that her heart was already beating with the force of a jackhammer.

When she reached the reception area, a young man in glasses looked up from a computer. "Isadora Patras?"

She offered an unsteady smile, trying to hide the fact that she was sweating and winded. "You must be Seth."

The man smiled and came around the desk to shake her hand. "It's a pleasure to meet you. Mr. Patras said you'd be in early and instructed me to show you around."

She nodded. "I appreciate ... you coming in early to welcome me." Her hand pressed above her hip where a cramp pinched.

Showing off a natural gift to neutralize situations, he casually handed her a glass of cool water, which she desperately needed.

"I'm always here before seven. Mr. Patras starts his day before dawn, so I'm usually swamped by sun-up with emails and instructions."

She smiled. It was interesting getting a glimpse

of her brother's life from this side of the glass. She recalled a time when Lucian didn't get out of bed until noon. "Thank you for the water. When do the elevators get inspected?"

"We expect them to pass inspection by the end of the day."

Seth showed her around and she was impressed by how luxurious the space was.

"This office is yours." He held open a glistening door. "We'll get someone out today to etch your name on the glass."

Etching seemed so permanent. She stepped inside and did a three-sixty, not expecting her office to be so, well, *big*. It was enormous with a panoramic view of Folsom and a beautiful Parisian settee on the back wall.

"The furniture arrived last night, but your brother said you can exchange it for something else if you don't like it. If you approve, we'll order a few chairs to match."

Unsure if Lucian was showing her special treatment or if this was how he welcomed all his employees, she simply nodded. "It's lovely."

"The conference room is across the hall and you have a meeting there at noon. Did Mr. Patras go over the details with you?"

"He said we'd be reviewing job candidates with Jamie Callahan and Slade and Sawyer Bishop, is that correct?" She privately hoped certain people had a scheduling conflict and couldn't attend.

Seth grinned. "That's the plan. I'll be in and out, too."

Hiding her trepidation that *everyone* would be in attendance, she gave a shaky smile, "I'll be there."

"Wonderful. I have to get back to my desk, but you go ahead and settle in. I supplied your drawers and left a briefing by your phone about the company—just Mr. Patras's mission statement and some other information to help you familiarize yourself with his vision. If there's anything else you need, let me know. I'm extension two."

"Thank you, Seth."

When he left, she slowly strolled past the window, glancing down at the bustling sidewalks and out at the horizon. In the distance she could see the peak of the Patras Hotel.

She moved to her desk and carefully lowered herself into the leather seat. Lifting the phone from its cradle, she dialed her brother's cell.

"Patras," he answered.

"It's me."

"Do you like the furniture?"

It took her a second to organize her words. She was so grateful for the job and all he'd done to make her feel welcome, she didn't know how or where to start. Overwhelmed seemed a good way to put it.

This was an executive office and, although she

was semi-qualified, she had zero experience. Big offices came with big expectations.

"I'm a little worried about nepotism," she said and laughed, not expecting those to be her first words.

Lucian's deep voice chuckled into the phone. "Fuck nepotism, Isa. We don't explain ourselves to anyone. It's our name on the building."

Her fingers glided over the leather blotter on her desk. "This office is gorgeous, Lucian. Not just mine, but the entire building."

"Wait until it's finished."

"You do realize most HR directors are put in glorified storage closets."

He laughed. "That's not how we do things here. You'll see. Did Seth show you around?"

"Yes. He's very helpful."

"Until we get you an assistant, feel free to use him for whatever you need. He'll help you get acclimated."

"I'm getting an assistant?"

"Of course. What kind of shit show do you think we're running here?"

It was surreal. For the first time in her thirty years of life, she actually felt like an adult. "Thank you, Lucian—for everything."

He was quiet for a beat. "This will be good for you, Isa. I like the idea of us working together."

"Me too."

"Okay, I gotta run. I'll see you in a few hours.

Congratulations on your new job."

"My *first* job," she corrected with a smile as she hung up.

She passed the morning reading over the information Seth left on her desk, her perception of her brother growing to immeasurable heights with every page. Not only was Lucian's vision for the company solid, his passion for starting something that created opportunities for others was evident in every word of his mission statement.

When she finished familiarizing herself with his vision, her intercom buzzed. "Ms. Patras."

Her finger clicked on the call button. "Yes, Seth."

"I'm ordering lunch for the meeting. Is there anything specific you like to drink?"

"Water is fine."

"Any specific brand?"

"I'm not picky."

"You got it. The others will be arriving in a few minutes. Lunch should arrive shortly."

Her heart stuttered in her chest. "Thank you, Seth."

"You're welcome."

She looked at her door and a chill crept over her skin, causing all the tiny hairs on her arms to rise. Gathering a blank notebook and pen, she set them on the edge of her desk and went to the restroom to freshen up.

As she ran water over her hands, her fingers

trembled. Looking at her reflection, she tried to measure the changes in her appearance over the last few years.

Her hair was shorter, but other than that she thought she looked the same. Would he?

Breathing unevenly, she glided her hands down the sides of her pencil skirt, and inspected her blouse. Her eyes held her stare in the mirror. "You've earned the right to be here as much as anyone else."

Leaving the bathroom she returned to her office to collect her things. Her brother's voice echoed from the hall followed by male laughter. Determined not to make a fool of herself, she drew in a steadying breath and exited her office, coming face-to-face with her past.

"*Isadora*," Sawyer said in a startled voice, his halting steps stilling the progress of the other men.

"Hello, Sawyer. Slade." She smiled at her brother and turned her attention to Shamus. "Jamie."

"Well, isn't this a pleasant surprise," Shamus said leaning in to kiss her cheek.

"Men, meet our new Human Resources director," Lucian announced, his evident pride causing her to flush.

Slade laughed. "Another ingenious choice."

She glanced at Sawyer who looked as if he'd

seen a ghost. He didn't appear to share everyone else's endorsement of the new HR employee.

"Shall we?" she asked, hiding her nerves and waving a hand toward the conference room.

"After you," Slade offered and she led the way, her heart kicking like a rabbit foot against her ribs.

Out of the corner of her eye she marked the notable changes in Sawyer's appearance. His hair had faded from its recognizable darkness to an overall peppered mix of white and softer browns. It hurt, knowing he'd changed so much, and wondering what took place in his life to bring about such a difference. Perhaps it was simply genetics, but what if stress had caused his hair to lighten? All this time and she still couldn't curb her innate reflex of concern for him.

His familiar fragrance reached her lungs and her motions turned jagged as they entered the conference room. She moved to the opposite side of the table, but she couldn't escape the nostalgic smell.

Lucian tossed her a sidelong glance and smiled. "You ready?" He gave her elbow an encouraging squeeze.

The men settled around the table, Lucian at the head, Shamus at the foot, and Sawyer and Slade across from her in the middle. She set her notepad in front of her and folded her hands, wishing she had a larger shield at her disposal.

Seth entered the room and went over the

lunch order with Lucian. Her brother gave his assistant a list of files to fetch for the meeting.

"You cut your hair." Sawyer's voice traveled across the table and her gaze slowly lifted. "It suits you."

"Th—thank you."

Looking at him was a mistake. Their gazes seemed to literally lock. He seemed as unable to look away from her, as she was unable to peel her focus from him.

"How have you been?" he asked, knowing perfectly well they had to keep the conversation casual.

Seth left the conference room and Lucian jumped right into motion, saving her from answering.

"Okay, let's start with the Leningrad lists while we wait for Seth to get back."

The next hour was spent reviewing resumes while Isadora compiled a detailed spreadsheet of pros and cons for each candidate. Once her eyes were on her work she didn't look across the table again. She hadn't expected to see so many applicants in one sitting, but she supposed that was how companies found the best men or women for any job.

Finishing off another stack, Lucian looked at Seth who was typing notes into a laptop. "Let's take an intermission and eat. Seth, you want to bring in lunch?"

He shut the laptop and left the room. Lucian stood and stretched. Slade seemed to watch her brother and follow his lead.

Shamus twiddled a pen between his fingers and reclined in his chair. "You like it so far, Isa?"

Her gaze moved to him and she smiled. "I do. It's been a busy afternoon, but I think it's great so far."

"Switching from Italy to your brother's domain has to be a jolting change," he teased.

"You went to Italy?" Her attention jerked to Sawyer who was watching her carefully.

"Toni and I went this summer."

His mouth was still the same, full lips surrounded by the threat of dark stubble.

"Did you ... enjoy it?"

Who didn't like Italy? *"Era il posto più bello che avessi mai visitato,"* she answered, showing off her grasp of the language and letting him know she found it beautiful.

He grinned, the simple expression cutting through her clothing and striking a nerve deep in her heart. *"Non bello come te, bella."*

Not as beautiful as you, bella. Her chest warmed as his words went right to her head and other places.

What was he doing? She wasn't sure if she wanted to laugh or cry.

"Now you've lost me," Shamus interrupted, reminding them of his presence. "This Irishman's going to see what's taking Seth so long with lunch."

A panicked throb filled her chest as Shamus left the room and she slowly turned back to Sawyer. He shouldn't look at her like that in mixed company. But now they were alone.

She cleared her throat. "How have you been?"

Her gaze traveled over every visible inch of him. She couldn't stop cataloguing differences—improvements. His hair, though more light than dark, looked incredible on him. His eyes wore creases she couldn't recall being so prominent. He looked like he'd lost a few pounds and that worried her, but all-in-all he was still her Sawyer.

"I've been well. Busy. Taking Slade on as a protégé definitely helps. It's interesting working with him on a professional level."

"Lucian said he bought a house."

Sawyer nodded. "Just outside of the city. He prefers the metropolitan pace over the ease of country living, so I'm not sure he'll keep it."

She shook her head. "I'm sorry. I can't stop staring. Your hair..."

He chuckled. "I know. I'm getting old."

"No, you're not. You're still handsome."

His gaze locked with her, a strange expression frozen on his face. "Are you ... dating?"

"No. I did for a while, but I hardly have the time anymore. I just graduated."

His smile was a mixture of surprise and awe. "I

heard. That's wonderful, sweetheart. You should be proud of yourself."

She wanted to tell him about everything he missed, and find out what he'd done for the past four years. She needed to know if he'd dated and explain to him that he was wrong about her, that she was cold and incapable of loving anyone else.

It hadn't occurred to her how much time had actually passed until she felt this momentary opportunity to catch him up. The probably only had another minute or so before the others returned.

"Sawyer—"

"Lunch is served," Seth announced, entering the room with a large lunch tray and the men at his heels.

As they gathered around the table, sorting out the containers and locating plates and napkins, Sawyer's gaze held hers. There wouldn't be time to tell him all she wanted to say. He might prefer it that way.

A dish was placed in front of her, breaking her eye contact and when she looked back his focus was elsewhere. Of all the things running through her mind, she was least prepared for the onslaught of emotions. They were supposed to be over, but nothing had ever felt so unfinished.

Part Two

Sawyer

15 Incerto

"UNCERTAIN"

SAWYER COULD BARELY DECIPHER a single word on the resumes in front of him. All afternoon he'd been distracted by her smell. At lunch he'd been consumed with curiosity about what she'd been about to say. He hadn't tasted a single bite of his food.

The meeting was expected to be long, but at the moment he didn't give a damn about the future of Lucian's company. He only cared about the four years he'd missed.

Who had she been with? What had she done? Did she think of him as often as he thought about her? He wanted to kick everyone out and fuck her right on the conference table—erase any memory she might have of someone else.

She looked incredible. Her hair was shorter

and her eyes a bit wiser. He'd forgotten how beautiful she actually was.

The moment he saw her in the hall, his entire system took a hit. Years of telling himself he'd done the right thing flushed down the drain after one glimpse of her. He was a fucking idiot for letting her go.

And now... Now he would have to see her constantly if their companies merged and Lucian bought out his father's stake in Leningrad. How would he survive that?

His gaze again drifted to her hands, still shocked to not see a diamond on her finger. She mentioned dating, but said school kept her busy. What about Italy? Did she take a lover with her? That was supposed to be *their* trip.

The pencil in his hand snapped in two and her brown eyes flashed at him. He casually turned and tossed the broken wood into the trash bin. "Give me a pen, Slade."

His son slid him a pen and Sawyer refused to look up at her. This meeting had to end soon.

How many men had come into her life? How many actually appreciated the gift she was in their hands? He sure hoped Lucian was keeping an eye on his sister's best interests.

His molars locked at the thought of her with someone else. It was enough to throw him into a rage, but what had he expected? He told her to go find a husband, a future, someone who could give her all the things she wanted. He'd done right by her in the end.

Or had her plans changed? She *was* starting a career.

He quickly did the math, counting the birthdays he'd missed. She just turned thirty. Single and thirty and starting a career. Maybe she wasn't the same innocent woman he'd sent away.

She looked older—better. Her body had ripened and her eyes held a sort of confidence that wasn't there before.

The longer he stared at her the more his body responded to her nearness. She didn't spare him another glance. As her hand dragged a pen across the page, taking notes as Lucian rambled, he watched her face. White teeth pulled at her plump lower lip. Her tongue slipped over the impressed divot, smoothing it out, and he inwardly groaned.

Fuck. He shoved the resumes at his son and stood. "Excuse me."

Lucian paused and frowned at him. Everyone else's attention turned to Sawyer as he stood there like a juvenile fool getting a hard-on in the middle of class.

His gaze avoided Isadora. "I'm afraid I have to take a rain check on the rest of the meeting. Slade will follow up with me about whatever I miss."

"You okay?" Lucian asked.

He glanced at his watch. "Just a scheduling oversight." He turned to Slade. "Let me know when you're wrapped up here and we'll ren-dezvous later. My apologies."

Grabbing his suit jacket off the back of the chair, he rounded the table and left.

When he reached the hall, his heart was pounding. Catching his breath, he adjusted his clothing and walked at a steady pace toward the elevators, perfectly aware that he was fleeing, but what choice did he have?

His finger pressed the button and he waited impatiently for the doors to open.

"They're out of commission until the inspections are finished."

"Shit," he hissed under his breath, recognizing her voice. Drawing in a steadying breath, he blanked his expression and faced her. "Another oversight."

Her relaxed focus made him twitch. She was too calm, too unbothered by their running into each other.

The corner of her mouth pulled into a half-grin. "Do you really have an appointment?"

Convinced of his own bullshit, his spine stiff-ened, a defensive scowl tightening his brow. "Do you think I'd lie?"

Her luscious lips twisted into a teasing smirk. "Yes."

He shut his eyes and sighed. Fuck. He just wanted to get out of there.

Meeting her perceptive gaze, he gave up. "I

didn't expect to see you today. How are you so calm?"

"I had a heads up. But if it makes you feel better, I didn't get much sleep since Lucian mentioned you'd be at the meeting."

He chuckled. "It helps a little."

She glanced over her shoulder and back to him. "Is this going to be a problem, us running into each other at work?"

Absolutely. It's going to be torture. "We're adults."

She nodded. "I'm glad you see it that way."

Her words implied him viewing her as an adult was something new. "Isadora..."

"Don't ruin it, Sawyer."

He swallowed back whatever warning he was about to give. "You're sassier than you were the last time I saw you."

"Because I'm not that girl anymore."

He studied her for a long while, searching for a glimpse of the vulnerability he used to find in her eyes. Her stare crossed his and skittered away. *There it is.* That was all he needed to see. "You're still you."

She loosely crossed her arms over her chest, either shielding herself from scrutiny or hiding the fact that her nipples were hard. Too late. He'd caught the twin peaks the moment they pressed into the silk of her blouse.

"I hold a lot more respect for myself, now. Demand it too."

He shook his head, finding it hard to assimilate to the hard act she seemed to be putting on. Was that for his benefit? He didn't like it. "I assumed you'd be engaged or dating."

She smiled. "I'm done waiting for other people. The things I can't control..." She shrugged. "I know what I want." Her stare intensified and his lips parted as there was no misreading the implication in her eyes.

They hadn't spent all this time apart just to go back to where they were. "Nothing's changed for me, Isadora."

"I figured you'd say that." She glanced at the elevator. "Toni left for college yesterday. I'm going out for a quiet dinner after work, to celebrate my first day. I'll be dining alone at Vogue. My reservations are for five-thirty if you want to join me."

Was this some sort of test? Vogue was in her brother's hotel. Lucian lived at Patras. Was she trying to test his limits?

"I'm afraid I have plans," he lied, immediately regretting his words when another glimpse of vulnerability flashed in her eyes.

"Oh. Of course." Her gaze lowered and she took a step back. "Well, you should probably get going then. I have to get back."

Something was off about her. Where was his sweet Isadora? The one who gave so much of herself and looked at him with such ... love? "Isadora, wait."

She slowly turned back to him and ... there it was. There was the woman he was looking for. Soft, gentle, modest, and true.

"I... I don't have plans."

"I get it, Sawyer. I have to go." She turned away.

He watched her until she disappeared into the conference room. Fuck. Now he'd upset her and there was nothing quite as torturous as knowing he'd hurt someone he...

He pivoted and shoved the door to the stairwell open. What the hell was the point of today other than to complicate his already complicated life?

When he returned to his office, he sat at his desk with nothing to do. His entire afternoon had been cleared so he could attend a meeting he'd skipped out on. He glanced at his cell, noting it was almost four. His fingers drummed on the surface of his desk impatiently until it was nearly five.

He couldn't wait any longer. Scooping up the phone he dialed. "Isadora Patras, Please."

"Who should I say is calling?"

"This is Sawyer Bishop. I need a name from one of the resumes she reviewed today." And why the hell was he explaining himself to reception? He pinched the bridge of his nose and waited.

"Isadora speaking."

God. Her voice was like honey, so warm and smooth. "It's Sawyer."

"I know. Seth told me."

He grit his teeth. How the hell could she act so casual about everything? She *was* acting. Treating him as if they had no history. He didn't like it. "Pick a different restaurant."

"Why?"

"Because you know we can't meet there, Isa. It's your brother's hotel and he dines there regularly."

"Ah, but if we're just meeting as colleagues there's no reason to hide."

His head cocked as he realized what she was doing. This was her way of reading his intentions. Two could play that game, though fuck if he knew what the hell was going through that head of hers.

"I see. Well then, you tell me, should we meet at Patras or perhaps someplace more discreet?"

Let her be the one to decide *exactly* what they were doing. He wasn't going to dance like some puppet on a string. If she wanted to act fearless, fine. But she'd first need the courage to admit what it was she wanted.

"I'll text you an address."

"Just tell me." He hated texting. Whatever happened to talking on the phone like civilized people?

"Someone just walked in. I'll text you."

The call cut off.

Staring at his phone, he waited. A few minutes later it beeped.

Your place. 6:00.

His breath caught in his throat, his body warming by the second. He asked for direct—and he got it.

Or was she choosing his place out of old habits and the desire for privacy? She might not even be thinking about sex.

But he was. "Fuck."

He opened the text screen to reply, but nothing came to mind. After deliberating for an extremely long time, the most he came up with was *I'll see you then.* He shut off his phone and stuffed it in his pocket.

16 Desiderio

"DESIRE"

AT SIX O'CLOCK SAWYER WAS GLUED TO his front window watching the edge of his driveway. Did she still drive a Volvo? He waited impatiently, his mind in an all-out guessing game of how their evening would go.

A sporty, ice-blue Mercedes turned onto his property. The sleek and luxurious convertible suited her and he smiled. She looked good in expensive things. She looked good in anything.

She looked good in nothing...

He met her out front and got the door. "You got a new car."

"It's actually one of my dad's. Mine's getting new tires. I still have the Volvo."

His brows lifted. That Volvo was almost fifteen years old.

She followed him into the house and he wondered if he should have ordered dinner ahead of time. His head was up his ass today.

"I figured I'd wait to order in case you wanted something special."

She placed her purse on the hall table and looked around. "You painted."

"A while ago."

"Who picked this color? It's an orange, right?"

He always forgot she was colorblind, probably because she never complained about it. "It's sort of a burnt sienna, called something obnoxious like Tuscan Dawn." He chuckled, because he hadn't liked the color then and it hadn't grown on him since. "My decorator picked it. She said it would grow on me."

"Has it?"

"I actually think I dislike it more now than I did then."

She laughed. "Stick with blues and grays. You always gravitate toward cooler tones. This is too warm for you. And get a new decorator. You know they're not doing a good job if a colorblind person can give them pointers."

He laughed. "You just know me better."

She looked over her shoulder, edging her way toward the den. Were they going to talk about trivial bullshit or real issues? She sat on his couch and he joined her, unsure how close he should sit.

"How was your first day of work?"

"Really busy. And exciting. Do you have

wine? I brought a bottle but I left it in the car. I can go get it."

"I have wine." He stood and went to the kitchen.

"You still have all the same boring books," she called as he searched for a wine key. "You really need to fire that decorator."

He uncorked a bottle of Chablis and let it breathe. "I'm used to her."

"She fills your house with things you don't like."

He poured two glasses and turned, coming up short when he found Isadora standing in the kitchen. He handed her a glass.

"To your first day of work."

"Cheers." She clinked her glass to his. Her stare stayed on his face as she took a long sip.

After she swallowed, she asked, "So what made you change your mind about seeing me?"

"I... Let's go back to the den."

Once they were both seated on the couch she looked at him expectantly. He eyed her suspiciously, wondering how she seemed so *over* their past when she hadn't necessarily moved on. Or maybe she wasn't over it at all and that's why she was here.

Enough dancing around the unknown. "You said you had dated?"

"Mmm." She nodded, swallowing another sip of wine. "Tyrian, the guy I met at Vivian's wedding. We went out for a few months, but I ended things."

"Why?"

"He was a great guy, but he wasn't *my* guy."

"Has there been anyone else?" He hated how badly he needed to know, certain if she said yes he'd suffer more than he already was.

"No. I mean, I had a cup of coffee here and there with some people from school. A few Italians bought me drinks. But nothing serious. Honestly, I haven't had the time to date. And I don't miss it."

He frowned. He was speaking to Isadora, but this wasn't her. She was so ... self-assured, so unbothered by being single. In a way it put her on his level and for reasons he didn't want to examine that intimidated him. He'd sent her away so she could find better. Maybe she was grateful they'd broken up. Maybe she now believed he was right —she *could* do better than him.

"It's a shame about Vivian and her husband. I didn't expect that." *That's how you respond?* For the first decent conversation in four years, he was certainly botching the shit out of it.

Isadora didn't miss a beat. "I admire her. I mean, there's a girl who went to school, became a doctor, fell in love, and figured out she'd married wrong and fixed it right away. No tears over spilt milk. A lot of women would suffer through, but Vivian got out as soon as she realized her mistake.

In time, no one will even remember she was married and she might still find the right man."

She spoke about a marriage dissolving as if nothing substantial was lost. A relationship had ended. A commitment gone, vows broken. What happened to the girl who believed in fairytales and romance? He'd wanted her to grow and experience new things, but this cool façade didn't suit her. She was either hiding or something major had changed her.

Out of things to say—not that he was showing off his clever conversation skills—he stood and went to refill his wine.

When he returned, her shoes were off and her feet were tucked under her legs. He froze in the doorway, taken off guard by how familiar and right she looked on his couch.

"What's wrong?"

"Nothing." He couldn't stop staring. She looked so at home. Perfect. As if she belonged there.

Her back straightened and he sensed the ice queen mask sliding back into place. "Do you want me to leave?"

"No." The words came quick, without thought, his heart objecting before his brain had a chance to weigh in. "I want..."

You to be yourself with me. He missed her.

She placed her wine glass on the coffee table

and stood. A stampede vibrated in his chest as she stepped closer.

"Do you want me to stay?"

Fuck. Fuck him for letting his dick lead him right back to where they'd been four years ago. She was playing him, using all her youthful charms against him when he should know better. Nothing had changed.

He took a step back. "Why don't you tell me what you want?"

A shaky smile curved her lips. "I want to stay, but that doesn't mean I will."

"What *does* it mean?" Enough with the cryptic signals. "I'd appreciate it if you could be direct, Isadora. I'm not sure what this is and I don't want any misunderstandings." He did want her though.

"Okay." She also took a step back. "I want you, Sawyer. Not just tonight, but for as long as it suits me. I don't want to wait around for Mondays and I don't want you lecturing me about husbands or babies. I want to live in the *now* and worry about tomorrow when it gets here."

That was certainly more direct than he was used to. "Are we talking about tonight and the occasional—"

"As long as it suits me."

She seemed to think she held all the cards. He glanced down the front of her body. All right, she held most of them. But that didn't mean she was the only person with conditions.

"What about discretion?"

"Does it matter at this point?"

"Yes. There's your position with the company and I want this merger with your brother. Until that happens everyone has to be on their best behavior."

"The merger or the buyout of Leningrad?"

"Both. First, Lucian will buy your father out and then we'll merge if all goes accordingly. A lot of time and money went into this deal—your brother's and mine. I don't want to jeopardize that at this point."

The buyout would be within the next year, but the merger could take much longer. Did he really have the energy to go back to where they were?

Lucian still had to get his company off the ground. Sawyer had no doubt, like everything else Lucian touched, this company would be a success. But his family's stake and his son's future wouldn't be secure until then. Once her father was out and Slade was partnered in, Sawyer could step back, and he didn't have to worry about his personal conduct.

She lifted her chin and looked him directly in the eye. "Fine. On one condition."

"What's that?"

"You treat what we have as a relationship. That means we communicate and you don't decide anything without me."

He'd thought he'd done the right thing, and maybe he had, but now he wondered if it had been four years wasted. When he ended their relationship he'd been a fucking mess, but he dealt with it, gave her time, and she seemed to handle it better than him.

She could still meet someone better suited for her.

Fuck that. He wanted her. His gut twisted as if he were about to commit a crime with a life sentence. If they did this, went back to what they had, he couldn't hurt her. He couldn't hurt either of them. It wasn't a decision to be made lightly.

If he were being honest—noble—he shouldn't have her at all. Nothing changed. They would always be in different stages of life. He was winding down and she was just beginning. They were on two different timepieces with gears that only sometimes overlapped.

This time, it might be her who left *him*. Letting her go was one thing—the right thing—but losing her forever... He might not survive that.

She let out a sigh. "If you can't agree to my conditions, just say so."

He looked at her—*really looked.* She was the whole package, even more than before. His affection hadn't waned. He still wanted to do right by her, even if she didn't see it that way. If her priorities had changed and she no longer wanted marriage and family, that changed everything—got rid of a good deal of his guilt.

"I'm only going to ask this once, but I need an honest answer. Do you still want a family and children?"

"Yes, but no one's offering that right now. I also want you, maybe more than the fairytale."

Well, she gave him honesty. Like that made his decision any easier. Fuck him and his selfish soul. If he was any sort of decent man, he'd send her away.

She was everything and deserved the world on a platter, not a single want gone unanswered, but he'd never be able to give her everything. She'd be sacrificing and eventually their relationship would turn into a filthy regret.

Thirty. Fifty.

Forty. Sixty.

She'd never want him once he passed seventy. The less painful end—for both of them—would be walking away now.

"You do realize I turned fifty this year, Isadora."

"Unless you're asking for a belated cake, I don't see why that's relevant. Your age never bothered me."

"Well, I was young when we started," he joked.

"It was seven years ago, Sawyer. Knock it off."

He arched a brow, still unsure if he liked or disliked this new sassy side. Maybe he wasn't truly grasping all the changes in her. Here was his Isadora, not asking, but *telling* him, exactly what she wanted. Perhaps her eyes were wide open this time.

He might never be okay with his decision, but his mind was apparently already made up.

"Fine. We treat this like a relationship, but it remains private until everything's settled with your brother."

"A *monogamous* relationship," she corrected. "Not even a plus one at events."

If only she knew. There had been no one in his bed or across from his table in four years. "Not a problem."

He enjoyed a woman's company, but no woman had ever been able to get him to bend the way Isadora could. Not since Chelsea was alive. There had always been something irresistible about Isa. She was special.

The silence of the house became a noise within itself. She smiled nervously at him. "So we're done negotiating?"

He laughed, finding her statement so very *Patras*. "Unless you have any more conditions."

"Just one."

He braced himself, unsure if he could concede another principle. He was already breaking so many of his rules, namely, to let her live a happy life and not interfere. But at this point, he knew he'd agree to anything. "Let's hear it."

"Make love to me."

His body tightened as blood rushed to his cock. Jesus. There was definitely something to be said for her tenaciousness.

His guard slipped and he smiled. Placing his glass next to hers on the table, he stepped toward her, unable to resist putting his hands on her a moment longer.

"Bella." He jerked her body to his and gave her a brief second to change her mind. When she made no objection, he lowered his lips to hers.

Her mouth fit against his like a memory he'd never forget. She tugged him closer and deepened the kiss, her eagerness adding fuel to the already scorching fire in his blood. His body firmed as his hands dropped to her hips, massaging greedily.

"Upstairs," he whispered, tugging her by the hand toward the hall.

"Here." She pulled him closer to the sofa until they stumbled to the cushions and her body cradled his weight.

His hands coasted over her prim and proper work attire as he hungrily kissed her, showing her exactly how much she'd been missed. At the office he'd been able to see the precise points of her nipples pressing through the thin silk of her blouse. He wanted to rip it off of her now.

Hiking up her fitted skirt, he worked the lace of her panties aside, sinking a finger deep into her core. She arched and moaned, breaking their kiss as his lips moved down her throat and his finger pumped into her.

She was so wet, so responsive. As he fucked his fingers into her tight pussy her scent swept to his nose, filled his lungs, and his desire rushed forward with unstoppable force.

"God, I fucking missed you," he hissed, yanking her blouse open and unveiling her breasts.

He shoved her bra out of the way and stared. Supple peaks tipped in dark scarlet. He captured a tight nipple in his mouth and sucked hard.

She cried out, running her fingers through his hair and holding him close. Her other hand tugged at his belt. He shoved her skirt higher and yanked her panties down her legs, forcing her thighs wide.

"Scoot forward." He cupped the back of her knees, dragged her to the edge of the couch, and dropped to his haunches.

She gasped as the heat of his tongue found her center and stabbed deep. "Oh, my God, *yes!*"

Her legs curled over his shoulders, as he tasted her. So familiar.

He sank two fingers deep and closed his lips over her clit. She cried out again, as her pleasure broke free in a show of such exquisite beauty he nearly came himself.

Stark desire stole through him as her body subtly shook. He kissed a trail up her stomach, back to her breasts. Her arms wreathed around him and she pulled his mouth to hers. Urging him on top of her, she fit her hand into his pants to free his cock and stroke him against her sex, guiding him with gentle presses until he finally sank deep.

His eyes closed as he let out a curse. She felt like home.

Burying his face in her hair, he caught his breath. Easing back, he stared into her eyes and nearly lost himself in the trust he found staring back at him.

"Isadora."

Her soft smile twitched as her cheeks flushed. *There* was that familiar innocence he loved. He pulled her mouth to his and kissed her with gentle affection as he thrust into her, claiming everything he'd lost as his once more.

Her eyes opened slowly, a glassy sheen giving away her bottled up emotions. That was the woman he wanted, *his* bella. She could save the act for someone else.

"Don't pretend to be someone else with me, bella. Where's my girl?"

"I'm here," she whispered, a tear slipping past her lashes.

He traced the moisture away with his thumb. He wanted to hold her, take care of her, protect her, but she was stronger and different now. Or was she?

"You're still my bella."

Her mouth curved into a smile. "I'll always be your bella."

He thrust hard. A static melody of pounding flesh mixed with their moans. He growled, unable to get close enough to her, doubling his speed.

When he was near finishing, he reached between them, teasing her clit, and she shattered once more. His release pumped into her and she held him tight, his shoulders trembling under her fingertips, an unnamable emotion cocooning his heart.

He pulled her into his arms, tighter than any man would hold a paramour, and it scared the living shit out of him. How had he gone without her for so long? Never again.

La Vita Segreta

"SECRET LIFE"

SAWYER POURED coffee into two mugs and passed one to Isadora. Her smile was shy as she looked up at him, cradling the ceramic cup in one hand and holding the blanket from the couch to her chest with the other. He found it hard to believe she was back in his life after countless days of lonesome hell.

"This is good. I missed your coffee."

He grinned and sipped from his mug, unsure if they should discuss what just happened. Other topics flitted through his head but they all seemed too casual. When he woke up this morning, he never expected the day to end like this, with her inhabiting his space again.

Now that the edge was off, his mind bombarded him with more unanswered questions. He needed to know what brought about so many changes in her, if her experiences were positive or negative.

"I should—"

"Why did you break up with that man?"

Appearing startled by his question, she placed her mug on the end table. "I told you why."

"There has to be more to it."

"You really want to talk about that, Sawyer?"

He shrugged. "Was he good to you?"

"He was a gentleman."

What the hell did that mean? "Did you get along?"

"We got along great, but he wasn't enough for me."

Rabid curiosity burned inside of him, desperate to understand exactly what she meant. He'd insisted she find someone more appropriate. But knowing someone else had known her in a carnal sense ...

It hurt and he didn't like it. More than hurt. It felt like a part of his heart had been violated.

She reached for his shoulders and the blanket fell away. Her naked body pressed into his. "I'll tell you whatever you want to know, so long as you keep your secrets to yourself. I can't bear the thought of you with anyone else. I know I'm stronger now, but I'm still breakable."

Running a finger along her delicate cheekbone he looked into her dark eyes. "I won't break you, bella." The thought of causing her any more pain was unbearable.

She smiled, but something shifted in her face. Maybe she was right. It was bad enough knowing she'd been fine without him. He could live without the details of how she'd managed. Better to focus on the now.

She was back now. He missed hearing about her days and that was what he should ask about, her day-to-day life now.

Antoinette was in college, yet he still pictured her as a little girl. He remembered the day Lucian left for college, how hard it had been on Isadora, yet she appeared to be taking her sister's departure in stride. He hated missing so much.

He didn't need the details of her experience with other men, but wanted to know everything else. "Tell me about Italy."

Her face lit with affection as she fell into reminiscing anecdotes of her and her sister's adventures across the globe. He laughed and listened and let her stories carry him to a familiar place he hadn't been in some time.

Isadora's heart was a wide-open part of her. The longer he let her talk, the more she opened up to him. He missed her stories. Being welcomed back into her life was perhaps the greatest surprise of his.

This time was easier. Familiar. And he promised never to take her for granted again.

It was never discussed, why they'd broken up. Sawyer sometimes privately wished her a proper future, loving her enough to know she deserved more than he could offer, but he was too selfish to let her go again. Having her back in his life felt right.

Though her schedule was busier, especially once Lucian's company really took off, they always made time for each other. They no longer only met on Mondays, but whenever they desired. At the office, when their paths crossed, there was an unspoken tension between them, but Isadora made professionalism an art form, so no one ever suspected they shared a life outside of their careers.

She never complained about their clandestine status, nor did she breathe a word about loving him. Perhaps she no longer did.

Once the cooler months started so did the usual winter events. Isadora attended some, but not all. Slade continued to ease into his role, taking over the reins and that meant Sawyer had to introduce him to hundreds of colleagues.

One evening, after a local charity event for St. Christopher's, the homeless shelter Chelsea had supported with great passion when she was alive, he and Slade stopped for a drink at a local bar.

Sawyer was disappointed in this year's fundraising efforts and knew that was partly his fault. If they didn't make some changes the shelter wouldn't make it another winter.

"It's difficult, doing so much and still seeing so much suffering. It can burn you out. Make you jaded." He needed Slade to understand how necessary the shelter was, why it couldn't close. It was about more than a promise he'd made to his late wife. It was about compassion, second chances, and survival for those less fortunate.

"You can't beat yourself up, Dad. Think of how many residents leave for better options."

"Unfortunately, we don't hear the success stories. We just have to assume they're out there. The number of those in need keeps increasing and the charity events aren't bringing in half of what they used to. Your mother was always so good at charming people to open their wallets. I'm failing her."

Slade patted his arm. "You're not. She'd be happy to know you kept with it. I remember going there as a kid and watching her sit and talk to them. She never saw them as different. Not everyone can be as open minded."

He frowned at his son's choice of words. "They *aren't* different. Some of them once had beautiful homes and luxurious lives. Everyone's only one crisis away from bankruptcy in this country. And sometimes loss isn't related to money at all."

His mind again went to Chelsea. Losing his wife had been the shock of a lifetime. He would've given up everything he owned to just have one more day with her.

In the beginning, it was a trial just to get out of bed in the morning. If not for Slade, he would have never made it through his grief. But grief like that never really went away. It certainly lived longer than people. Exactly why he refused to love anyone that deeply ever again.

Slade looked at him as if he could read his thoughts. "You know it's been twenty years, Dad. No one would blame you for moving on."

"Love's too complicated. It has the ability to lift you up and cut you down in one fell swoop." He paused to sip his cocktail and flag down the bartender for a refill. "When your mother died... It broke something in me that can't be fixed."

Slade slid his glass forward as the bartender approached. When they were alone again, he asked, "Don't you want to be happy?"

"I *am* happy."

"Dad, you haven't been with anyone in years."

Shifting the attention off himself, he asked, "What about you? You haven't brought home a girl since high school."

"My needs are met."

Sawyer chuckled. "I get that, but what about a family? Don't you want children someday?"

"No."

Startled by his son's immediate rejection of the possibility, Sawyer frowned. "Since when?"

"Since always. I might get married one day, but there won't be kids in my future."

"How can you say that?"

"Because I'm a realist."

Jarred by his announcement, he took a moment to process the idea that the Bishop name might die with them. For a split second he wished he could give Isadora a child, but that would never work. It seemed like the perfect solution, but it wasn't—just more selfish thinking on his part.

He'd be nearly seventy by the time their child graduated high school. The older he got the more responsibilities would rest on her shoulders. He'd be lucky to see their kids reach Slade's age. It was simply out of the question.

He watched one child grieve a parent. He wouldn't do that to another, leaving Isadora with that sort of unbearable loss, the helpless position of explaining to a child that there was no way to bring a parent back.

"Dad, are you listening?" Slade waved a hand in front of Sawyer's face.

"I was thinking. Sorry."

"I said, you should get on one of those dating sites. At least then you won't be spending all your nights alone at the house."

Sawyer chuckled, not realizing how pathetically his son viewed his social life. "How do you know I don't have a gorgeous woman in my bed every night?"

"Come on, Dad."

"You never know. She could be waiting for me at home right now. Naked."

"If you're not going to be serious, forget I said anything."

Thinking of precisely who waited for him, he checked the time and tossed a few bucks on the bar. "You're right. I'll take your advice into consideration. But I have to get going."

There's a beautiful woman waiting for me...

On the drive home, he considered confiding in his son the next time the topic of dating came up. He tried to imagine how Slade might react to his relationship with Isadora. They always got along well and Slade could possibly keep the information to himself. But nothing stayed secret forever, and Slade wasn't his biggest concern.

His worry was *her* family.

The older Lucian got the more he used his aggression as a weapon of intimidation. While Isadora saw a thoughtful industrialist in her brother, Sawyer knew the truth.

Lucian was a son of a bitch to work with. Smart as a whip, but a real cut throat when it came to doing business and he didn't hesitate to destroy any opposition that stood in his way. Not only that, the kid had a temper that could rival his father's.

Sawyer had seen both Patras men use their power to resolve personal vendettas. They were extremely territorial and if anyone dared to infringe on what they viewed as theirs, there were sure to be consequences.

The last thing Sawyer wanted was the wrath of a Patras interfering in with his life. And he didn't want Isadora to deal with that sort of backlash either.

While she might be able to reason with Lucian, Christos would be furious. There was no reasoning with that man. His daughter was smart, beautiful, *and* wealthy. Christos viewed those qualities as bargaining chips meant for his personal benefit. The man had despicable disregard for his children, which was the primary reason Sawyer kept an eye on them after their mother died.

He could still hear Christos's words from many years ago. They'd been disturbing enough for Sawyer to maintain the illusion of a friendship with his partner, long after his feelings for the man turned to hate.

"Useless daughters! My son will probably be the death of me, but my daughters..." Christos had laughed as though Isadora and Antoinette were as inconsequential as lint. "Let's just hope they're beautiful. My only hope is marrying them off so someone else can support them.

"The older one's attractive enough. Let them screw whomever they want, but marriage is a business. Their mother never understood that. It's the

only way a father can get a return on an investment like daughters. You're lucky you only have a son to worry about, Sawyer."

He'd listened to several rants of the same degrading tone. Enough that Sawyer always felt he had no choice but to keep an eye on all three Patras children. While Lucian had the luxury of being a son, he still suffered. His father had a different form of cruelty for him.

Christos would never approve of his daughter settling with Sawyer. There would be no heirs or advancement of any kind.

Sawyer was quite successful, but not to a Patras standard. And at this point in life, he had little ambition left. This was it and it was a far cry from what Christos expected his daughter to achieve for him whether she was aware of that or not.

That was exactly why he never misled Isadora with words of love. He cared deeply for her, yes. And when they made love he always made sure she felt his affection, but he never wanted to vocalize any promises that would take away from her future or cause her trouble.

He didn't give a shit about pleasing Christos, but Isadora did. She'd always craved her father's approval and settling with Sawyer would guarantee she never earned it. Plus, she was born to be a mother. It was simply her nature.

As he pulled into the driveway his mind returned to the same position it had held for years.

Their relationship was complicated, too complicated to involve others. They were happy the way things were and that should be enough.

And, in a strange way, the clandestine tone of their liaison worked. It made the flame flicker hotter than ordinary affairs. Hiding created a fast, furious, and scorching thrill that built a hunger unlike anything else. His body warmed just thinking of how hot they could get.

Isadora was wild, untamed, and utterly enchanting. It was almost impossible not to love her. Almost.

His deep affection lent itself to looking out for her, his mind certain their time would eventually end and she'd settle down with someone more suitable. But, for now, he savored every passing moment.

As he entered the house he smiled at the energy in the air, sensing her presence the moment he walked through the door. "Bella?"

"Upstairs," she called.

He climbed the stairs and saw his bedroom door cracked, light seeping into the hall. Pressing it open, he grinned.

Sitting with her back against the pillows, she held a novel in her hands—some silly love story she'd been obsessing over. She wore a college T-shirt and *his* reading glasses.

Folding back her page, she closed the book and smiled at him. "How was the shelter meeting?"

"The usual. I grabbed a drink with Slade afterward."

"I figured."

He emptied his pockets and hung his clothes on the garment rack. As he approached, she placed her book aside and crawled to the edge of the bed to greet him.

Sawyer touched the rim of his glasses and chuckled. "You need to go to the optometrist. You'll ruin your eyes wearing mine."

Rising on her knees she wreathed her arms around his shoulders and kissed him. "I don't know what you're talking about. My vision's perfectly fine."

Yet she was always stealing his glasses. "They look better on you anyway."

"Mmm, flattery will get you everywhere."

Her lips teased his jaw as she pulled him down to the bed. If only others knew how good he actually had it.

18 Distanza

"DISTANCE"

AS THE YEARS CARRIED ON, his son stopped worrying when Sawyer was going to get back out there and Isadora's family gave up hounding her about finding a future husband—though her father made comments on the rare occasions he called. Life was good and time moved faster than usual.

Lucian had finally drawn up the paperwork to buy out Christos's portion of Leningrad and Sawyer was anxiously awaiting the invitation to combine the company with Patras Industries. The second generation was taking over, which meant he could finally pull back at work and allow Slade to take the wheel, though it was easier said than done.

As he pored over the contract in bed one night, seeing firsthand just how having Lucian involved would overshadow much of their family's contributions, he sighed.

"Problem?" Isadora asked.

He had to tread carefully. Isadora had become a familiar part of her brother's affairs and ranked one of his most loyal employees. She was good at her job and Sawyer didn't want to complicate anything for her.

"No. Just realizing this is definitely going to change things. I've grown used to running Leningrad with your father away. Lucian will want to be a lot more involved."

"But you'll be partners. He's not taking anything away from you."

"Slade will be a junior partner as well. I trust my son, but one senior partner doesn't equal a senior and junior partner. Things never work as easily in threes."

"Are you saying you don't trust my brother?"

He didn't touch that one. Lucian's first priority would always be Lucian.

He sighed. "It'll be nice when I'm retired and they can worry about this nonsense." She snorted and he glanced at her over the rim of his glasses.

Stretching close, she kissed his cheek. "I know you, Sawyer. You need to work. It's in your blood. Take a vacation and stop acting like you're some obsolete cog in a company you practically created."

"Your father created it."

She rolled her eyes. "You've run it for the last twenty years. Without you, Leningrad wouldn't exist."

"For all your father's faults, I don't think he ever expected his own son to disembowel his businesses the way he has. There's practically nothing left of his legacy."

Her focus returned to her novel as she adjusted on the pillow next to him. She turned a page, her response to her family's ongoing feud seeming more indifferent than ever.

"Bella?"

"I have no sympathy for him."

Frowning, because Isadora had always strived for her father's approval, he worried he'd missed something. "You okay?"

Flipping the book to her lap, she huffed. "That man cares nothing for me. Why should I waste a single worry on him?"

He frowned. Where was this sudden anger coming from? "Did something happen?"

Her lashes fluttered and she returned to her book. "No, he just called last week on my birthday to lecture me about Toni changing her major again."

Her father hadn't wished her a happy birthday? He sighed and shut his eyes. She let the man get away with so much, it was utterly disgraceful that he couldn't even remember his kid's birthdays.

His hand closed around hers. "Bella, your father loves you."

She gave him a strange look he didn't recognize. "When people love you, they tell you."

Her words pierced something fragile between them. They were no longer talking about her father. "You know I care deeply for you."

She looked at him, expression guarded. "I know."

He stared at her, hoping she really understood how much.

She broke eye contact and shut off the bedside lamp, turning on her side and facing away from him. He silently sighed and shut off his lamp as well.

Lying beside her, he pressed his lips to her shoulder. "Your father's an asshole."

"Just what the world needs, another asshole."

He frowned, unsure if she was implying he, too, was an asshole. Rolling to his back, he stared at the ceiling.

The following night, as he waited for her after work, their dinner growing cold on the table, he feared his clumsy words might have done more damage than a quick conversation could repair.

By seven o'clock he was convinced she wasn't coming. Dumping their plates in the garbage, he shut off the kitchen lights and went to the living room in search of a distraction. Nothing on television appealed. Frustrated, he pulled out his cell and dialed her.

They didn't do this. They didn't say they would be somewhere and stand each other up. If that was the way she wanted to behave—

"Hello?" she answered, sounding frazzled.

"I threw our dinner in the trash."

"I'll be right back," she said to someone he couldn't see. A few seconds later, she whispered, "I'm sorry. Something came up."

"A call would have been nice, Isadora."

"Please don't be mad. It's been a terrible day."

Sitting up, his anger slipped away as concern gnawed at his gut. "What happened? Are you all right?"

She exhaled into the phone. "No. I mean, I'm fine, but Lucian's girlfriend was in a horrific accident."

"Monique? Is she okay?" Slade often spoke fondly of the woman.

Isadora's whisper was so hushed he could barely make out her words. "She died."

His mind blanked at the shocking news. The girl was in her twenties. She had her whole life ahead of her. Lucian was likely crushed.

"What? How?"

And Slade... The three of them were very close. He was torn between speaking to Isadora and calling his son.

This must have happened after work, because

he saw Slade that afternoon and he seemed fine. Either that or he hadn't heard.

"It was a motorcycle accident. It's awful, Sawyer. Lucian's in shock, I think."

"Where are you now?"

"We're at Slade's."

He sat up. "Slade's?"

"The accident happened around the corner. Thank God he was here. He seems to be more help to Lucian than I am. I know she's been a part of my brother's life for years, but I hardly knew the woman. I feel terrible. I always assumed I'd have the chance, but..."

"I'm sorry. Please tell your brother I'm so sorry for his..." His words cut off. She couldn't do that without people wondering how he found out. "I'm sure word will get out and I'll speak to him soon. What a dreadful situation. Is there anything I can do for you?"

"There's nothing to do. I'm not even sure why I'm here. The two of them are just sitting in silence. Slade's taking it pretty hard. He's a good friend, Sawyer."

It didn't take long for his son to call. Sawyer expected as much. Yet, nothing prepared him for the desolate look in Slade's eyes when he came to Sawyer's home that night.

"I don't understand this, Slade. I know the three of you were close, but... Did you love her?"

His son looked at him through red-rimmed

eyes, his throat working to swallow back words that Sawyer wished he would share. "No," he rasped. "I loved what she brought out in my friend."

Sawyer analyzed those cryptic words for days, never fully understanding the grief of his son. Was the woman that good for Lucian in Slade's eyes? That didn't make sense when Isadora believed they were poorly suited. Surely she knew her brother better than his son. Perhaps Slade really had loved Monique, but was too ashamed to admit the truth. Regardless of the cause, his son's sorrow was a palpable ache he couldn't soothe.

Nothing was the same after that day. The death of Monique left Slade so stricken with grief every other relationship suffered. Lucian was also affected, but hid his personal feelings well.

Isadora also sensed the imbalance in the boys. While Lucian was moving on—or more accurately blazing forward—Slade's ambition seemed to vanish. He often stopped by the house uninvited, and that added another complication to Sawyer and Isadora's relationship.

Sometimes a sense of no control could drive men to wild extremes. Not the desired temperament of the new generation that held the reins in Folsom. And certainly not the circumstances Sawyer wanted to combat at this time of his life.

For weeks it was a touch and go game of phone tag between him and Isadora, her asking if she could see him, and him making excuses because his son was once again sitting in his home. Just sitting.

"I wish you would talk to me, Slade. I can't help you if you refuse to explain this to me."

Slade's blue eyes were flat, his expression devoid of emotion as he stared at the distant wall. "No one can help me."

"Maybe you should speak to someone, a grief counselor or something." At this point he was convinced Slade and Monique had been having an affair behind Lucian's back and his son was simply too ashamed to confess the truth. "You know, I'd never judge you, Slade. Sometimes we can't control who we love."

His sharp gaze flashed to his face. "What do you mean by that?"

Sawyer frowned. "I'm just saying ... sometimes our hearts are more powerful than our common sense."

"I think," he quietly said, "Loving the wrong person can only lead to a broken heart. I knew better, but I couldn't help it. My heart couldn't help it."

"Does Lucian know that you loved her, Slade? He might understand—"

His son glared at him, cutting off his statement. "I didn't love her."

"Then who?" Maybe he was missing everything. All of this coincided with Monique's death. He assumed...

Sawyer drew in a long breath and slowly sat back, the flicker of an explanation flitting through his mind. "Is it Lucian?"

"I have to go." Slade stood and Sawyer rushed after him as he moved to the front door.

"Slade, wait." He didn't know what to say, wasn't even sure if he was on the right track.

Slade never gave any indication that he might like men. On the contrary, Sawyer had only seen him date women. Lucian, however...

Dear God, the man was so blatantly heterosexual there was no way to misinterpret his orientation. His heart broke for his son. "Slade ... Lucian's not gay."

His shoulders worked as he faced the front door, each labored breath cutting through the thick silence. Finally, he said, "Neither am I."

Sawyer never broached the subject again, figuring that Slade would explain things when he was ready. As time went on, he dismissed the assumption that his son was in love with another man, but he did wonder if they had both shared a connection with the woman that died.

Nothing made sense and even things that had always been, suddenly seemed uncertain. Slade and Lucian's relationship shifted, resembling that of enemies more than friends or business partners as the months went on.

Lucian Patras, Slade Bishop, and Shamus Callahan were rapidly recognized as names no one fucked with. All three men were in a brutal race to the top, but only Shamus seemed capable of being pleasant along the way. Even Isadora noticed changes, as concerned for her brother as he was for his son.

"I can't seem to get through to him," Isadora complained to Sawyer one evening. "Lucian's so cold and closed off since Monique died. Everything has to do with business. That's all he cares about."

"It's what he loves, bella. I imagine he's trying to fill a void."

"But it's been over a year. He can't shut love out completely."

"I'm sure your brother's ... having his needs met. Maybe right now he's using work to cope. Let that be his mistress for a while. Give him time."

"I'll never understand men. Why love something that can't love you back? He's turning into my father."

Sawyer didn't mention that she loved him despite his refusal to return the sentiment. After so much time he believed she knew he loved her, but he'd yet to say the words.

It was a confusing time, tension running high between his son and her brother and neither he nor Isadora were clear on why that was. Lately, there were a lot of things Sawyer seemed in the dark about.

The following week he stepped into his son's office and waited for Slade to get off the phone. When he ended the call, Sawyer asked, "Where's the paperwork for the Gerard deal?"

"Gone. We sent it out yesterday."

Sawyer's brow lowered. "Who the hell signed it?"

"Lucian already signed off. I handled our portion."

Sawyer scoffed. Nothing like being removed without permission.

"Next time we agree on a deal that size I want to see the final contract."

"I don't have time for this, Dad—"

"Make time."

"*What do you want from me?*" Slade barked. "We have a job to do and sometimes I think I'm the only one doing it! Two senior partners and I'm the only one here every day. You skip out whenever you want and Lucian's getting his brains sucked out by some gold digging whore!"

Jarred by Slade's venomous response, he held up his hands. "Slade, take a breath."

"I don't need a fucking breath, I need to wrap up this deal so I can move onto Chrysler & Ro. since I'm the only one who seems to give two shits about what matters."

This shift in his son had started after the death

of Monique and had only gotten worse with time. He wanted to help him, but he didn't know how.

Leaving the office, he let the door hang wide and marched directly past reception into Lucian's office.

"Mr. Bishop, you can't go in there," the secretary called.

"This is my fucking company," he snapped and barged into Lucian's office.

"I'll call you back." He hung up the phone. Lucian raised a brow, and waited for an explanation. He was alone, but clearly in the middle of something.

"The Gerard deal required my signature."

Lucian closed his laptop. "No, it required a partner and an under signer. I signed and Slade handled the rest."

"You know, it would be nice if my presence wasn't completely ignored around here. Slade said you're dropping the ball on Chrysler & Ro."

He cocked his head. "Slade's not thinking clearly."

"He says the same about you."

"Do yourself a favor, Sawyer, and don't involve yourself in issues that aren't yours."

He knew then that whatever was going on with his son absolutely had to do with Lucian.

"Fine. But just remember, you were in diapers when your father and I started this company and I won't stand for my authority being undermined."

Lucian's dark gaze fastened to his as he slowly rose from his chair. "I apologize if us moving ahead on a time sensitive deal somehow hurt your *feelings*, Sawyer, but this isn't a fucking daycare. I might have been a child when you started here, but I'm senior partner now. Next time you come in my office throwing a fit like a toddler, you better be holding a box of your toys, because your next step will be out the fucking door. Do we understand each other?"

His molars locked as rage burned through his body. "You can't get rid of me that easily. I'm not Christos." And he'd be damned if some spoiled shit took credit for his life's work.

"Find someone else to unruffle your feathers. I have work to do." He pressed the intercom. "Laura, get me the Chrysler & Ro. paperwork."

Furious, Sawyer turned and gripped the door.

"And Sawyer?"

What you little prick? "What?"

Lucian's voice was deceptively calm. "I've accomplished plenty of things that weren't *easy*. A challenge will never stop me from getting my way."

He left and slammed the door. That was the last time he overlooked something. Since the buyout, his position seemed more obsolete than ever. And as it came time to finalize the merger, Sawyer's instinct told him it wouldn't be as simple as they'd all hoped.

He wanted to be present every chance he could, but his obligations weren't simply tied to Leningrad. Winter had arrived with record breaking wind chills and they were scrambling to keep St. Christopher's open—at least until the spring. That sometimes took precedence over work. Peoples' lives were at stake and it wasn't looking good.

Every time he returned to the office things seemed worse than he'd left them. Lucian was becoming one of the most ruthless, unsatisfied entrepreneurs Sawyer had ever witnessed. His aggression wasn't selective, either. If Lucian said black, Slade said white. Whatever was going on between them wasn't going to just go away.

He knew things were the nastiest they'd ever been the day his son barreled into Leningrad with a black eye.

"What the hell happened?" Sawyer barked, seeing Slade's face.

"Stay out of it, Dad." His son went to the ice bucket in the corner of his office and threw a few cubes into a linen napkin.

"Did Lucian do that? That kid's out of hand."

"He's not a kid," Slade snapped. "He's a grown man who's having his brains sucked out of his dick."

Sawyer's preoccupation with the shelter had cost all of them. He somehow felt responsible for this rift between them, believing if he'd been more aware of what was going on he might have been able to stop it before it spun out of hand. Too late.

His authority at the company was slipping and the doors of St. Christopher's were now permanently closed. He was failing his son, failing Chelsea, and if Lucian didn't settle down, he'd soon be failing Isadora, because he was going to go ballistic on the man. She'd never forgive him.

He should have sat down with the both of them months ago, but he never expected things to get this volatile. "You two have to work this out. You're more than partners. You're friends."

"Fuck our friendship."

Sawyer's concern extended beyond business. Isadora would hear about this altercation. Lately, they'd been discussing coming out as a couple, but this fissure between their families would cause another delay. "Fuck!"

His son scowled and winced, pressing the ice to his eye. "Why are you so pissed off?"

Frustrated with the entire situation, he paced. "When I put years into something and see it getting destroyed over some pissing match you two can't work out, I'm entitled to get angry. Whatever's going on between the two of you has to stop. Our families have too much history for this bullshit."

"You're acting like this is all my fault!"

He didn't care whose fault it was. "I'm not in the mood to go up against the Patras name."

Slade's face darkened with pent up rage. "This isn't about his fucking name. It's about him!"

Slade didn't get it. He was still new. He didn't understand how that family worked. "Don't let your ego overshadow the fact that their name will always carry more power than Bishop. They're kings. They always win. I want this worked out and I want it worked out quickly."

Slade scoffed. "Thanks for taking my side."

"I am on your side!" He'd heard enough. This was not the way grown men conducted business. "All of this was created for *you*! I'm trying to protect you by teaching you that sometimes we have to concede to the bigger wolf. I don't care if you have to tuck your tail and beg, you will make this right."

"Fuck that! I get that this was once Christos's company, but now it's *ours*. I'm not going to be some fucking callboy who follows Lucian's lead when we're the ones running the company. I'm not afraid of him."

Sawyer laughed without humor. "You should be."

He left him there to think about his advice, but his son was a stubborn man with costly pride. It got so bad, Lucian rarely ventured into Leningrad anymore, but that didn't mean he wasn't watching closely.

Though he and Isadora rarely bickered, the recent tension between their families infected every part of their lives over the next several weeks. She heard about it through whispers in the HR department at her office and, no matter how much he tried not to let Slade and Lucian's issues come between them, she brought it home anyway.

"I don't understand why you can't say something to Slade," she argued. "He's your son!"

"And Lucian's your brother, but I'm not holding you responsible for his actions!" he snapped. "Did you ever think this woman he's seeing might be bad for him?"

She drew back as if that couldn't possibly be the cause. "Evelyn? What does she have to do with any of this?"

"According to Slade, she has everything to do with it. Since she's come around there's no reasoning with your brother. He's off his game and it's affecting his work."

She scoffed. "My brother's worked his entire adult life to build an empire. He's overcome more heartache than anyone should have to face, and he never lets his personal life affect his professional one. If his relationship is overshadowing his work, well, maybe it's about time!"

"He thinks he loves that woman, Isadora. But everyone else can see she's using him."

She shook her head slowly, something close to pity flashing in her eyes. "He's in love, Sawyer. Maybe if you knew what that felt like you'd understand."

Now she was turning this on him. "This isn't about us."

"They're our family. How can you sit there and say it's not about us?"

"It's a personal issue between Slade and Lucian, Isadora. Keep Human Resources out of it."

"Because I'd only care about their relationship if it affected my job? You're an idiot." With that she stormed out of his house and didn't call him for a week.

He didn't know what she wanted aside from the impossible. Things were shifting, slowly, like a dusting of snow that posed the threat of an avalanche. He wasn't sure how to slow time or go back to the way things were, but he sensed a collapse approaching.

19 *Vendetta*

"VENGEANCE"

THEY'D TAKEN on a new kid at Leningrad, a real prodigy with a gift for investment. Slade had initiated the hiring and Sawyer was intrigued the moment he heard the name.

"Hughes, did you say?" It had been years since anyone spoke that name with any sort of reverence. "This is *Crispin* Hughes's son?"

Slade nodded. "He's young and green, but his instincts are spot on."

"His father was a crook," Sawyer reminded.

"Well, his son's honest and hungry for success. I lost my wallet, and the kid, not knowing who I was, chased me down six blocks to return it—all its contents still inside. I believe he's trustworthy."

Sawyer eased back in his chair. Ultimately, he'd leave the decision up to Slade, but it was a curious situation. After Crispin Hughes killed himself, the family vanished off the map.

"Where did he work before this? And why isn't Isadora Patras handling the paperwork? She's supposed to do all our hiring now."

His son grimaced. "I'm choosing to leave all Patrases out of this decision. Lucian's head's up his ass and I want Hughes on our team. I don't want his sister filling him in."

Sawyer's guard went up. "Need I remind you we still play for the same team?"

"That might change."

The leather of Sawyer's chair creaked as he swiped the application off his desk. Business was business, but there was something unsettling about hiring someone behind their partner's back —though it did happen on occasion. Lucian had brought in several new employees without consulting with them first.

If this kid was all Slade said he was, it would be foolish to let him slip through their fingers.

"Christos Patras despised Hughes." Maybe he was getting hung up on historic events that no longer mattered. "Let's hope the vendetta died with this kid's father. You say he's a prodigy?"

"Definitely someone we want to grab before anyone else does."

Sawyer slid the application back onto the desk. "Then we should act fast. I'd like to meet him."

"I'll bring him by next week."

Slade had been right about the kid. Parker Hughes had an aptitude most hires spent years working up to and still couldn't achieve. His instincts were flawless and his drive was unstoppable.

As green as he was, the clients didn't seem to care. He was a young, good looking twenty-something year old, who knew exactly how to close a deal and get what he wanted. But Sawyer couldn't figure out exactly what he was after. The kid wasn't as enamored with wealth as most men were in their company.

However, it didn't take long for Sawyer to realize he should have trusted his first instinct and cleared the position with Lucian. Their partner was outraged when he found out about Hughes. They'd had an incredible quarter, with profits higher than they'd seen in decades, but Lucian wanted Hughes gone and made that clear the day he stormed into Leningrad making threats and looking like the devil himself.

Lucian then left for France, an unexpected trip they were all grateful for. He'd been a tyrant and they all needed a break to think their options through.

It was a tough call. Hughes knew how to make money and did so with little consequence. They were all benefitting from his contribution to Leningrad, but Lucian had laid down a severe ultimatum. Either the kid went or Patras would buy out the Bishops—which he could easily do.

Thinking of all he'd worked for, the legacy he'd hoped to pass on to his son, their personal relationship with the Patras family, and his private relationship with Isadora, Sawyer saw no other option than to go over Slade's head and salvage their ties to Patras—if they weren't already severed.

He'd called Hughes into his office and informed him that he was being let go. "This wasn't an easy decision, Parker. You're an incredible asset, but we're making some cutbacks and your lack of seniority with the company has to be taken into account. I hope you understand."

"I understand no one else is being cut and you just lied right to my face. What, Patras didn't have the nerve to fire me himself?"

It was the first time Hughes had ever shown a shrewd side in Sawyer's presence. "Your issues with Lucian Patras are not my concern."

The kid's green eyes reflected an inappropriate level of indifference as he smirked. "Of course they aren't. I got what I came for anyway."

Sawyer's head cocked, unsure what his cryptic comment implied. "There's a non-compete clause in your contract."

"The contract that's now null and void since you're dismissing me from the company without cause? Read the fine print, Bishop. I'm not an idiot. You're *breaking* our contract. I can do whatever the hell I want. Patras knows that, which is exactly why I threaten him. Unlike him, I'm indebted to no one."

The irony was the kid was right. He could fuck all of them by pulling his clients and investing in his own business.

"This shouldn't be personal. If I had a way to keep you on, I would."

"But then you'd be breaking the first commandment of business. Thou shall not piss off a Patras. Believe me, it's personal." He stood. "Have one of the secretaries forward my things to my address. I wouldn't want anyone accusing me of taking something I haven't earned."

He walked out of the office and Sawyer stood, hating to leave things on bad terms. Hughes might be new, but he wasn't someone a wise person would taunt.

Lucian was a fool not to realize the kid would now become their competition. It was better for them to maintain the impression of an alliance.

"Parker, hold on a second."

When he reached the hall, Hughes was already at the elevator bank. The metal doors parted and the sight of Isadora in their building distracted him. What was she doing here?

He glanced at Isa only to gesture for her to give him a minute. "I could write you a recommendation for a better company."

"Excuse me," Hughes growled, shoving past Isadora and stepping into the elevator.

She frowned and quickly stepped out of the way, looking back at Sawyer in confusion.

Hughes stabbed his finger into a button. His shrewd glare clashed with Sawyer's. "I'm done working for you people. But I'm sure this isn't the last I'll see of any of you."

The doors closed and Sawyer gave up. "I'm sure," he mumbled.

Isadora's gaze bounced between him and the elevator. "What was that about?"

Letting out a huffed breath, he massaged his brow. "A good opportunity lost." Letting all thoughts of Parker Hughes go, he smiled at her. "What brings you by?"

Keeping her expression professional, she stepped closer and handed him a thick file. "Lucian wanted me to deliver these to you."

He flipped open the cover and glanced at the buy-out forms. He passed them back. The cocksucker sure didn't deliver empty threats.

"Tell him the situation's been handled. These aren't necessary."

No need to involve her in the whole Slade, Lucian, and now Parker Hughes saga—an ongoing drama even he didn't completely understand. But in every battle, someone had to surrender. This time it was Sawyer. He just wanted peace.

"Good," she said, clearly having read the contents.

"Bella..."

He wanted to tell her things should be better now, but that was a promise he wasn't sure he could keep. Their relationship had been tense for months because of familial issues and it was wearing on the both of them. They needed an evening where work stress wouldn't intrude.

"Can I see you tonight?" he asked quietly.

She held the file against her chest like a shield. "I can't." Her gaze skated to a nearby filing cabinet and then to a nearby woman making a phone call on her cell.

Sawyer frowned. "What's going on?"

Her mood, like everyone else's, seemed altered. She'd been unreachable lately, withdrawn and appearing sad for reasons he couldn't identify. "Do you want to talk in my office?"

"I have to get back. I have an interview in twenty minutes. But you should know..."

He waited for her to finish the sentence, but she seemed to be having difficulty getting her words out. "Tell me."

Her lashes lifted and her brown eyes locked with his like a bad omen as his gut twisted. What the hell was going on?

"This is my last week working in the city, Sawyer."

Startled, he couldn't hide his shock. *Why?*

"I'm taking some time to go back to school. I'll still attend company functions and oversee certain tasks, but I'll mostly be working at home."

"When did you decide this?"

"I've been thinking about it for a while. This past year has left a bad taste in my mouth and I don't like the job anymore."

"You love your job."

"Not anymore. I'm tired of being addressed like I'm a glorified coffee fetcher. I'm the head of a department and everyone assumes I was given the position out of nepotism, which might actually be true. No one will ever respect me so long as I work in an environment my father or my brother created."

"Isa, people respect you." He wanted to go somewhere private where they could discuss this.

"No." She shook her head. "They fear my name and the men who share it. That has nothing to do with me or what I deserve."

It was an enormous decision and the fact that he was just hearing about it now—at work as if he were just an ordinary colleague—showed how much distance had come between them.

"Let me see you tonight. Please. We can talk about this in more detail once we have privacy."

"There's nothing to talk about. I've made up my mind. I'm meeting with an adviser tonight and the rest of the week will be spent training my re-placement. I have a few more interviews, but I think I found who I want."

It surprised him how much her decision bothered him. It felt like she was just giving up. "You worked so hard, Isa. You earned a degree and, until recently, you seemed to love working in HR."

"Sometimes you love things to no avail. I'm tired of giving my days to something that gives very little back."

"Isadora—"

Her expression shuttered. "I have to go."

He respected that she didn't want to have a private conversation in the hall of Leningrad. So he let it go. For now.

He watched as she returned to the elevator, waiting for her to look back, but she didn't. He was losing—losing his top employee, his authority at a company he'd dedicated his life to, the shelter he swore to always keep open, and losing her.

Returning to his office he scowled at his desk. In a flash of rage he swept everything off the surface and sent it clattering to the floor.

"*Fuck!*"

20 Ostacolo

"OBSTACLE"

"TONI'S IN HOG HEAVEN," Isadora told Sawyer over dinner. "The condo's stunning. Lucian really shouldn't spoil her like that, but that seems to be the only way he knows how to do things these days."

Moving his food around on his plate, Sawyer kept his thoughts about her brother to himself. Although Lucian backed off and he and Slade could now be in the same room together without nasty threats, everything had changed.

Isadora was living a separate life, attending night classes and meeting new people. He was happy she was pursuing her dreams—which now had to do with a Master of Arts in English—but her energy and zeal was devoted to a world he knew little about.

The sparse time they had as a couple due to

her class schedule was interrupted by other events he was no longer comfortable attending unless propriety demanded it.

Her brother's wedding, for instance.

He often wondered if Slade had been right. A little over a year ago, he'd told his son that sometimes men had to bend to the larger wolves in a pack. Sawyer had done just that, compromising his own beliefs to satisfy the ego of the alpha. Yet everything that came after that decision only proved to remind him he was becoming an inconsequential piece of the puzzle he'd created. He should have listened to his son, let Patras buy them out, and gone off on their own. Perhaps made Hughes a partner.

No longer hungry, he cleared his plate over the trash. "I'm going to take a shower."

Isadora, who had been in mid-sentence, paused. "Are you okay?"

"Fine. I just want to wash the day off."

He kissed her brow and left her to finish dinner alone. When he exited the bathroom she was waiting on his bed.

"What's going on with you, Sawyer?"

"What do you mean?"

"You were hardly listening to me at dinner. I know you've been stressed lately, but you've been in this sour mood for weeks."

"I'm fine."

She slid off the bed and gave the towel at his

waist a tug. "Let me help. I know how to ease your tension."

She pulled the towel away, but he wasn't in the mood. He hadn't been in the mood for days.

Looking down at his flaccid cock, he went to the closet. "Not tonight."

The room grew quiet. When he emerged in a pair of lounge pants, she wore an expression of concern. "We're in a rut."

"We're fine. I'm just tired." That had to be it.

"Do you want me to go?"

He wanted to get out of this fucking mood, but he couldn't figure out how! "No, I want you to stay."

As he brushed his teeth, she slipped out of her clothes and followed him into the bathroom. She used the sink when he was finished and they climbed into bed together. Once the lights were out, her hand skated over his thigh and reached into his briefs, but nothing was going on there.

"Isadora."

"What?" she giggled.

"I meant it when I said I was tired."

She accepted his excuse and rolled to her back. "Goodnight."

"Goodnight, bella."

The following afternoon he silently waited as a nurse ripped a blood pressure cuff off his arm.

"Pressure's a little high."

He awkwardly sat on the crinkling paper of an

exam table. After making a note in his chart, the nurse slid the clipboard into the holder by the door.

"The doctor will be in shortly."

Vivian Sheffield entered the room a few minutes later, appearing pleased to find him in her office. "Sawyer, it's good to see you." She grabbed his chart, but rather than read it, she smiled and asked, "What brings you in today?"

He hesitated, trying to tactfully explain his concerns. He'd known Vivian all her life and knew she was a good doctor, but sometimes it was difficult being direct with a medical professional when you knew them on a personal level as well.

"I've been ... more tired than usual."

She nodded, now flipping through his chart and making a quick note. "Any changes in your day-to-day life?"

"No. Things have been a little tense at work."

"Any symptoms besides exhaustion?"

He cleared his throat and her gaze lifted to his face. "I ... haven't been able to..."

This was fucking humiliating and he debated making up a lie and figuring out a different solution, but he needed to fix this *now*. Isadora was beginning to question his attraction to her and he didn't want her putting the blame on herself.

He cleared his throat again. "...perform."

Understanding dawned and Vivian nodded, placing the chart aside. "Well, that could be a number of things. Age can be a factor as well as stress. How old are you now, fifty-four?"

"Fifty-six."

"It's not uncommon for men to have a drop in testosterone at that age. Your blood pressure's a bit escalated as well. We can run some blood work to see if there are any other issues that might be coming into play."

Her explanations were similar to what he'd read online, but not necessarily giving him the solution he needed. "What about something I could take?"

She smiled. "There's that too. Would you like me to write you a script?"

"Please."

An hour later he was leaving the pharmacy feeling hopeful but old. Tucking the prescription into his pocket he backed out of the pharmacy parking lot and called Isadora through his Bluetooth.

"Hey, you."

"Bella." Today they were not going to argue. "Can I see you?"

"When?"

There was really no point in returning to the office this late in the day. "How about now?"

Seeming to sense what he had in mind, her voice took on a sultry tone. "I can be there in twenty minutes."

"Good. I'll see you then."

At the next traffic light he cracked open the bottle and swallowed a small, blue pill. When he pulled up at his house Isadora's car was already in the garage. He entered the house and found her sitting on the top step, wearing his robe, her bare legs delicately crossed and casting shadows over secret places.

Dropping his keys onto the table by the door he smiled up at her. "You beat me here."

"It's been a while since you called me in the middle of the day like that. I wasn't sure where you wanted me."

She was so beautiful, so sexy. His body responded in an instant, and relief swept through him.

"I want you everywhere," he rasped as blood rushed to his cock.

She gracefully stood, letting his robe slide off her shoulder onto the landing. Like a goddess, she came to him in a slow descent that had his heart pumping.

His cock was throbbing by the time she pressed her bare breasts to his front, her soft lips curving into an inviting smile. He lowered his mouth to hers. Heaven.

Her hands drifted over him, stroking his arms and sides, sliding over his clothes. He groaned as she cupped him through his pants.

"Well, *hello*," she whispered, fitting her hand over the bulge behind his zipper.

He wanted her and he wanted her *now.* A fire burned in his blood as he backed her to the wall, his mouth sealing over hers and taking greedily.

She lifted her knee, hooking a leg above his hip as he ground into her. His mouth closed over her pulse as he fit his fingers between her thighs and teased.

"Sawyer... What's gotten into you?"

"I've missed you."

It wasn't that he'd stopped wanting her. That would be impossible. He *always* wanted her. Things would be better now that he had the pills.

She arched into his touch and quivered as he stroked her folds, her body quickly responding in a carnal display of utter feminine perfection. His pulse raced with need and he had to get inside of her.

He unlatched his belt, fingers shaking with urgency, and turned her to face the wall. "I need to be inside of you, bella."

"Please." Her palms splayed on the wall, her bare ass pressing into his thighs. He gripped his engorged flesh, lining the tip up to her wet sex, and surged deep.

Her head fell forward as she moaned. He drilled into her. The long line of her spine accentuated her willowy body as it curved with his every advance. Her cries of pleasure echoed through the hall as he gripped her hips and buried himself to the root.

"Yes! Oh my God, *don't stop.*"

Relieved to have her again, have his body responding to her the way it always had, he found himself insatiable. More than hungry for her—he was starved.

She cried out, her sex contracting tightly around his swollen cock and milking his release hard enough to skew his vision. Seeing stars, he pulled out of her and rested his body against hers, caging her slender form with his as she shivered against the wall.

He blinked, literally blurry-eyed from the force of his release. "I needed that."

She sighed happily. "I'd say." Her body turned inside of his arms and she faced him, her lashes low and her smile a bit drowsy. "Wow."

Once they recovered, he went into the kitchen and made a plate of fruit and cheese, snagging a bottle of wine on his way up to the bedroom.

Isadora rested like an invitation across his pillows and his body had yet to flag. If he could get his eyes to clear he'd be golden.

"Thirsty?" he asked.

"Mmm," she answered, popping a grape into her mouth and holding out a glass.

They nibbled on fruit and quenched their thirst, then he moved the plate and wine aside. Her body rested in a tangle of tempting limbs and he could hardly believe he was ready to have her again.

Rolling her to her back, he kissed her slowly, tasting the wine on her tongue and taking his time exploring her curves.

She smiled up at him as he caressed her breasts. "You're awfully ambitious today." Her fingers curled around his heavy flesh and stroked.

"I can't get enough of you."

Realizing how worried he'd been that they might lose this connection, his relief was immeasurable. She was his comfort, his solace, his relief after the worst of days. He needed her and he needed this.

He pulled her body under his. "I want to make love to you all night."

Her thighs parted and he slid home, his eyes closing on a surge of ecstasy. "I'm going to hold you to that promise," she sighed, her nails dragging slowly down his back.

Sometime in the middle of the night he jerked awake to a strange sensation. His breathing was labored and, as Isa's body warmed his side, he recalled he wasn't alone.

Brow tight, his palm pressed into his chest where a dull ache formed, then sharpened enough that he bared his teeth as he winced. Isadora slept soundly beside him and he didn't want to disturb her, not if he didn't have to. Wincing again, he tightened his lips and swallowed a groan.

Fuck, that was a sharp one, but each wave waned before any real concern could form. Maybe it was just heartburn. Lying in the dark he waited for the ache to recede, but it seemed to spread through to the center of his back with every inhalation, intensifying until his hands trembled, then disappear for a few minutes. Another sharp twinge stole his breath.

Looking to his left, he debated if he should wake her, but the pain receded again, convincing him it was just anxiety or something mild. He'd wait it out, breathe through it, and eventually it would pass.

His mind turned over random thoughts—work, family, Slade, Isadora—until he was wide awake. It had been about ten minutes since the last wave of pain, so maybe he was out of the woods.

Slipping out of bed he went to the bathroom, uncharacteristically winded from the short walk. Short of breath, he kept his hand close to the wall for balance.

A sudden, sharp pain stabbed through the center of his chest and he doubled over against the vanity. "Jesus Christ."

He caught his breath and pressed the heel of his palm into his ribs. The pain stayed, not piercing, but radiating and pulling like a knot cinching tight around his lungs and shoulders. His heart thundered, beating at the back of his ribs as his skin beaded with sweat.

"Fuck."

He took a sip of water from the faucet and

opened the medicine cabinet, clumsily shoving items around until he found the aspirin. Small bottles rattled and clattered into the porcelain sink. Cracking open the cap with his teeth, he swallowed a pill and bent to wash it down with more water from the spigot.

His arms trembled as if he'd just lifted three hundred pounds. Splashing cool drops over his face, he caught his breath, the palpitation of his heart marking every half second and triggering his panic. Was this an anxiety attack or a heart attack? Sharp pain interrupted his decision and he shut his eyes.

Vivian had briefly reviewed side effects with him that afternoon. She'd mentioned something about possible chest pain, but nothing of this magnitude. This felt like a fucking elephant sitting on his chest, crushing his ribs, breaking his shoulders.

Sweat beaded on his brow as the throbbing ebbed and flowed. Maybe he should call someone, but didn't want to worry Isadora if it turned out to be nothing. He also didn't want to explain that these sensations might be the result of treating impotence.

If it got any worse he'd have to wake her. The waning ache subsided enough for him to breathe again, enough for him to believe this episode was not a life or death situation. But it was a terrifying slap in the face, one that left him shaken. He needed a few minutes to find his bearings.

He waited in the bathroom, drifting in and out of sleep as he slouched over the sink. It must have been close to an hour before the discomfort eased enough to dismiss his fears completely.

Sliding quietly under the covers he tried not to disturb Isadora, but she'd always been a light sleeper. Eyes still closed, she rolled to face him and draped her arm over his stomach, snuggling into his side.

"You okay?"

"Just getting a glass of water," he lied, pressing a kiss to the top of her head. "Go back to sleep."

She sighed and a moment later her weight sank into him.

He didn't go back to sleep. As he lay in the dark, the sun slowly rising and casting light across the shadows, he worried what these side effects meant in the long run, his thoughts taking a morbid turn.

If something happened to him, Slade would handle Leningrad. His estate was in order and he knew his son would be taken care of. But what about Isadora?

His blood chilled as he considered things no man wanted to think about. Who would look after her? Who would love her and keep her safe? She was capable of taking care of herself, but he wasn't ready to lose her.

Angry that his body was betraying him, he considered what would happen if he couldn't take the pills anymore. Maybe this was a one-time thing. They'd overdone it tonight and that might be why his heart reacted in such a way.

Nevertheless, his response scared him. It was a risk he wasn't sure he'd be willing to take in the future. He loved sex, but it would never be worth dying for. Maybe there was a different brand of pills he could try.

Maybe you should try dating someone your own age...

What the hell difference would that make?

He sighed, doing the same math problem he'd done nearly every day of the past decade. Their age difference had always been a factor, something he knew would someday become a burden, but he wasn't ready for that day to come. Not yet.

In the back of his mind he berated himself. This could all be a case of heartburn he was turning it into some midlife crisis. Tomorrow he'd give Vivian a call and see how things went the next time he took the medication.

Part Three

Isadora

Chapter 21

"Later on he will understand how some men so loved her, that they did dare much for her sake."
Bram Stoker
Dracula

"GOOD LORD!" Isadora shrieked, pivoting away from the den where her sister and Shamus were practically clawing each other's clothes off.

Despite everyone's warnings, Toni had finally gotten her wish and captured Jamie's heart. Lucian had been angry when he'd first learned his best friend was sleeping with his little sister, but eventually he got over himself and accepted that Toni was an adult and entitled to make her own decisions.

He just ... got over it.

That could have been Isa. If she and Sawyer had disclosed their relationship before the falling out at work, Lucian might have accepted their relationship and everything would be normal now. But it wasn't. Not even close.

She felt robbed. After years of carefully guarding her heart and hoping she and Sawyer might someday exist as a normal couple, her dreams were dashed. As things stood, their families had no interest in crossing paths—too many bridges burned.

Sawyer used to worry about her missing opportunities, but keeping silent as a couple over the years seemed the greatest missed opportunity of all. The Bishops—for reasons unknown to her—had betrayed her brother's trust and Lucian was not a man to overlook such things.

She didn't care what their reasons were. She hated that the two men she loved most in this world refused to work out their differences, neither one seeming to realize how much their actions affected her.

But she endured, keeping her brother in one part of her life and Sawyer in another. It wasn't what she wanted. It had never been what she wanted. But for the first time ever, she lacked the optimism to hope things might change for the better.

Everyone was in love. Her sister had Shamus. Lucian and his wife, Evelyn.

Isadora was the oldest. She should have been the first to marry, but the way things were going, she'd be the last—*if* it ever happened at all.

Having given the lovebirds enough time to compose themselves, she called from the hallway, "Can I come in now?"

"Yes," they both answered and Isadora cautiously entered.

"Get a room, you two. My house isn't an orgy den."

"Sorry, Isa," Shamus apologized, putting some distance between him and Toni.

"You're lucky it wasn't Lucian walking in here. Toni, fix your hair."

Her sister giggled, not a modest bone in her body.

"Lucian and Evelyn are getting ready to leave if you want to say goodbye." Once a month her siblings came over for a family dinner and those were the moments Isadora treasured.

On the weekends, she volunteered at the new homeless shelters, taking great joy in her brother's recently discovered passion for helping others— one of the many good qualities his wife brought about in him.

Her evenings were spent on campus as she was on the last leg of earning her master's degree. And when she didn't have class, she passed her nights with Sawyer.

But as time went on she found those intimate moments between them coming further and further apart. It was almost as if they were moving backward, sometimes barely spending one night a week together like they used to in the beginning.

Trying not to dwell on her personal life, she followed her sister and Shamus to the foyer to say goodbye to her brother and Evelyn.

"Are we getting together for lunch this week?" her sister- in-law asked.

Isadora truly adored the woman, finding her to be a breath of fresh air that their family very much needed. "Yes, one o'clock?"

"I'll meet you in the lobby."

It was their thing to meet at the hotel once a month to catch up on gossip. So many times Isadora had wanted to confide in Evelyn about Sawyer, but her sister-in-law was beyond loyal to Lucian. Isadora didn't want to burden her with keeping a secret from her husband.

They said their goodbyes and Isadora watched the four of them leave. When she shut the door she felt the weight of emptiness pressing in.

It was a rainy day, so distracting herself in the gardens was out of the question. She could go to Sawyer's, but feared her presence might not be wanted.

She didn't know what was happening to them. Sawyer had always reached for her in the middle of the night, but now he only reached for her on occasion. Some nights he claimed he was too tired to fool around. That was fine. She was satisfied just to be near him. But as his libido changed, so did their relationship.

After all the years they'd spent together, she never viewed their relationship as a solely sexual one. So why did everything feel like it was falling apart once the sex faded? It wasn't just sex.

Sawyer had never been easily irritated, but some nights she questioned why he invited her over at all. They'd watch television and snuggle, but when she tried to do more he either made an excuse or got frustrated, like she was some sort of deviant for wanting to fuck her boyfriend.

If she complained, he apologized, making more excuses about work, stress, and exhaustion. Then he'd do things to her, leaving her satisfied, but not the way he used to.

She wasn't an idiot and his behavior was beyond transparent. Foreplay was a poor replacement for making love, whether she reached completion or not.

If they were dealing with a situation a pill could fix, she assumed he'd address the problem. But things were only getting worse and she feared they were up against something bigger, something even she wasn't ready to talk about.

Their hot and cold love life was giving her emotional whiplash and her self-esteem was getting bruised from all the ups and downs. She knew they had to confront whatever was happening, but she was afraid of the outcome.

Grabbing her purse, she drove to his house, unsure what kind of mood he'd be in. She didn't want a fight. She was looking for a solution.

She let herself in and called for him. "Sawyer."

He came around the corner, a look of surprise on his face. "What are you doing here?"

"It's nice to see you, too." She put her purse on the hall table.

"I thought you had family dinner tonight."

"Everyone left." Apparently she was intruding on something. "Do you want me to go?"

"Of course not. I was just watching television. Come in."

She followed him to the couch, irritated that this was their best option. TV didn't allow for much talking and they needed to discuss things. "Let's go out."

He frowned at her. "It's ten o'clock."

"So. It's the weekend. Let's do something."

"Isadora, by the time we arrive somewhere it'll be almost midnight." By *somewhere* he meant a place where no one would recognize them.

She wanted to scream. She was sick and tired of all the obstacles cluttering their day-to-day life. Love shouldn't be this complicated. However...

Don't go there...

"What's happening to us, Sawyer? We never make plans anymore and you're always making excuses and claiming you're busy, but whenever I pop in you're just sitting around."

"That's not true."

But it was true. He seemed to direct all his energy toward things that didn't concern her. Then, when she got to spend time with him he was in decompression mode. It didn't make sense for him to be this burnt out from work alone.

Paranoia that something else might be going on had become a daily hurdle her brain tiptoed around. But the longer this went on the more suspicious his behavior seemed.

Glancing at him, she frowned. He focused on the television as if she wasn't even there.

Her worst fear slipped out, "Is... Is there someone else?" The words physically hurt to say.

He turned sharply and scowled at her. "Isadora."

"What? I don't know. Some nights I call and you don't even answer. I don't understand what's happening to us."

"How could you even ask such a thing?" he snapped, clearly offended.

"I'm sorry. I just worry I'm not enough for you anymore or that I don't satisfy you like I used to."

Shutting off the television, he stood. "You're more than enough for me. Are you staying over? I'm going to bed."

Hurt that he was brushing off a conversation

they clearly needed to have, she sighed. "I'm going home."

Another week went by without much more than a quiet dinner shared between them. At her wits' end, she did the unthinkable and checked his phone while he was in the shower, but there were only a few texts, none of them anything to get alarmed about.

Frustrated with his sketchy behavior, the next week she searched his medicine cabinet. It turned out she wasn't the only secret Sawyer was keeping.

Holding the answer in her hand she fought the urge to cry. That little bottle of pills represented so much.

She'd been blaming herself, questioning his feelings, and her self-esteem had been on a downward spiral. Not only that, this was a lie he'd been keeping between them, something he promised never to do.

Gritting her teeth, she sniffed and blinked back her tears. Marching into the bedroom, she flung the pill bottle at his chest and he caught it with a startled look.

"Did you think I'd care that you were taking them?" she'd shouted, glaring at him.

"What the hell were you doing in my cabinets?" he barked, chucking the bottle into a nightstand drawer and slamming it shut.

"Maybe I was searching for aspirin. I go in your cabinets all the time!"

"You were *snooping*!"

"Fine, I was snooping. But you won't talk to me about this and I don't know why. I tell you *everything* and it hurts to know you'd hide this from me. Did you think I couldn't tell?"

"It's none of your business!"

"Well it should be! I'm your—"

Her words cut off.

Over twelve years since they started this and she still didn't know what she was to him. She shoved the disturbing thought away and took a steadying breath.

In a calmer voice, she said, "Sawyer, I don't care that you need to take them."

"I don't *need* to take them," he growled. "My doctor gave them to me. Count them. They're all there."

"But... Then why do you have them?" If he didn't need them, wouldn't they be sleeping together?

"Jesus Christ, Isadora. Some things are just private."

"Is... Is it me?"

He sneered at her. "Stop making this about you. I told you, we're fine."

"We are *not* fine, Sawyer! I've put up with plenty and pretended it was normal, but not *this*! Some nights you fuck me and some nights you don't. If it's not a physical issue, I want to know what it is!"

"It's not you," he said between clenched teeth. "It's *me*. I'm fifty-six! It's exhausting trying to keep up with you. You're in your prime, Isadora. My prime was thirty years ago! I warned you something like this would eventually happen, but you refused to listen! The pills are precautionary."

Maybe he said more. She wasn't sure. The moment he'd described her presence in his life as *exhausting* she lost track of the conversation. Her vision blurred as she breathed slowly, wondering how he could say such a hurtful thing.

Flashbacks from before came hurtling out of her buried memories and she winced. She would *not* let him make this her problem. *No.* He was equally accountable in this relationship. They were going to talk this through until it was resolved. And he was *not* going to blame her for *his* lie.

Keeping her voice calm, she said, "I never expect anything from you, Sawyer. Not your commitment, your name, your money, or even your love. How dare you treat me like the source of your frustration? If you're tired of our relationship, then have the balls to say so. You hid this from me, knowing full well I'd blame myself. The only thing I ever asked of you was honesty, and you've been keeping this secret for how long?"

The sharp angles of his face softened and his shoulders lowered. He glanced at the nightstand. "You're right," he said slowly. "This isn't your fault. I've had the pills for months, but I don't like the way they make me feel. I should have thrown them away."

His apology sounded heartfelt and she could see he was embarrassed by this, but there was no need for him to feel ashamed. There had to be other options. Diet, maybe a change in routine. He was too young to go through something like this.

She crossed the room to comfort him and he held out a hand. The regret in his eyes the only warning that something more was coming. Something terrible.

Her blood turned to ice. She'd seen that look in his eyes before. "Sawyer—"

"I can't do this anymore, Isadora. I can't keep up with you—"

He's just embarrassed. "Yes, you can—"

"Stop and listen for once! Goddamn it!"

She jerked back. He never screamed at her like that.

He ran a hand through his hair and sat on the bed, seeming unusually winded. "We've been at this for years. I care for you very, *very* much, bella. But our time is done."

If he tried to pull her heart through flesh and bone, it would have hurt less than hearing those words.

He was upset, not thinking clearly. Maybe he was even feeling a little vulnerable.

"Sawyer, don't do this. There are other options."

"We have to stop ignoring the truth. Look at us. Our families no longer get along, we have to hide—"

"We don't have to hide *anything*." This was *their* life. "I'll tell them tonight if you want me to. I don't care who knows."

He shook his head. "Do you see the way people look at us when we're out? I watch them have a mental debate, trying to decide if I'm your father or some old pervert. You're thirty-six years old and you barely look twenty."

Who cares what strangers think? "Don't do this, Sawyer. We've tried being apart before. It doesn't work."

"Enough is enough, Isadora. Give me my pride and let what we've shared be enough. The longer this goes on—"

"You act as if you're eighty! You're fifty-six, Sawyer. Your age doesn't bother me any more today than it did twelve years ago."

"Stubborn," he mumbled.

"Who cares what people see—"

"*I do!*"

Her gaze jerked to the carpet. He would barely let her speak.

The anger in his tone was so unfamiliar. They were past the age issues. At least she was. Why wasn't he?

"You care about strangers' opinions more than you care about mine," she murmured.

"No, but I care enough about you to know when it's time to let you go. Ten years from now I'll be approaching seventy. You're wasting your life with me."

"You're rounding up and that's not fair."

"It'll come eventually, regardless."

Tears slid down her cheeks, but she didn't have the strength to wipe her eyes. "Why are you pushing me away again? Why can't you let me decide what's right for me? I've told you over and over again *this* is where I want to be."

"And I've never once told you this is where I want you."

Sharp agony knifed through her heart as his words sliced into her with the precision of an execution ax. She gasped as her spine seemed to bend at the blunt shock. He could steal her entire in the span of a breath.

Her arms closed protectively around her ribs, but it was too late. He stabbed her right through the heart.

"Bella, I've always hoped you'd find something more."

She gasped again, the impact of his words piercing her tender heart like sharp needles. "How can you say that after all this time?"

His gaze turned apologetic and his voice dropped low. "There's no doubt I've been selfish.

I'm human. But there comes a time when right is right. That time's now. The pills... That's just nature's way of reminding us how unsuited we are for each other."

"No." She staggered away from the bed, searching for a place to hide before he hit her with one more hurtful word.

They'd just been going through a rough time. She'd been busy with school and he was stressed out with work. There was nothing wrong with them as a couple, nothing that couldn't be fixed. "I'm not listening to this."

"It's not something I'm going to debate. I'm telling you, I'm done."

Something petulant unleashed inside of her, rejecting the sense that she had no control over the outcome. "No, Goddamn it! *No!*"

She couldn't bear to hear another word. He was suddenly in front of her, grabbing her shoulders and forcing her to settle.

"Listen to me, bella," he said sternly, demanding her attention. Cupping the side of her face, he brushed away her tears. "This is right. I know it hurts, but I swear to you, I'd never put you through a moment's pain if I didn't truly believe I was protecting you from something worse. Please, try to understand that, my beautiful girl."

She choked on a sob. Maybe if she gave him a few days he'd realize he was only repeating mistakes. They were miserable without each other.

"We've been down this road before."

"This time's different. Our relationship was never supposed to be permanent."

A broken whimper burbled and she painfully swallowed it back. "Why can't you just love me?"

His mouth formed a tight line as he silently blinked at her. Every passing second was an excruciating measure of the years she'd lost, loving him to no avail.

When it was clear he wouldn't say the words, she shouldered him off of her. "You swore you wouldn't do this. I stood right downstairs and you swore we'd talk through our problems, but you're pushing me away again."

"Some problems can't be resolved with communication."

Her head shook. There was no reasoning with him. Her hand opened over her heart in an attempt to subdue the pain. "I trusted you."

"You can still trust me—"

She scoffed. *"How?"*

"Please don't be angry."

She swiped at her lashes. "Don't tell me how to feel! Especially when I've *never* been able to control *your* feelings."

"Isadora, I don't want it to be like this. I'm not your enemy."

"I don't know how else to be!" she shouted. "It hurts, Sawyer—physically hurts to be pushed away by someone as emotionally handicapped as you. Chelsea's dead. Do you understand that? *Dead!*"

His face shuttered and she immediately regretted her hurtful words, but couldn't apologize for telling him the truth. He loved a ghost more than he would ever love her.

She gave him her heart and he broke it more than once. No one else had ever hurt her the way he had. No one else could.

He was the enemy. His power to do her harm was too great and unpredictable for her to combat anymore.

She took a staggering step back. "I have to go."

"Isa, please, try to understand that the last thing I want is to hurt you."

Her tearful gaze lifted to his face and she looked at him, truly saw him. Flaws, imperfections, faded charm. She'd spent her entire life fearful she'd make some unforgivable mistake, but his cowardice made her look like the bravest woman in the world. He would always be afraid of what people might think, like she was some black mark on his soul, a stain he placed but couldn't remove. He didn't deserve her.

Her head shook, the finality of his character doing irreparable damage to hers. "I would have given *everything* for your love. But you'd rather have nothing."

"Bella—"

"Don't! No more, Sawyer." With that, she

forced herself to look away and put one foot in front of the other until she was out the door.

Twenty-Two

> *"Forgiveness will cut a whole in half, divide and reduce beauty. Be warned, in every instance of forgiveness, some resentment remains."*
>
> *~Lucian Patras*

PERHAPS SHE WASN'T LISTENING, or maybe she figured no man could be that stupid. Three months had passed and she still assumed he'd change his mind, that after some time apart he'd come running back to her, proclaiming his love.

She was a fool.

They never ran into each other and her enormous, empty home, which she'd so blindly purchased, seemed drenched in loneliness. Just another miscalculation on her part, another assumption that everything would work out if she played by the rules.

All she ever wanted was a simple, normal life. Someone to love who loved her back. She'd trade every luxury to her name if only she could know what that felt like—even if just for a day.

She needed to get away, escape everything, and possibly never come back.

One afternoon while having lunch with her sister-in-law, Evelyn surprised her by taking her hand. "Are you okay, Isa?"

Forcing a smile, Isadora lied, "Of course."

Evelyn tipped her head to the side and gave an empathetic smile. "You know, when I first met you a few Christmases ago, I remember thinking you were the most beautiful woman I'd ever seen in real life, but there was something so sad in your eyes. You're always so cheerful and supportive of everyone else, but sometimes I worry we could be more supportive of you. If there's anything you need, we'll help you."

What she needed didn't exist.

She squeezed Evelyn's hand and her smile turned genuine. "I know you would help me. We're family. I've just been depressed lately. It's probably just winter blues." But it wasn't the weather. "I've been thinking about getting away."

"That's a great idea. Let us help you make the plans. You can take the jet and go to Lucian's island."

"Oh, I don't need all that. I was thinking more along the lines of a trip down the coast to a little bed and breakfast or something."

Evelyn emphatically shook her head. "No, we're pulling out all the stops. You worry about packing and your brother and I will take care of everything else. I insist!"

Her brother's island wasn't exactly what she needed, but it was a damn good substitute for reality. She lounged in the sun, worked on her tan, and gorged on novels. But after a few days she was ready to come home, the privacy of the island exploiting her loneliness to an insufferable degree.

It was a slow acceptance, but she had no other options. She was going to be alone and she needed to figure out how to live with that fact.

It was time to redefine her life again—something she had plenty of experience doing, but not with the optimism she once possessed. Still, she knew the process and forced herself to make all the right moves, believing that *eventually* the emptiness would get filled.

She called Seth and instructed him to message over all the invitations for their upcoming spring events. She intended to go back to work once she finished the last of her classes, but she didn't want to work anywhere she might cross paths with her past. That meant she needed to start networking other avenues and deciding how she wanted to use her notable education.

Putting together a resume was frustrating. The emblazoned *Patras* across the top mocked her.

No one would take her seriously in Folsom, because her male relatives had established so much clout before she had a chance to earn her own. Their name earned favors and attention, but it also jilted the competition. She could have been a school teacher or a middle-class nine-to-fiver, but her name raised the standards and her personality balked at heights.

After weeks of polite rejections, she had no choice but to return to a world she long ago tried to escape. It was different for men of power. They were recognized. Isadora was merely borrowing her brother and father's esteem in the eyes of those interviewing her. People either assumed she was too good for a regular job and wouldn't take it seriously or the job was too good for her and should go to someone who actually needed the income.

Her only solace came at night, when she sat alone in her big empty house and wrote down all the deep emotions she kept hidden inside. Her journal was a decade long, an adult woman's ramblings of a lost little girl.

Perhaps one day when she left this world someone would find it and see all she had to give, everything no one wanted to take. At least that would be something.

Lucian hardly attended social events since getting married. Stuck up affairs weren't Evelyn's thing and they often asked Isa to go in their stead. While Isadora wasn't a huge fan of lavish parties meant to occupy wealthy people's time, she did enjoy the events that actually served a purpose. When the stack of formal invitations arrived from Seth, she sorted through the piles and made the charity events her top priority.

As her schedule booked up she gradually found a level of equilibrium again. She wasn't happy, but she wasn't broken. She existed behind a façade of class and poise no one cared to see through. It was the armor she'd adorned the moment her mother died and it still fit well.

Everything was working rather well, this disguise of contentment she'd concocted, until her false confidence started to garner the unwanted attention of gold diggers. And they *were* gold diggers. Any man more interested in her name than her breasts was not a man she needed to know.

Perhaps Sawyer had broken more than her heart, because any sort of masculine attention grated on her nerves. She was jaded, cynical, and uninterested in men as a whole.

Throughout her entire life she'd been overshadowed by one indomitable personality to the next. Whatever species of human they wrote about in romance novels, she decided, was purely fictitious, woven fantasies that made little girls believe in things that were as nonexistent as unicorns.

Real heroes and shining knights didn't exist. So it was her job to save herself.

But the pathetic advances got worse and worse —fortune hunters dead set on cornering her and asking uncomfortable questions—always about her family's business. They came out in droves and could be as relentless as a swarm of wasps. It became such a problem, she was certain something had to be provoking so much attention. It certainly wasn't her.

"Do me a favor, Lucian," she said one afternoon when her brother stopped by the house. "Don't send any more of your colleagues to these functions with the expectation that I might fall desperately into their arms."

He frowned. "I have no idea what you're talking about, Isa."

She rolled her eyes. "Oh, come on. I know you and Evelyn have been trying to secretly set me up. It's getting tedious—and a bit insulting."

"Isadora," he said slowly. "*What* are you talking about?"

"Just stop, okay? Every time I attend a benefit or a gala, more men come up to me, introducing themselves as your colleagues, and asking me to dinner. Enough already."

He laughed. "Did it ever occur to you that if men are asking you out, it's because they want the pleasure. Evelyn and I have nothing to do with it."

"But..." That couldn't be right. It happened too often to merely be a coincidence. Although her father had always insinuated she should marry a sizable bank account, it had been years since he hounded her on the subject.

Lucian had to be lying. Either that, or his wife was doing this on her own.

"I know Evelyn thinks I'm looking to meet someone, but I'm not. Can you ask her to stop? It has to be coming from somewhere."

He gaped at her and scoffed. "What the hell is wrong with you? Why is it so hard to believe someone might be interested in you *without* any prodding? I assure you my wife is *not* contacting any men, on your behalf or otherwise."

"I..."

Men weren't interested in her. It was either her name or her money.

"Well, I don't like the attention. They're only talking to me because I'm a Patras."

He shook his head. "Yes, you're *Isadora Patras*. You're beautiful and nurturing and have the kindest heart of anyone I know. I can't, for the life of me, understand why you *still* don't see the value in yourself. Trust me, Isa, people like you for more than your name."

Changing the subject, she snatched a heavy, white invitation off the counter and smacked Lucian in the arm with it. "When were you going to tell me about this?"

He glared at her. "About what?"

"The opera house event! Lucian, you were voted *Man of the Year* and you said *nothing?* Did you expect us not to find out?"

He shrugged. "I don't need all that attention."

"But you're going, right?"

He let out a sigh. "I'm going, but Evelyn should be the one they honor. She's the one who got me involved with St. Christopher's."

She nudged him with her shoulder. "*Man of the Year*. Like your ego isn't going nuts over that title."

He snatched the invitation from her and arched a brow, his mouth twisting into a boyish grin and reminding her of when he was young. "It *is* pretty impressive."

The opera house's white tie gala was Folsom's most formal event of the year. Each year the proceeds went to a different cause. This year all donations were going to the homeless shelter.

Isadora had been a volunteer at the shelter since it reopened, so she was quite passionate about the cause. However, four generations of Bishops had chaired on the board of the old St.

Christopher's church, so she suspected Sawyer would be in attendance. As much as she hated the possibility of running into him, she couldn't miss an event that honored her brother.

Toni and Shamus were in some sort of disagreement, so Isadora decided her sister would be the perfect buffer for the gala. Although she didn't want to see Sawyer, she needed to look her absolute best in case he saw her. For the first time in her life, Isadora put great thought into her attire, pulling out all the stops and sparing no cost.

Ball gowns were *de rigueur* for woman, no exceptions made. Full-length, white opera gloves were also expected. It was probably wrong that she bought a dress the exact shade of Sawyer's eyes, but it was one of the few colors she recognized and pale enough to be in theme. The men were expected to wear tuxedos with white accessories down to their pearl cufflinks and gloves.

Toni refused to tailor her gown according to some silly tradition. And while she stuck out like a sore thumb, she looked radiant in a crimson antebellum gown that covered one shoulder and fell into a cascade of roses at the hip.

"I feel like a cupcake," her sister laughed, as they took the wide marble steps up to the opera house entrance.

Antique sconces flickered on every wall, illuminating the grand interior staircase leading to mezzanine seating. Invitees were dressed to the nines. Dapper men loitered in the lobby, sharply adorned in designer tuxedos, as women graced their arms like debutantes at a royal affair.

A quartet played while guests ascended the steps. They were required to give their name in order to pass, the long celebrated event boasting an "invitation only" VIP guest list of the most elite men and women on the east coast.

"You look fine," Isadora told Toni, as her sister continued to fuss with her extravagant gown. "You're lovely." The train of her skirt might have been a little too much, but her sister didn't need to hear that.

"Hey, isn't that Emily Cornerstone, the actress? I loved her in *Don't Come Knocking Twice.*"

"Who?" Evelyn asked, not sharing Toni's affinity for A-listers.

Pretending to look at the actress, Isadora scanned the crowd for Sawyer, pausing at every silver head her gaze passed.

While she hoped he wasn't there, she also didn't want to be caught off-guard. Better to spot him first so she could avoid crossing paths.

The evening opened with cocktails and buttered hors d'oeuvres and by the end of the first hour they were moving to their seats. Their family owned a mezzanine box and Lucian was eager to get to their private balcony.

"Let's head upstairs." He maintained a territorial hand on his wife's hip.

Wanting to freshen up before the main event, Isa excused herself. "You guys go ahead. I'll catch up."

Toni frowned as their brother and Evelyn followed the crowd. "It's starting in five minutes, Isa. Lucian's giving his speech soon."

"I'll be there. I need to use the restroom."

"Okay." Her sister followed their brother as the lights dimmed, signaling the guests that it was time to take their seats.

Bedecked men and women flowed through the wide corridor to their seats and Isadora traveled down the extensive hall, eyes searching for a restroom.

Instruments hummed from the pit as a prelude to the evening. The halls were almost empty when she left the bathroom. The balconies quieted as people settled in and the orchestra echoed from below.

The prelude concluded and the halls were silent except for her shushing skirt. A woman's voice resonated from the stage, welcoming guests.

She needed to get back to their box or she'd miss her brother's speech. There was a round of applause followed by Lucian's recognizable, deep voice.

"Damn it," she hissed, pausing at a random archway to watch from someone else's balcony.

He looked magnificent in his tuxedo, so much a man to admire. Her heart pinched with pride as she allowed herself to take a small bit of credit for the incredible person he'd become. Gone was the ruthless young opportunist he'd been, and now a palpable sense of contentment flowed in place of his vengeance.

"Not many of us know what it is to go hungry," he began, voice strong. "But some of us do. Some of you have taken quite a journey to get here tonight."

He smiled the way he often did when in deep reflection. "Some of us wear courage like a second skin, making it all the more difficult to detect. There's a woman here tonight, I won't give her name, but she's the most courageous woman I know. She didn't start her life at the top, yet she sits amongst us like a queen in her own right. She played a silent role in keeping St. Christopher's doors open."

The audience sat silently, hanging on his every word. If someone dropped a pin, she imagined the sound would echo through the theater.

"There are a lot of privileged people here tonight. But with privilege comes great responsibility. Your generosity ensures that the less fortunate have a roof over their head, food in their bellies, and coats on their shoulders. Your generosity feeds hope. It fuels an unwavering belief that every member of this community deserves a second chance. The woman I mentioned... She survived many cold winters with little more than flicker of hope to keep her warm.

"That's real courage. It's a fire that burns through the darkest hour but remains bright enough to lead a person home. It's going against *all odds* and holding onto the faith that you can always be more tomorrow than you are today. Your generosity meets more than basic needs. Your generosity keeps that flame alive, lighting the way to a better future. You are *all* honored guests this evening."

He lifted the crystal award he'd been presented for his work on the new homeless shelters, three more built just that year.

A grin teased at his lips. Turning his gaze toward the upper balconies where their family sat, he smiled.

"I humbly accept this honor on behalf of every donor in the room tonight, but I dedicate it to *you*, the queen amongst us that let that little fire guide her all the way home."

Uproarious applause broke and Isadora blotted her eyes. A reoccurring gratitude filled her chest as she, too, was overwhelmed with appreciation for the generous people here tonight, the ones that gave Evelyn the tools to rise above adversity and find a home in her brother's heart.

Wanting to catch Lucian back at the box and see Evelyn's reaction to his speech, she turned and came to an abrupt stop, the breath knocking out of her lungs so fast it obliterated the smile from her face and left her dizzy.

Sawyer.

But he wasn't alone. He was speaking softly to a woman who looked to be in her late fifties. The woman laughed and cupped his cheek lovingly.

Isadora's stomach lurched. A scream bubbled in her throat, as he leaned in and pressed his lips to the other woman's. A crushing ache exploded in her chest as his arm wrapped around her, pulling her close, holding her the way only a lover would.

He drew back, smiled and whispered something in the woman's ear.

They looked right together. Well-suited. Happy.

Every admitted truth killed a part of her soul, piercing her fragile heart like a sharp, lethal thorn.

The woman laughed over some intimate secret and Isadora could bear no more. Closer and closer she moved until she was standing not two feet away from them.

The words formed in her head, almost without volition. *"You son of a bitch! How could you? Too old to date? Can't get it up? Guess those pills don't bother you so much now!"* She glared at them. *"Or maybe it was just me!"*

Something cold fell on her breast, and she jerked, as if coming out of a dream, her lips locked tight around her clenched teeth. She was facing her worst nightmare and unlike the enraged voice in her head, her heart was too broken, too shocked, to voice a single sound above a whimper.

Another tear fell, slipping silently down her breasts and disappearing behind the bodice of her gown. The way he looked at her... Smiled...

Oh, God...

She wished she had the courage to say every horrible thing running through her mind, slap him, and rip out that woman's hair, but thirty-six years of instilled manners, and a fear that she might actually let her true self show, kept her silent. They hadn't spotted her and she still stood thirty some feet away, unnoticed, her fingers pressing into her lips to hold her pain inside.

She watched them from a tortured prison made of invisible walls that separated her from everyone else. And she hated herself for not having the courage to tell him exactly what he deserved to hear.

How could he do this? He couldn't be with me, but he can be with someone else? It hasn't even been a year!

A sob burbled in her throat, nearly slipping out. She needed to get out of there before he saw her. *Run!*

Pivoting, she hiked up her gown, and bolted toward the nearest exist. She was an absolute disgrace, sobbing and wheezing, unable to do more than walk at a clipped gate in her tight bodice and heeled shoes.

So many attempts to be a strong woman and he'd brought her to her knees in a matter of seconds, cut her down to exactly what she was. Nothing.

She was such a fool! Such an absolute idiot, because despite all he'd done, she *still* loved him. She foolishly let him have this power over her heart and she hated herself for being so naïve.

He'd clearly gotten over his little blue pill phobia, because he was obviously in an intimate relationship now. Nausea churned and she gasped through her rushing tears.

Her mind replayed the image of him kissing that woman, a cruel carousel that spun round and round in her mind, ceaselessly beating at her until she wanted to rip out her memory and forget everything she ever knew of Sawyer Bishop.

Wiping her gloved fingers over her face, the pale silk smudged with damp mascara. She berated herself for giving her life and heart to a man who never appreciated it—never wanted it.

A sob broke from her throat, disrupting the silence of the halls. She was losing it. She needed to run faster. Get the hell out of this place.

Seeing the sign directing the way to the front entrance, she quickened her strides. Music played and guests were starting to mingle their way into the halls. Soon the entrances would be clogged and she couldn't let anyone see her like this.

Taking the turn at a breakneck pace, she raced

around the corner and cried out as her body was thrown backward, her face colliding with something hard as her heart lurched and her body careened, the back of her head smacking painfully on the floor.

A burst of white light exploded behind her eyes and the chandeliers swirled above her as her body collapsed in a disgraceful heap of tears and silk on the floor.

"Shit!"

Her head throbbed as her body was fully laid out on the carpet. She blinked, literally seeing stars.

Her hearing funneled in and out, making it difficult to focus on what the man above her was saying.

"Jesus, are you okay? I'm so sorry! I didn't see you and—"

Mortified, she adjusted her gown to cover her legs. "I'm fine. It was my fault. I wasn't looking where I was going."

She babbled nonsense, her focus on nothing other than getting up and getting out. Heaven help her. Guests were filtering into the hall.

She awkwardly shifted her upper body off the carpet, strands of hair coming undone from her French twist as a woozy sensation stole her breath. Voices carried and her skin burned hot with embarrassment, her humiliation the only distraction from the pain of the fall.

"Let me help you—"

"I assure you, I'm fine." She searched for her shoe and wedged it on her foot.

"You're trembling. Please, let me help you." The man held out a hand and she stilled, her vision finally clearing enough to make out his features.

Arresting eyes of an indiscernible color gazed upon her with unfeigned concern. There was something about those eyes, something... She'd seen eyes like that before, but for the life of her she couldn't recall where.

"Please," he insisted softly and a strange calm came over her.

Her hand slid into his as he gently, without much effort, pulled her to her feet. He reached down and collected her clutch. "You dropped this."

His voice was deep, thick, the sort that filled a woman's ears and did strange things to her body.

"Th—thank you."

"There's a bench over here. Why don't you have a seat for a moment and find your bearings."

She glanced at the bench, her thoughts disjointed. She was tempted to rest, when only a second ago she'd wanted nothing more than to run.

Her attention pulled between those eyes and the sound of nearing company. "I... I can't."

"Please. You really busted your ass and—*shit*."

She drew back as he reached for her face. "What are you doing?"

"You…"

He swiped a finger across her mouth. He hadn't bothered with the white gloves required that evening, nor did he bother to ask before invading her personal space.

"Your lip's cut."

Her fingers rushed to her mouth, which was sore and puffy. As she pulled her fingers away a dark blotch mixed with the smeared makeup marring her silk gloves. "Is that blood?"

"I'm sorry. Are you going to pass out? Shit, please don't faint. I'm really sorry. I know I keep repeating myself, but I feel terrible."

"Oh, God." Wooziness softened her knees. She probably looked a wreck.

"Let me find you some ice. Are you here with someone? Is there anyone I can call for you?"

She shook her head, amplifying the ache radiating through her neck and skull.

He led her to the bench, those familiar eyes studying her so closely she felt uncovered in some strange way. Naked.

He lowered his tall body to the bench, his knee brushing hers through the silk of her gown. His brow creased as he examined her face.

"Your pupils are even. We crashed pretty hard. It looks like the start of a bruise along your chin. If you wanna take a swing at me to make it even I'd totally understand."

A numb, disjointed laugh slipped past her swollen lip. He wanted her to *hit* him?

"It's not your fault. I was moving too fast." She frowned, wondering why everything suddenly seemed eerily calm when she'd been a frantic mess seconds ago. Maybe she had a concussion.

He appeared unharmed. "Are *you* hurt?"

"Nah. You got my jaw pretty good, but I think you took the brunt of it. You should really get some ice on that lip."

She frowned at the lapel of his white tux where a smudge of what might be makeup tarnished the ivory fabric. Her attention pulled from his jacket as voices flowed into the hallway.

She was shivering and couldn't stop shaking. "I think I'm okay now. I should go."

He caught her wrist. "Just give it a few minutes. I'll get you some ice and—"

"I can't stay." She stood, but her legs were so unstable she inelegantly dropped back to the bench in a swish of silk and tulle.

"Easy," he said softly, supporting her arm. "Who's here with you? I'll call them."

"No." She didn't want to explain herself to anyone. "I just need to leave."

"The party's just starting."

"I..."

She frowned, unsure why this man was so determined to help her. She must look horrifying for him to be *this* concerned.

"I can't stay. Thank you for waiting to see if I'm all right, but I'm fine now. Just a little shaken."

"Then let me take you somewhere to get some ice on that lip. I'd hate to say it, but it's getting worse. The longer you let it go the blacker the bruise will get. Then I'll be left in social ruin, branded the man who knocks over beautiful women at white-tie events. Do you really want to do that to me?"

She laughed again and winced as her lip pulled. It wasn't that funny, but the way he said it, with such self-deprecation, struck her as comical.

Something in his expression told her he really didn't care what other people thought about him. He gave a sheepish grin and his whole face came alive. She must have really whacked her head.

"You have a great laugh," he said, those eyes steadily staring into hers. What color were they? Too light to be brown. Certainly not blue.

"Thank you." She was suddenly warm, but still shivering.

"If you can't stay here, let me take you to across the street. There's a small bar. A drink might calm your nerves and you can put some ice on that lip. Please." He stood and held out his hand.

"You shouldn't have to leave on my account. I

can ice it when I get home. I'm steadier now. You stay."

He shrugged. "These sorts of events really aren't my style anyway."

There was something strange about him, different, yet so convincing, she immediately believed he was telling the truth. Her hand slid into his as he pulled her up with little effort, steadying her before allowing her to take a step. Once she found her footing he released his hold and her skin prickled.

"Don't forget this," he said, tucking her clutch into the crook of her elbow. "M'lady?" He held his arm out to her, the gesture of a true gentleman.

Conscious of her surroundings and not fully trusting her wobbly legs, she accepted his aid and allowed him to lead her down the grand staircase at a slow pace.

Her heart jerked as familiar faces filled the common areas. She lowered her face hoping not to be noticed.

"Are you hiding?" he murmured, keeping his gaze forward.

"I don't want them to see me," she confessed, her focus on the entrance several yards away.

"Keep your head down and stay by my side." He guided her hand to his other one as his arm slid around her back, placing her in the protective shelter of his body. "Laugh like I just said something funny."

A fake chortle slipped past her throat as more guests closed in.

"Good. No one's paying attention. We're just slipping out to get some air. Watch your step."

The fresh evening breeze was a blessing. It filled her lungs, but each breath was laced with something else, something rich and comforting. Once they crossed the street, she realized the scent was coming from him.

"We made it." His hold fell away leaving a cool chill in its place.

He held the door to the small establishment and she stepped inside, not recognizing the dimly lit bar. "I've never been here before."

"No? They have comfortable seating in the back, couches and books for anyone interested."

"Books at a bar?"

"Some stories require something stronger than coffee."

He led her to the back and it was like something out of a sitcom. Vintage furniture was arranged at various angles, providing intimate nooks and crannies for people to converse or read.

He directed her to a small table by the rear wall. Shelves stacked from floor to ceiling, full of battered old books. A bow window overlooked a small patio with an illuminated pond.

"This is so charming." It was as if she'd stepped into a dream.

"It's one of my favorite places."

Since arriving at the bar time seemed to stand still. She'd gone from her worst nightmare to this hidden, peaceful corner of the city she didn't know existed. It felt safe here. "Do you read?"

"As often as I can." He glanced to the front of the bar. It seemed they were the only customers at the moment. "Let me go see about getting you some ice. What do you drink?"

Should she have a drink? Maybe a cab would be the better thing to order. Although, the thought of going back out there, leaving this hidden nook...

"I suppose a glass of chardonnay is merited."

He nodded and disappeared to the front.

Chapter 23

"And on her lips there played a smile as holy, meek,
and faint as lights in some cathedral aisle."
Henry Wadsworth Longfellow
The Quadroon Girl

WHILE ISADORA WAITED for her rescuer to return, she admired the titles filling the wall. Her memory travelled from the other side of the street like a sketchy etching she couldn't quite envision.

She probably hit her head harder than she realized.

He returned a moment later, carrying three glasses, one containing ice, the other her chardonnay, and something dark for himself. Sitting beside her, he opened a linen napkin and filled it with ice, folding it carefully.

She watched his hands, noting the various scars and how efficiently he went about concocting a knotted pouch of ice. Maybe he was a doctor.

"Here we go." He gently turned her chin, pressing the cool napkin to her lips. She winced and he grimaced. "Sorry."

She didn't know why she let him touch her, but nothing inside of her wanted him to stop. Blinking, she watched as he carefully inspected the damage.

His face was close enough to see the shadow of hair darkening his jaw, tiny little follicles of soft brown. There was a knick on the bridge of his nose, and a healed over slice close to his right eye. Her gaze drifted away when his assessing stare collided with hers.

Her lip only stung slightly, but her chin was starting to throb along her jaw. She really smacked into him, yet he didn't appear wounded at all.

"Rough night?" His voice was so temperate, coaxing like an old friend, yet was almost positive she'd never met him before in her life.

He had the calming effect of an empath. "It wasn't the best."

"Money, love, or respect?"

Such an odd question made her chuckle, but

she supposed those were the three things most is- sues stemmed from. "Love."

He nodded in understanding. "Who is he?"

In all her years, she'd never uttered a word about him to anyone. So many moments of happi- ness and heartache bottled up inside. Perhaps she was in shock.

"He was the love of my life."

The words fell out of her mouth quietly, a great unburdening that held more weight than any other admission she'd ever pronounced. God, it felt good to say it out loud.

"Were you his?"

Her gaze lowered. "I thought I was, but... He's with someone else now."

"Sometimes," he said slowly, still pressing the ice to her lip as his gaze studied the damage. "We think everything we feel is all that can be felt. But people can love more than one person. It might feel like your heart's breaking, but maybe it's just making room for other things. Growing pains, if you will."

She blinked at him. "Did you just make that up?"

"Yeah. But I believe it."

"It's lovely."

It was a comforting theory. Perhaps Sawyer's relationship with this new woman didn't have anything to do with his feelings for her. Maybe they were two separate emotions, two parallel lines running a similar course, never meant to cross. But she still hurt.

He smiled. "I think this is good for a while. It stopped bleeding." He lowered the napkin and reached for his glass. "Did you ever read Dr. Seuss?"

What a strange question. "Of course."

"Well, remember the Grinch, how his heart grew? I think that's more accurate than people realize. Our hearts can love so many things, so many people. It's naïve to think the first time we fall in love will be the most epic love of our life. It seems a waste of life to only love one person that deeply and never give your heart to anyone else. Stingy."

She agreed with him, but still found herself the one exception to the rule.

She'd never love anyone but Sawyer and he'd done irreparable damage to her heart. "Unless people are so careless by the time they're through, the heart's spoiled for anyone else."

His smile twisted with understanding. "Growing pains. Don't underestimate the heart's resilience. Time heals."

"Do you honestly believe that? I've loved him for most of my life. I don't think my heart knows how to stop loving him."

He hesitated, but then said, "I lost my mom when I was just a kid. I know that's different, but she was the only person I ever loved at that point. Losing her felt like taking off a warm coat I'd worn all my life. I'd reach for it and it wouldn't be there. I assumed the pain would never ebb. It was a hollowness I couldn't escape, no matter how hard I tried."

"I know that feeling." She'd first experienced it after losing her own mother. Losing Sawyer was somehow worse, because he was gone, but still there.

"A lot of people know some form of heartache," he said. "But over time, the pain eases and you realize your heart still beats. So long as it's beating, it can love again. I promise. It might be a person or a story or a work of art that steals your affection, but eventually something other than sadness will take your breath away."

It was as if he knew exactly what to say, exactly what she needed to hear. She wanted to give him some personal detail back so he'd keep talking to her.

"I lost my mother when I was a teenager."

"It's a tough thing, but we've managed this far, haven't we?" He gave her a grin like a soldier might share with a veteran who fought the same war, but never shared a word, their similar experiences enough of a bond to overshadow uncrossed paths.

She smiled. "You have an interesting way of putting things."

He sat back and studied her. She couldn't imagine how disheveled she must look.

"Do you want to talk about him? Maybe it'll help. I'm a good listener."

Her mouth opened, about to spill her most intimate secrets, but she caught herself and snapped her lips shut. What was she doing?

"I don't know you."

"And I don't know you. Maybe not knowing each other will make it easier to talk. I was planning to spend my night in an opera house with five hundred strangers. What's the difference between that and chatting with just one?"

A lot. "Intimacy."

"Does intimacy bother you?"

Her face heated. "I don't discuss my personal life with anyone. I never have."

"That's a good quality, but it can get exhausting bottling so much inside." He laughed to himself. "I think you and I might have a few things in common."

He didn't seem like a cautious person by the way he was speaking to her. She wasn't exactly sure how to read him.

"You don't act shy."

"*Private* is a better word. People see what's on the surface and assume they have a person figured out." He glanced at the shelves behind him. "Books are always judged by their covers, so I've mastered showing people only what I want them to see, letting them assume they know what's on the inside. When their egos are satisfied they lose interest."

"So you spend your life performing for others?"

"No, I don't concern myself with others on most accounts, but I know how to keep them away. Give them what they expect and they think they have you all figured out. Most people have incredibly short attention spans."

Her stare narrowed on him, wondering if he was performing now. "I don't judge books by their covers."

He tilted his head, giving her a skeptical smirk. "No?"

She shook her head. "Book covers bore me. I'm colorblind, so I have no choice but to go by what's inside."

"No kidding? You can't see any color?"

"Blue. Everything else is sort of flat and dull. Shades blend together."

He twisted and searched the shelves, pulling a book down and placing it on the table. "What do you see?"

It was *The Wonderful Wizard of Oz*—one of her favorites. "A lion. I can make out the pictures and words, but it's all sort of ... yellow, I guess."

His mouth twitched as if he were hiding a pained grin.

"It's not yellow, is it?"

Offering a regretful smile, he said, "No. It's

green. His mane's red. I guess you're not a fan of the movie."

She laughed, perfectly aware of the moment *The Wizard of Oz* switched from black and white to color, but not used to people so candidly questioning her about what qualified as a disability. "Actually, it was one of my favorites growing up."

"Really?"

She nodded and sipped her wine, careful not to bump her lip. "I used to watch it over and over again, thinking one of those times my eyes would see what Dorothy saw. Eventually I gave up."

His brow pinched. "I wish I could show it to you."

She smiled, thinking about how many times she wished she could see what everyone else saw. It was worse when she was young. Now, she just accepted it. Holding out hope only led to disappointment.

She'd read an article about some special glasses being designed for people like her, but she doubted they worked as well as the creators intended. It was better to accept what was rather than hold out for some unrealistic fantasy that would never compare to the real thing.

"Emerald used to be my favorite color," she told him. "I have no idea what it looks like, but I knew if there was an Emerald City it had to be beautiful."

"It is."

Something shifted, leaving her feeling too exposed. Her gaze drifted to the table. "So, you were saying you're an introvert."

"I like my privacy and try not to concern myself with other people's opinions whenever possible."

"You must love dressing in something as generic as a tux."

He chuckled and flashed a grin. "It does keep things on an even playing field. It's amazing how differently people treat a person when they swap out a designer suit for tattered blue jeans."

"Do you do that, dress down to mess with people?"

She'd never been in public wearing anything less than a well put together ensemble, coordinated down to the stockings on her feet. All of her life she'd depended heavily on boutique saleswomen and her sister to make sure she didn't clash or look like a fashion emergency.

"I dress down for myself. Ambiguity's nice, but if I need to accomplish something and a suit carries more influence, I'll put on a suit." He shrugged, his relaxed posture a total contradiction to his pressed attire. "If I want to escape responsibility for a while, an old sweater and jeans does the trick."

"Which is the real you, the suit or the sweater?"

"The sweater."

For some reason she was glad he'd said that. She'd met enough tuxedos in her lifetime, but she'd never really spent time with the sweater sort.

She glanced over his shoulder. "Did you read any of these books?"

"I've read all of them. Sometimes I leave novels here for the next person. That one there..." He pointed. "That was mine."

She slid the book from the shelf. "*Lord of the Flies*." Her hand brushed over the tattered cover, pausing over a butterfly.

"Can you see it?"

She nodded. "It's blue. I read this a long time ago. I forget it now."

"Take it with you."

She glanced at him, guilty before even committing the crime. "I can't do that."

"Why not? It's mine."

"But you donated it. Taking it now would be like stealing."

"Do you want me to ask permission? I'm sure they'd let me pay them for it."

"No, that's all right." She could buy her own copy if she felt like reading it again. She slid it back onto the shelf and sipped her wine.

They sat silently for a moment and his attention drifted toward the entrance of the bar. "Do you hear that?"

She turned her ear in the same direction. "Hear what?"

"The music coming from the opera house. When I was younger I'd sit outside and listen to the shows. I think I've heard everything from *Madama Butterfly* to *Otello*, sitting right on those steps."

Two of her favorite operas, but she couldn't imagine only hearing them. There was something magical about witnessing the performers come to life on the stage and transcend time, creating a world out of nothing more than props, ambiance, and their own talent. Why would anyone want to miss seeing that?

She took a moment to appraise her company, feeling like something was a little off about him. His tuxedo looked like Oxford, but it was difficult to tell in the dim light. He didn't wear any jewelry and his cufflinks were plain.

There really wasn't anything extravagant about him, aside from his tux, which in all truth could have been rented. However, he'd been inside the opera house when they met, which meant he'd somehow earned his way onto that guest list.

"Have you ever *watched* an opera?"

The side of his mouth lifted into a half grin. "No, but I have a vivid imagination."

"You *were* on the guest list tonight, right?"

He laughed. "Do you think I swindled my way inside?"

Maybe. He hadn't been seated at the start of the evening. Perhaps he snuck in when those monitoring the doors were preoccupied. Realizing how foolish that sounded, even in her own head, she blushed.

"I was invited," he assured, smiling. "I've invested a lot of my time with the people of St. Christopher's. It's important to me that it remains open."

So he was a philanthropist. "I've never seen you there. I volunteer whenever I can." She wondered if he knew Sawyer, if he was on the board with him.

Recalling Sawyer sent a punch to her heart, still painfully tender. Her hand started to shake and, as she reached for her glass, chardonnay sloshed over the rim onto the lap of her gown.

"Dear lord, I'm a train wreck tonight."

She reached for the napkin, forgetting it was filled with ice, and sent melted chips pelting across the table. Shutting her eyes, she pinched her nose and drew in an exasperated breath.

"Hey," he whispered softly. "It's just water and wine."

Exhaling slowly, she swallowed and gave him an apologetic look. "I'm not usually like this. I'm typically the calm one, the steady, put together one."

"Everyone loses their balance once in a while."

She studied him for a long moment, wondering who he was and where he'd come from. She wanted to ask his name, but only if she could avoid giving hers. She didn't need the label of Patras interfering with the authenticity of their conversation. "Are you always this patient with people?"

"I've been known to have an off day."

She liked the way he defined things. "That's what this is for me, an off day."

"Maybe it's not. Maybe this is just an ordinary day and all the others were off. This might be the real you you've been hiding behind a shield of elegance and propriety. People hide all the time, but sometimes, no matter how much armor we wear, a few bullets get through."

"A shield like a tux?"

"Maybe ball gowns are your sweaters," he teased.

Her gaze went to the pristine white tie at his throat where stubble had started to grow. She glanced at her gown and thought about how much effort she put into her appearance tonight. All she wanted was to look unbroken on the outside, so much so that no one would notice how shattered she was inside.

She certainly used clothing to boost her shaky courage, but tonight that wasn't enough. Maybe it stopped being enough a long time ago.

If this wasn't her, then who was she? Was any of this real? Was she the heiress in a ball gown attending affairs, hiding in the shadow of her impressive brother? Or was she her own person?

"I don't know who the real me is."

"Well," he said softly. "I think she's probably kind. Gentle with other people's hearts. Pretty. She's read the classics, which tells me she has a romantic soul. And she's fragile, but too focused on where she's heading to consider herself breakable. How am I doing so far?"

She blinked at him, unsure how a perfect stranger could assess her with such detail in such a short time. But he gave her too much credit. "You forgot to say transparent."

"No, I didn't. People probably think they know you from what they see on the outside, but I bet there's a lot more going on under the surface."

His fingers brushed her discarded glove resting on the table. Her chest tightened as he touched the smudges of makeup, blood, and tears. So exposed, yet she didn't move a muscle to hide away the evidence.

"Some people wear tuxedos while others wear silk gowns," he whispered. "It's all about illusions. And you, m'lady, have it down to an art form, I think."

"I'm not that complicated," she rasped, finding it difficult to draw in a full breath. The wine was getting to her. Her skin felt flushed and warm.

He flashed his teeth in a confident grin. "I think you're one of those people who knows exactly what others anticipate from you and excel at meeting their expectations. Keep the cover simple, hide the story inside. Which is probably why tonight, when something clearly upset you, your first instinct was to hide. Protect the illusion at all costs for the sake of others."

"I wasn't hiding. I wanted to leave."

His eyes watched her and her skin prickled, that strange sense of exposure taking hold again.

He was right. She ran off to hide, not from the man who hurt her, but from those who wouldn't understand her response, the people who always expected her to be the unshakable one.

"It gets exhausting," he confessed. "I did it for a while, at the start of my career, but then I realized even business can get too personal and I didn't want to pretend to be someone I'm not anymore."

"I've done that."

She thought of Tyrian and how badly she wanted to be the girl perfectly satisfied with a charming, emotionally available, well-mannered guy. But she couldn't. Without passion, there was no point.

Her lashes lowered, the shameful truth whispering past her lips. "It can feel like layers of your soul's scraping away, like you're trying so hard to please others that you're losing yourself in the process."

"Was it a job?"

"A guy. A long time ago. Not the one from tonight."

"How long did it last?"

"About three months. You?"

"Mine was a job and it barely lasted a year."

"At least you weren't pretending in order to find love."

He laughed. "That's not necessarily true. I thought success would make her love me, but her heart belonged to someone else. In the end, when I saw the way she looked at him, I realized, for all my affection, I never looked at her that way."

"You let her go?"

He shrugged. "There are varying levels of love and my feelings for her made a mockery of the word. Sometimes we love what's comfortable, what's familiar, and when it's gone we panic. I didn't have to let her go. She was never mine."

"You're quite the philosopher. Interesting, too. I imagine that helps with your success." She wasn't sure what he did for a living, but knowing he was on the guest list proved he was a successful man.

"Thank you. Occasionally I try."

He was definitely charming, not because of the way he spoke, but *how* he spoke. He might even be a bit of a romantic. "If you had to choose between love or money which would you pick?"

"Love, all the way," he answered quickly. "I respect money and everything it can do. It's a necessary evil. But even the richest man is limited in terms of love."

Another view they had in common. Yet, here they were, dressed like royalty, in the back corner of a bar covered in books.

Maybe they were just hypocrites. It was a lot easier to say money didn't matter when you had plenty in the bank.

"Can I get you another glass of wine?"

She glanced at her cup, surprised to see it empty. "If you don't mind staying a while longer."

"Are you kidding? This is way more entertaining than the night I expected." He stood and took their glasses to the bar.

She should text Toni and let her know where she went, but the overwhelming thought of having to explain herself kept her away from her phone. Maybe just a little longer. She felt safe here, like she could hide and catch her breath before facing reality again.

Two glasses of wine turned to three and eventually she lost count. The longer they talked the more comfortable she became around him. He was witty and sweet and charming in an unobtrusive way. There was something about him that soothed her, made her want to learn everything about him and trade secrets, even if they never saw each other again.

People dressed in gowns and tuxedos filtered into the bar, reminding her of where they were and how long they'd been missing. She reached in her purse to check the time on her phone, shocked to see it was almost midnight.

There were a few missed calls and texts from Toni asking where she was. Guilt slithered through her pleasant mood and she reluctantly accepted that she couldn't hide forever. She should get back.

"Thank you for helping me tonight."

"Please don't thank me. I feel terrible I knocked you over."

She shrugged, sort of glad they bumped into each other. "Accidents happen."

His hand brushed hers and her stomach tightened, as she stared at his fingertip grazing her knuckles. A whoosh of butterflies exploded in her stomach and her gaze jumped to his face. He gave a shy smile and she understood their chemistry wasn't one-sided.

"I had a great time getting to know you," he said softly, his gaze holding hers.

Feeling winded though she'd been sitting for some time, she whispered, "Me too. It was sweet of you to bring me here and..." She gestured to the damp napkin. "The ice."

"My pleasure." His hand slowly pulled away.

She fidgeted, unsure how to say goodnight and thank you without seeming awkward. "People are probably wondering where I am."

"Him?"

Her smile fell. "No, he doesn't even know I'm here. My family, though ... I just left without telling them." She gestured to her phone. "My sister texted me about a hundred times."

"Ah. If you want to stay and talk a while longer I could take you home. You could let her know you're safe."

Her lips parted, a curious feeling twisting inside of her. "I should probably go home with her. I insisted she come with me tonight."

"Does she live with you?"

"No, but she's spending the night."

"Then you should probably let her know where you are," he said, gesturing to her phone.

Reaching for it, her hands trembled, her mind protesting that she wanted to stay. She texted Toni letting her know she was at the bar across the street.

Her phone buzzed back and she slipped it inside her clutch. "She'll be here in a few minutes."

"Can I see you again?"

Fear and nervous excitement took hold. She wanted to see him again, but she was so afraid she was leading herself towards another letdown. He wasn't like the other men she knew, yet she couldn't put her finger on what made him so different.

Her phone vibrated again. "Excuse me."

She pulled it out and read the text from her sister saying they were crossing the street now.

Feeling suddenly rushed after such relaxed conversation, she collected her gloves and stood. He stood as well, a pulse of energy beating between them.

She wasn't ready to say goodnight. Turning, she saw her siblings working their way through the late night rush at the bar. "I had a really nice time tonight."

He smiled, his anxiousness seeming to shadow hers. "Me too…" He laughed and shook his head. "I don't know your name."

She laughed as well. How strange to share so much with someone, but never share their names. "It's Isadora."

Reaching in his pocket, he pulled out a plain white business card with a phone number. "It was a pleasure to meet you, Isadora. I'm—"

Evelyn's voice cut through the air. "*Parker?*"

Isadora turned as her sister-in-law stared up at her companion and Lucian scowled.

Toni took inventory of everyone's expression, seeing their brother's clear dislike for the person Isadora had spent the evening with, and a slow silent *ooooh* shaped her sister's mouth.

They knew each other? How?

Evelyn laughed, her expression the absolute opposite of her husband's. "Holy. Shit."

TO BE CONTINUED…

**The story continues in Two Billion Enemies!
Read *Two Billion Enemies* Now!**

**Claim your FREE book when you subscribe
to Lydia's newsletter!**
Click here to sign up for Lydia Michaels'
Newsletter.

Are you follow Lydia Michaels?
Stalk her on TikTok, Instagram, Facebook,
Goodreads, and BookBub!
TikTok @LydiaMichaels
Instagram @lydia_michaels_books
Facebook @LydiaMichaels
Goodreads
BookBub

Show Your LOVE
*If you enjoyed this book, please don't forget to leave a
review.*

LYDIA MICHAELS' READING ORDER

MCCULLOUGH MOUNTAIN
Almost Priest
Beautiful Distraction
Irish Rogue
British Professor
Broken Man

Controlled Chaos
Hard Fix
Intentional Risk

JASPER FALLS
Wake My Heart
The Best Man
Love Me Nots
Pining For You
My Funny Valentine
Side Squeeze

CALAMITY RAYNE
Calamity Rayne Gets a Life
Calamity Rayne Back Again
Calamity Rayne Gets Hitched

THE SURRENDER TRILOGY
Falling In
Breaking Out
Coming Home

RUTHLESS BILLIONAIRES
One Billion Secrets
Two Billion Enemies

MASTERMIND
Blind
Untied

NEW CASTLE
First Comes Love
If I Fall
Something Borrowed

ADDICTED TO YOU
Crush
Bang
Throb

THE ORDER OF VAMPIRES
Original Sin
Dark Exodus
Prodigal Son

STAND ALONES
La Vie en Rose
Simple Man
Sugar
Breaking Perfect
Hurt
Tennessee Honey
Protege

About Lydia Michaels

Lydia Michaels is the award winning and bestselling author of more than forty titles, a certified life coach, and transformational speaker. She is the consecutive winner of the 2018 & 2019

Author of the Year Award from *Happenings Media,* as well as the recipient of the 2014 *Best Author Award* from the *Courier Times*. She has been featured in *USA Today, Romantic Times Magazine, Love & Lace*, and more. As the host and founder of the *East Coast Author Convention,* the *Behind the Keys Author Retreat,* and *Read Between the Wines,* she continues to celebrate her growing love for readers and romance novels around the world.

In 2021, Michaels released the groundbreaking, non-fiction series, ***Write 10K in a Day,*** to commemorate her career in the publishing industry. She looks forward to many more years of exploring both fiction and non-fiction writing, teaching about the craft, and learning from the others in the author community.

Lydia is happily married to her childhood sweetheart. Some of her favorite things include the scent of paperback books, listening to her husband play piano, escaping to her coastal home at the Jersey Shore, cheap wine, *Game of Thrones*, coffee, and kilts. She hopes to meet you soon at one of her many upcoming events.

You can follow Lydia at www.Facebook.com/LydiaMichaels or on Instagram @lydia_michaels_books

<u>Read By Mood</u>
Billionaire Romance
<u>Falling In</u> | <u>Sacrifice Of The Pawn</u> | <u>Calamity Rayne</u> | <u>Blind</u>

Contemporary Romance
<u>Wake My Heart</u> | <u>The Best Man</u> | <u>Love Me Nots</u> | <u>Pining For You</u> |<u>Almost Priest</u>| <u>My Funny Valentine</u> | <u>Side Squeeze</u> | <u>Almost Priest</u> | <u>Beautiful Distraction</u> | <u>Irish Rogue</u> | <u>British Professor</u> | <u>Broken Man</u> (LGBTQ) | <u>Controlled Chaos</u> | <u>Hard Fix</u>|<u>Intentional Risk</u>

Emotional Favorites
<u>La Vie en Rose</u> | <u>Simple Man</u> | <u>Wake My Heart</u> | <u>Sacrifice of the Pawn</u> | <u>Crush</u>
Romantic Comedy
<u>Calamity Rayne</u>

Erotic Romance
<u>Breaking Perfect</u> | <u>Protégé</u> | <u>Falling In</u> | <u>Sugar</u>

First in Series
<u>Almost Priest</u> | <u>Falling In</u> | <u>First Comes Love</u> | <u>Wake My Heart</u> | <u>Crush</u> | <u>Original Sin</u>

Paranormal Vampire Romance
<u>Original Sin</u> | <u>Dark Exodus</u> | <u>Prodigal Son</u>

LGBTQ+ & Menage Romance
Broken Man (MM) | Breaking Perfect (MMF) |
Crush (MMF) | Hurt (Non-Consensual) | Protege

Sexy Nerds & Second Chances
Blind | Untied
***Teacher Student, Workplace, and Age-Gap
Love Affairs... Oh my!***
British Professor | Pining For You |Breaking
Perfect | Falling In | Sacrifice of the Pawn

Single Dads & Single Moms
Simple Man | Pining For You | First Comes Love |
Controlled Chaos | Intentional Risk

Dark Tortured Hero Romance
Hurt

Non-Fiction Books for Writers
Write 10K in a Day: Avoid Burnout

www.ingramcontent.com/pod-product-compliance
Lightning Source LLC
Chambersburg PA
CBHW050954210726
48287CB00004B/1213